CLAIMING SARAH

ACE SECURITY

BOOK 5

Susan Stoker

Montlake
Romance

Text copyright © 2019 by Susan Stoker

Published by Montlake Romance, Seattle

www.apub.com

Amazon, the Amazon logo, and Montlake Romance are trademarks of Amazon.com, Inc., or its affiliates.

ISBN-13: 9781542008051
ISBN-10: 1542008050

Cover design by Eileen Carey

Cover photography by Wander Aguiar

Printed in the United States of America

CLAIMING
SARAH

Chapter One

"I seriously don't have time for this shit."

Sarah winced, but kept her eyes on her purse sitting in her lap. She was exhausted after a grueling twelve-hour shift, but hadn't even considered calling off the meeting. She *needed* this.

She'd come into the Rock Hard Gym right on time and told the receptionist who she was and that she had an appointment with Cole Johnson. The young woman had looked surprised but told her to take a seat and she'd go talk to the man.

Sarah had sat on a surprisingly comfortable chair in the lobby of the gym as the receptionist walked past her, partway down a hallway to the left of the lobby, and entered an office.

She'd closed the door, but it didn't latch, making it easy for Sarah to hear the conversation between the woman and Cole.

"Is Trina around? Can she take this for me?"

"You said she could leave early today, remember? It's her birthday, and her boyfriend wanted to take her out."

"Damn. That's right. Where's the schedule?"

"Last I saw it, it was on the corner of your desk, but that was about five pounds of papers ago."

Sarah heard the humor in the college-aged woman's tone, but couldn't even muster enough energy to smile. The weight of the world seemed to be sitting on Sarah's shoulders, and she wasn't sure she could keep up her usual sunny disposition.

The man she had an appointment with and the receptionist continued speaking.

"God, this place is a mess. How long is her appointment supposed to be for?"

"I think it's scheduled for an hour."

"Damn. I literally don't have an hour. I have an interview in thirty minutes."

The receptionist must have given him a reproachful look, because Cole said defensively, "Hey, I thought I was free. And besides, he couldn't come in until now because of his other part-time job."

"What do you want me to tell her?"

"Tell her I had an emergency come up, and see if she can reschedule."

Sarah had heard enough. The last thing she wanted was to be a burden to anyone. But she also wasn't going to sit around any longer and listen to this guy make up excuses and lies for why he didn't want to keep their appointment.

In order to prevent the poor receptionist from having to lie to her, Sarah quietly stood and headed for the front door of the gym. It was probably for the best anyway. It was getting dark outside, and she hated to be out and about after the sun went down. She didn't feel safe.

Not that she felt particularly safe any time of day anymore.

She was pushing open the doors when she heard the receptionist call out her name. For once, Sarah didn't bother to be polite. She kept going without turning around.

Castle Rock, Colorado, was a pretty small town. The downtown area was eclectic and welcoming. There was a park at one end and a small Italian restaurant she'd heard wonderful things about. A coffee shop was across from Rock Hard Gym, and there was a bar called Rock 'N' Roll a few spaces down as well. Several other independently owned stores made up the rest of the downtown area.

Looking around, Sarah didn't see anyone lurking about. She took out her key chain and hooked her middle and pointer fingers through the eyeholes in the cute metal cat head. The pointed ears stuck out and would seriously hurt anyone who tried to grab her as she made her way to her car. One of the nurses at the hospital had the self-defense tool on her own key chain, and Sarah had ordered it the same day she'd seen it.

Hating that she felt so vulnerable and unsure—she never used to feel this way all the time—Sarah picked up her pace as she hurried toward the parking lot at the end of the block. Even though it wasn't quite dark yet, the overhead lights illuminated the sidewalk. Every step felt as if she were walking through molasses. She was exhausted after working all day and wanted nothing more than to climb into her bed and sleep for eight hours straight.

"Sarah! Wait!"

Surprised at the sound of someone calling her name, she turned and saw a man jogging down the sidewalk toward her.

She should've been running away rather than letting him approach. She didn't know him. Had never seen him before. She would've remembered if she had. But she could only stare as he got closer. He was taller than her five-seven by at least half a foot. He had black hair and a closely cropped beard. The focused attention in his green eyes kept her rooted to the spot.

He was wearing a pair of sweatpants and a black T-shirt with some sort of logo in white on the front. His arms were covered in tattoos, but she couldn't see what the designs were, as he was moving too quickly. His biceps bulged as he jogged toward her, and she had no doubt he was muscular all over.

Her fingers tightened on the modified brass knuckles in her fist, and she held her breath as he got nearer. She should've ignored him. Should've kept walking . . . but she was fascinated by how much he immediately reminded her of her father. Not necessarily in looks, but in the way he stared at her, as if she were the only person currently on the face of the earth. She hadn't been on the receiving end of a look like that in ages.

The first time she'd met her dad, when she was six, he'd gone to his knee in front of her and promised she'd be safe with him. Something about the look in his eyes had made her believe him on the spot.

And she was seeing the same promise in the eyes of the man coming toward her. That was crazy . . . wasn't it?

"Sarah, right? Sarah Butler?" the man asked as he stopped in front of her.

Sarah nodded.

"I'm Cole Johnson." He held out his hand.

Sarah looked down at it and swallowed. She didn't want to do this, but she couldn't be rude. She uncurled her fingers from around the self-defense weapon and switched it to her left hand. Then she reached out and shook Cole's hand.

His fingers were warm, and she could feel the calluses on his palm as he gently pumped her hand. "I'm sorry," he said in a soft tone. "I'm assuming you overheard my conversation with Carrie."

It wasn't a question, but Sarah nodded anyway. Cole was still holding her hand, as if he were afraid the second he let go, she'd bolt.

"I've told her a million times to make sure my office door is shut when she comes in to talk to me, but obviously she forgot."

Sarah tugged on her hand and wasn't sure Cole was going to let go of her for a second. But he finally loosened his hold enough for her to reclaim her hand.

She wasn't sure what he wanted to hear, so she kept her mouth shut. Mike and Jackson had told her often enough that if she didn't have anything nice to say, she shouldn't say anything at all. She'd taken their words to heart and very rarely said the things she was thinking.

Cole apologized again. "I was a dick. I'm sorry. In my defense, my partner has been out of town for the past week, and I'm drowning in administrative stuff that she usually takes care of. I also didn't know it was you. Carrie didn't give me your name when she said you were here. That's not a good excuse, though."

Sarah pressed her lips together and nodded. He was right, it wasn't a good excuse. They had an appointment. It wasn't as if she'd walked off the streets and demanded he spend an hour of his precious time with her.

He winced. "Look, you have a right to be pissed. I want to make it up to you. Come on back to the gym, and we can talk."

Sarah took a deep breath and found her voice. "It's okay. You're busy and don't have time right now. I'll just come back some other time."

Cole regarded her for a long moment before saying astutely, "I have a feeling if I let you go right now, you won't be back."

Sarah refused to feel guilty. He was right, she had no plans to come back to Rock Hard Gym for the self-defense lessons she so badly needed. But she wouldn't lie to him either. So once again, she kept her mouth shut and simply stared back at him.

Cole sighed. "Look, I can't lie, I'm busy. I've got a million things going on, and I double-booked my schedule tonight. But the day I'm too busy to help a woman who needs self-defense lessons to feel safe is the day I might as well quit and find another occupation. Also, I'm the boss, but I suck at delegating. You coming back and talking to me right now will save me from having to do other administrative work I've been putting off."

She eyed him skeptically.

He smiled—and her knees almost gave out from under her. She'd thought he was good-looking before, but when his lips quirked upward in a genuine smile, he was drop-dead gorgeous.

"Please?"

"What about the interview you've got set up?"

Cole shrugged. "I'll have Carrie do it. She's the one who'll be working with him. I've got the questions I'd planned to ask printed out already, so I'll just give them to her, and she can conduct the interview. It'll be fine."

Sarah hesitated. Her bed called out to her. She wanted nothing more than to go home and bury herself under the covers.

"Please? I'll feel terrible all week if you don't let me make this up to you," Cole begged.

She sighed. "Fine."

"Great!" Cole exclaimed. He stepped back and held out a hand, indicating the sidewalk behind him. "After you."

With the oddest feeling that this decision would somehow change her life, Sarah fell into step with the man beside her as they headed back to the gym.

~

Cole silently blew out a breath of relief. When Carrie had informed him he was off the hook, that his appointment had just walked out the door, he'd panicked. He realized Carrie hadn't shut his office door when he'd been ranting about not having time to see anyone, and the woman had obviously overheard, gotten offended, and left.

Turning away women who wanted self-defense lessons wasn't his usual MO. He always went out of his way to help however he could. Especially considering his best friend had been in a situation where she'd been stalked and terrorized for years. Felicity was safe now, and had recently gotten married to Ryder Sinclair, half brother to the Anderson triplets.

Logan Anderson had personally asked Cole to handle Sarah's lessons, and he'd agreed without hesitation. The thought of her leaving without getting the help she obviously needed was abhorrent.

He hadn't lied to Carrie; he didn't have an hour to spend with a new client, but he hadn't known it was *Sarah*, and he'd never forgive himself if something happened to the young woman because he'd turned her away. He couldn't help but notice—and approve of—the brass knuckles she had in her fist. Yeah, they were in the form of a cute little cat, but the points of the ears on the metal gadget would definitely do some harm and give her a chance to get away if it came down to that.

He'd run after her, and luckily, she'd agreed to come back to the gym.

The walk was done in silence, which gave him an opportunity to study the woman beside him. She had brown hair, currently up in a haphazard bun, and beautiful hazel eyes. He would bet everything he had that they'd change colors based on the light around her. She was wearing a pair of wrinkled scrubs, indicating that she worked in the medical field. Her shoulders were hunched, and she made sure to stay far enough from him so their arms and hands wouldn't accidentally touch.

They arrived back at the gym, and Cole held open the door for Sarah and followed her inside. His professional gaze assessed her overall form from behind. She was very different from the carb-hating, protein-loving clients who frequented the gym. She might not have the muscle strength to execute some of the more advanced self-defense moves, but she could still do some damage to someone intent on doing her harm.

Ignoring the way Carrie was staring at him in shock—he'd never run down a client before, begging her to let him help after claiming he had no time to see her—Cole gestured for Sarah to go down the hall into his office.

He winced at the mess when he entered behind her. Felicity was always giving him crap about the condition of his office, but it hadn't ever bothered him . . . until now. Until he wanted to impress this woman for some weird and unknown reason.

He hurried past her to the small love seat against the wall and gathered up the papers that were on the cushions. "Please, make yourself comfortable. I need to go give Carrie the questions for the interview."

He stood patiently in the middle of his office, waiting for her to sit. She lowered herself gingerly to the very edge of the couch, as if she were ready to bolt if he so much as twitched in her direction. She was still gripping her keys in her left hand, and Cole hated that. Not that she was prepared to defend herself, but that she felt she needed to arm herself against *him*. He didn't know her story, only the little bit that Logan had told him, but he had a feeling whatever she was worried about was bad.

"We really can reschedule, Cole," she said, raising her eyes to his. "If this is going to disrupt everyone, I can come back later."

"It's fine," he said, trying to reassure her. "My staff is used to things being crazy around here. I'll be right back."

He waited until she nodded, then dropped the papers he'd collected from the couch onto his desk, shuffled a few of them around until he found the interview questions, and headed out of the room.

He was back less than five minutes later, and saw that Sarah hadn't budged from her position. She was still perched on the edge of the cushion and still had her keys in her hand. But now her eyes were closed— and he could see her torso swaying as her body struggled to stay upright.

Cole watched her for a beat, unexpectedly filled with emotions he hadn't experienced in a very long time.

It was more than concern for a woman who was obviously at the end of her rope. There was something about Sarah—her wariness, her vulnerability—that touched him deep inside. She immediately reminded him of Felicity. Uneasy, scared, hanging on by a thread . . . but he sensed a spine of steel, stronger than even *she* could ever know.

However, even after spending only a few minutes in Sarah's presence, Cole knew she was very different from his best friend.

Felicity never hesitated to tell someone what she thought. If someone pissed her off, they knew it. She wasn't mean about it, but she had no problem speaking up. She also frequently walked through the gym scolding the patrons for not cleaning the equipment after they'd sweated all over it. If someone told a story and had their facts wrong, she was the first to point it out. She was outgoing and outspoken, even more so now that the stalker who'd been after her for more than a decade was no longer a threat.

Sarah seemed far more subdued. She'd had every right to read him the riot act, but she hadn't. She'd politely let him off the hook, even though he'd been a dick. Yes, he was tired and overworked, but that didn't give him the right to be an asshole. And he had been.

"Sarah?" he said quietly as he pulled a chair over and sat in front of the couch.

He might as well have yelled the word for the effect it had. Her eyes popped open, and her back went ramrod straight. He saw the second she realized where she was and who had spoken, as her body sagged in relief, even though she quickly hid her emotions. "Yeah?"

"I'm sorry I took so long."

"No, I'm sorry for falling asleep on you. It's been a long day."

Cole found himself wanting more information. He wanted to know where she worked, what she did . . . if there was anything he could do to make her day better. But instead, he got down to the reason she was there in the first place. The sooner they finished up here, the sooner she could go home and get some sleep.

"I don't have a lot of information on your situation. You were referred to me by Logan Anderson. All I know is that you have an ex-husband who's been harassing you?"

She shook her head. "No, I haven't ever been married."

"Oh, I'm sorry. Logan must've misunderstood," Cole said. It was possible. Ace Security got a ton of emails and messages every day asking about their services. When Logan had emailed Cole to tell him about Sarah and ask if he would teach her some self-defense, Logan probably got her case confused with one of the others he'd been looking into. But for some reason, whatever was going on with her had struck a chord in Logan, if he'd reached out for Cole's help.

Ultimately, it didn't matter if an ex-husband or boyfriend was harassing her, or a perfect stranger. She could end up just as dead no matter who was making her life hell.

Sarah swallowed hard. "I just . . . I need to be able to protect myself . . . just in case."

Cole waited for her to go on, but when she simply sat on his couch, silent, he realized she was done talking. That was all she was going to give him. If it had been anyone else, he probably would've been relieved and finished up quickly by scheduling a time for their first lesson.

But this time, Cole pushed for more. "Who's harassing you, Sarah?"

She stared at him for a long moment, and Cole did his best to try to make himself look as nonthreatening as possible, which was kind of a joke, considering his tattoos and muscles.

Finally, she took a deep breath. "It's stupid."

"If someone has done something to make you feel like you need to take self-defense classes, it's not stupid."

"You aren't going to think it's anything to be nervous about."

"Why don't you let me be the judge of that," Cole told her, even more worried now. He had a feeling if she was downplaying the threat against her, it was probably way worse than he'd imagined.

"It's just that . . . I've been to the cops, and the guy I talked to flat out told me there was nothing he could do, and that I was likely imagining danger where there wasn't any. Even my coworkers think I'm crazy."

Cole leaned forward. He wanted to cover her hands with his own in comfort, but settled for doing what he could to reassure her with words. "If that little voice in your head is telling you that you're in danger, then you are. There've been plenty of times in my life when I've sensed something was off or wrong, and have been proven right. But regardless, whether you're imagining things or not, that's not my place to say. If you want to learn how to protect yourself to feel less vulnerable, then I can teach you the skills to do just that. It's not a matter of me believing you or not. But with that said . . . you can trust me, Sarah. If you tell me you're in danger, then I'll one hundred percent believe you."

"Why?"

Her question was blunt and to the point, and she looked right into his eyes as she asked.

"Because my best friend was stalked for over a decade by a man who others thought was perfectly normal. Because I've seen case after case Ace Security has taken on where men have sworn up and down that their ex-wives or girlfriends were batshit crazy, and the police didn't believe them . . . and in the end, they were proven correct when they were attacked by the same women authorities deemed 'normal' and 'docile.'

"Because most importantly, when I look at you, I can tell you're at the end of your rope and you need help. Let me help you, Sarah."

She didn't cry. Didn't wring her hands. She simply began to talk.

"I met Owen Montrone six months ago. His mother was in the hospital where I work and was very sick. I was nice to them both, as I am to everyone. Owen is . . . slow."

"What do you mean? Mentally handicapped?" Cole asked.

"Not really. I mean, I'm not sure. I think he just has a really low IQ. His mom told me he was in special classes throughout his school years, and he's lived with her for his entire life. Anyway, he seemed lonely in the hospital. A little lost. I went to lunch in the cafeteria with him once, after his mom pleaded with me to spend some time with him. A few weeks later, I heard his mother died. Not long after that, I started getting letters from Owen.

"I wasn't sure how he got my address, until I mentioned it at work. The receptionist said she'd given it to him when he'd called one day. He'd told her he wanted to thank me for all the help I'd given his mom, and she thought it was sweet. She was reprimanded, but by then it was too late. After the letters, the gifts started arriving. And I've sometimes seen him around . . . in the same places I shop and eat out. I've asked him to please stop, but he hasn't."

"What kind of gifts?" Cole asked.

"Flowers. Candy. Stuffed animals. You name it."

Cole's brow wrinkled. "Anything blatantly threatening?"

"No."

The word was said with a hint of hostility, and Cole understood why the police had basically patted her on the head and sent her on her way. "And the letters?"

"They're rambling, but there's nothing sexual or otherwise hostile in them. Nothing that the police decided was in any way a threat. He just talks about his day and how I make him smile and stuff like that. The cops told me it sounds like he has a crush on me and is probably harmless." Her knuckles turned white as she clenched her hands together in her lap. "But they're wrong," she said quietly. "Don't ask me how I know. It's a weird vibe I get when I see he's sent something, but I know they're wrong."

"I believe you," Cole said.

Her eyes met his, and he couldn't miss the hope he saw there.

"Even though all he's done is give me presents and notes?"

"You asked him to stop, and he didn't. He sounds like he's obsessed," Cole told her. "He can go from being nice to enraged that you haven't returned his affections in a heartbeat."

Sarah nodded.

"No means no. That goes for someone asking for a date, not just for sex. It doesn't matter if it's a guy or a girl saying no. You told him that you weren't interested in dating. That you wanted him to stop with the gifts, and he hasn't. I'd be more concerned if you *weren't* worried about this guy."

Her shoulders sagged in relief. "So you'll help me figure out what to do if he ever decides the notes and gifts aren't enough?"

"Absolutely. I'll do everything I can to help you, and that includes getting Ace Security involved if it comes to that."

"I hadn't realized the costs involved," Sarah said. "I think that's why Logan contacted you in the first place."

Cole leaned even closer, and satisfaction crept through him when she didn't back away. "I know Logan and his brothers, and believe me when I tell you that, once they hear what the cops told you and the facts of your case, money won't be a factor."

"Thank you," she said.

Cole nodded, then stood and walked to his desk. He rummaged around for a minute before pulling out his appointment book and holding it up triumphantly.

"You know, there are these new things that came out a few years ago called computers. You can even keep your schedule on them so you don't get overbooked."

Cole blinked at her teasing, then beamed. He much preferred this side of her to the scared, defeated woman he'd first met. "Really? Maybe you can walk me through how they work sometime."

Still smiling, Sarah just shook her head at him.

"My partner should be back next week, so I'll have a lot more free time. How does next Monday sound to start your lessons?"

"Good. I work until five, though."

"That's fine. Maybe six thirty, to give you time to grab dinner before you get here?"

Sarah shook her head. "If it's okay, I'd rather do it right after work. Before it gets dark."

Cole didn't like the implications, but kept his mouth shut . . . for now. "Okay, I'll pencil you in for five thirty. If you're early, that's cool, and if work runs over and you get here a little after, it's okay too. Sarah?"

"Yeah?"

"Thank you for giving me a second chance. I'm usually not so harsh."

"It's okay," she said quietly. "You aren't nearly as mean as most people I come into contact with."

With that bombshell, Sarah stood. "I'll see you next week."

"Next week," Cole echoed. He followed her out of his office and watched as she smiled and nodded at Carrie and disappeared out the front door.

His mind already wandered over the things he wanted to know about her. Which hospital she worked at and what she did there, why people were mean to her . . . why she felt the need to always be so nice.

By the time he realized he should've walked her to her car, it was too late.

Shaking his head at his stupidity, Cole vowed to do better.

Making a mental note to talk to Blake and Alexis and see what they could find out about the assbagger Owen Montrone, Sarah Butler, and her situation, Cole took a deep breath before tackling the ten million other things he still had to deal with before he could call it a night.

PRAISE FOR SUSAN STOKER

"Susan Stoker knows what women want. A hot hero who needs to save a damsel in distress . . . even if she can save herself!"

—CD Reiss, *New York Times* bestselling author

"Irresistible characters and seat-of-the-pants action will keep you glued to the pages."

—Elle James, *New York Times* bestselling author

"Susan does romantic suspense right! Edge of my seat + smokin' hot = read ALL of her books! Now."

—Carly Phillips, *New York Times* bestselling author

"Susan Stoker writes the perfect book boyfriends!"

—Laurann Dohner, *New York Times* bestselling author

"These books should come with a warning label. Once you start, you can't stop until you've read them all."

—Sharon Hamilton, *New York Times* bestselling author

"Susan Stoker never disappoints. She delivers alpha males with heart and heroines with moxie."

—Jana Aston, *New York Times* bestselling author

"Susan Stoker gives me everything I need in romance: heat, humor, intensity, and the perfect HEA."

—Carrie Ann Ryan, *New York Times* bestselling author

"Susan Stoker packs one heck of a punch!"

—Lainey Reese, *USA Today* bestselling author

CLAIMING
SARAH

DISCOVER OTHER TITLES BY SUSAN STOKER

Mountain Mercenaries Series

Ace Security Series

Delta Force Heroes Series

Chapter Two

Sarah was feeling pretty good about the outcome of her visit to Rock Hard Gym by the time she got home. It hadn't started out well, but she actually liked Cole Johnson. He'd apologized right off the bat and, once she'd explained her situation, seemed genuinely concerned. She was relieved that she might learn a few things to help protect herself . . . just in case.

But that good feeling disappeared in a flash when she saw the huge box sitting on her front step.

She hadn't ordered anything recently—so she knew instantly who had left the package.

Frustration and fear shot through her. Not wanting to deal with whatever Owen had sent this time, she unlocked her front door and shoved the box inside the house, but left it in the foyer without a second glance. She'd been hungry, but simply seeing the gift made her appetite vanish.

She hated that Owen continued to show up at her house. Hated that he even knew where she lived.

Trudging through the living room, she headed straight for the stairs. There were tons of things she should be doing, including house chores, but she couldn't muster up the energy to do them.

Her house was way too big for her, but it was the only home she'd ever known and contained all she had left of her dads. Mike and Jackson

Butler had adopted her when she was six. She had been scared of her own shadow at the time, and had already lived in three previous foster homes.

Back then, she hadn't known what being gay meant, or that it was highly unusual for two men to be allowed to adopt a child. She only knew when Mike took her in his arms, she wasn't scared anymore. And when Jackson smiled at her with his slightly crooked teeth, he somehow made everything all right.

After they'd passed away, their smell had slowly faded from the house, and last year Sarah had finally found the strength to start going through their things to donate what she could. She still slept in the same room she'd slept in most of her life, refusing to move into the master bedroom.

But as time passed, the house was less and less the comfort it used to be. It needed a paint job, the carpets needed replacing, and the grass was perpetually too long. She was finally to the point where she could admit that it was too much for her. Not only that, but with Owen showing up to leave her "presents," she didn't feel safe rattling around in the big house. There were too many places for someone to hide if they wanted to.

How Sarah wished her dads were still around today. They never would have let Owen get away with what he was doing. They would've confronted him and made him stop with the gifts and letters way before now. Jackson and Mike had been her champions and protectors from the second they'd opened their home to her. She missed them every day, but never as much as she did right now.

Fighting tears, Sarah went into her room and, after making sure her curtains were shut tight and no one could see inside, stripped off her scrubs and headed down the hall to the guest bathroom. She took a soothing, hot shower, standing under the spray long after she was clean.

Feeling marginally better, a little more like the optimist she usually was, Sarah put on her robe and climbed into bed. It was early, but it wasn't as if she had anything she needed to do. Besides, she had to get up at four fifteen in order to get to the hospital in time for her shift at five. She had one more day with a twelve-hour shift, then she had a couple of days off.

As she lay in bed, her thoughts drifted to Cole Johnson.

She'd been ready to blow him off, to see if she could find someone else to teach her self-defense, but then he'd gone out of his way to restore her faith in him. After hearing him talk to his receptionist, she'd gotten an image in her head of an older, pompous business owner who felt he was way more important than anyone else. But seeing him had been a pleasant surprise. He was young, probably around her age, and good-looking. *Very* good-looking.

He probably had women falling all over themselves to gain his attention. He was surrounded by fit women all day—surely one of them had caught his eye. Cole Johnson was probably very busy, both with his work and his social life.

She, however, had virtually *no* social life. She worked odd hours, and when she did have time off, Sarah found herself either catching up on chores she'd put off around the house or sitting on the couch, binge-watching one show or another.

But even before she began working as a nurse, she hadn't been a socialite exactly. She'd studied hard in high school, trying to make her dads proud of her, and that had continued into college as well.

After graduating with her two-year degree, Sarah had immediately found a job as a nurse's assistant. She'd been working in the field for almost ten years now. She loved her job and really didn't want to do anything else. Many of the nurses she worked with had encouraged her to go back to school to get her nursing degree, but honestly, she was happy with the level of responsibility she had now. She also got to spend more time with the patients and their families, to share in both their joys and sorrows.

Sarah tried to think back to the last boyfriend she'd had—and winced when she realized it had been years. Literally. Josh—no, John—had been the last, and that was . . . four years ago.

She shook her head. She wasn't really surprised, as her fathers had been killed around the time she'd broken up with John, and she'd had to deal with the cops, lawyers, and her grief. But still.

She'd lived in Parker, Colorado, since the day Jackson and Mike had taken her into their home. The suburb of Denver had been home almost her entire life, but she enjoyed working at the hospital in Castle Rock. It wasn't as crazy as the hospitals in Denver, and it only took her around twenty minutes to get to work. Castle Rock had grown on her. She liked the small-town feel.

But because she hadn't grown up in Castle Rock, she didn't know any of the small-town gossip.

One day at work, Sarah told one of the nurses about Owen, and she suggested Sarah contact Ace Security. She'd gone on and on about how the brothers who owned it, triplets, had grown up in the area before moving away after graduation. The nurse had also been more than happy to tell Sarah how the boys' mother had murdered their father, and about the trouble each of their girlfriends had run into.

She'd even good-naturedly complained about losing her chance to hook up with one of the infamous brothers for good, after a half brother showed up and immediately became infatuated with a woman who was being stalked.

Sarah realized that Cole's partner must be the woman who had married the last Anderson brother.

Thinking about Cole again made her blush inexplicably. He wasn't the kind of man she was usually drawn to. He was a lot taller than she was, and his eyes seemed to bore right into her as she spoke. So many times, men either looked over or through her, as if she wasn't important enough for their time and attention. But not Cole. She'd had his *entire* attention, and she had known he was listening to her. The air of intensity surrounding him was a surprise. His tattoos also made him look badass, but he'd definitely treated her with care.

And before meeting him, she'd figured he'd be in shape since he ran a gym . . . but she hadn't really understood what *in shape* meant.

Cole's biceps were almost too big for the T-shirt he'd been wearing. In fact, she'd never seen such large muscles on anyone before. The plethora of tattoos accentuated that strength. His thighs were even more muscular; she could see that he definitely filled out the sweatpants he was wearing.

But what really surprised her was how she'd felt while standing next to him. She probably should've felt uneasy. He could easily squash her like a bug; she wasn't exactly in shape herself. But instead of being scared of his obvious strength, she'd felt safe.

No one would dare mess with her when Cole was by her side.

It was an uncomfortable thought.

Sarah had taken care of herself for much of her thirty years of life. She'd never thought about being with someone simply because of what they could do for her. But the second her eyes met Cole's, it was as if everything inside her had just sort of . . . melted.

It was disconcerting.

And the reason why she hadn't hesitated to go back into the gym with him.

With anyone else, she knew she would've firmly but politely told him she'd changed her mind and then gone on her way. But there was something about Cole that made her want to let him fight all her battles for her.

Which was stupid.

And dangerous.

The only one who could keep her safe was herself.

Relying on someone else would only end badly.

Then her thoughts turned back to Owen, as they had way too often recently, and she wondered what he might've left her this time.

It was big.

Shit. What if he'd decided to get her a puppy? He'd hinted in his letters that he could see the two of them getting married and living happily ever after with a bunch of kids and dogs.

He wouldn't.

Would he?

Sarah had no idea if Owen realized he was terrorizing her. She guessed he didn't.

Knowing she wouldn't be able to sleep until she'd at least checked to make sure there wasn't anything alive in the box he'd left for her, Sarah threw back the covers and grabbed her cell phone, just in case. She headed back down the stairs, making sure to turn on every light she passed.

No way was she going to lurk about her house in the dark. She wasn't crazy.

She grabbed a pair of scissors on her way to the front foyer. Her eyes landed on the box, and she took a deep breath.

Moving slowly, she carefully slid the scissors along the tape holding the box shut. She peeled back the flaps—and stared down at the contents in confusion.

Reaching inside, she lifted the surprisingly heavy object and put it on the floor next to the box. She didn't worry about fingerprints or anything like that. She knew who'd sent the gift and whose fingerprints would be on it.

Sarah stared at the homemade wooden dollhouse for a long moment.

It was incredibly detailed and probably expensive. It was obviously custom made. She sat on the floor in the middle of the foyer and stared at it in consternation.

One side of the house was missing, allowing her to see inside and play with the dolls if she wanted to. There were three rooms: one large open space on the first floor, and two smaller rooms on the second. A female doll was propped up in the kitchen in front of the stove, and a male doll was sitting on the couch nearby, facing a television.

The walls of the house looked like logs, and the roof was thatched. There wasn't any detail that had been overlooked, from the tiny dishes in the sink to the rugs on the floor and the pictures on the walls. The furniture was made of wood and painted by someone who was obviously very patient and detail oriented. A miniature bed was neatly placed in one room upstairs, and a desk and computer were sitting in the second room, obviously an office.

Sarah's mind raced. It was an unusual gift . . . and it made her extremely uneasy. It wasn't outwardly threatening, and it matched the love notes Owen had sent her, the ones in which he'd talked about them getting married and living happily ever after.

A draft of cold air seemed to come out of nowhere. Goose bumps broke out on Sarah's arms, and the hair at the back of her neck stood up. Grabbing her phone, she clicked a couple of pictures of the house. The cops weren't exactly interested in her case, but maybe if Cole's friends decided to help her, they'd want to see this.

Sarah quickly picked up the dollhouse and packed it back into the box. She'd take it to the hospital tomorrow and donate it to the children's ward. She certainly didn't want it.

Deciding to leave all the lights on, Sarah practically ran back upstairs to her room. She closed and locked her door before climbing back into bed. Placing her phone on the small nightstand, she lay on her side and stared at it for a long moment.

She literally had no one to call. She had a lot of acquaintances at work, but they were "work friends." Not the kind of people she'd call when she was scared or just wanted to chat. Her dads were dead. She didn't have any siblings.

For the first time in ages, Sarah felt completely alone. She'd been an orphan for a while now, but tonight, she really felt like one.

If she up and disappeared tomorrow, would anyone notice . . . besides Owen? She had a feeling he was the only one who would care.

Closing her eyes to try to stop the tears, Sarah realized it was no use. Crying silently, she finally fell into a restless sleep.

Chapter Three

"Hey, Cole! How'd the week go?"

Cole looked up from the desk and mock-scowled at his friend and co-owner of Rock Hard Gym. "You are never allowed to leave again."

Felicity chuckled. "That bad, huh?"

Cole sighed and studied Felicity. She looked good. Of course, he'd always thought she looked good, but seeing her relaxed and happy underscored just how stressed she'd been the entire five years he'd known her. Marrying Ryder Sinclair definitely agreed with her . . . as did not having to be on the lookout for the crazy asshole who'd stalked her for so long. "It was just a crazy week. How was Chicago?"

Felicity smiled sadly. "Difficult, but good. It was hard seeing my mom's grave, but it was also cathartic. I didn't have to hide in the shadows this time."

"That's a relief." Cole stood up, walked over to Felicity, and took her in his arms. As he was hugging her, he realized that she was about the same size as Sarah.

The thought didn't really surprise him. For days, his mind had wandered back to the intriguing and stoic woman he'd met the week before.

Felicity pulled back and glanced at Cole. "What?"

"What, what?" he returned.

"Something happened while I was gone, didn't it?"

"Lots of things happened," Cole said.

Felicity's eyes narrowed, and she stepped back and put her hands on her hips. "Don't mess with me, Cole. You look . . . *weird*. What happened?"

"Gee, thanks," Cole quipped.

"I'm not messing around," Felicity said, her voice dropping. "You look . . . super serious. And you're not usually serious. Unless you're trying to convince me not to leave town." She smiled to let him know she was joking, then said, "What's up?"

Cole sighed. "I met someone. A girl."

Felicity's eyebrows went up as she gasped and put a hand on her chest. "A real live girl? Be still my heart!"

"Shut up," Cole told her, slugging her lightly on the arm. "I'm pretty sure she's in trouble."

All humor left Felicity's face. "What's wrong? Should I call Ryder?"

Cole shook his head. "No need. I've got a meeting already arranged with everyone at Ace Security."

"Really?"

"Yeah."

"She must be in a world of hurt if you called in everyone."

"That's just it. I'm not exactly sure what her situation is. I've only met her once, but she told me enough to make the hairs on the back of my neck stand up."

"Who is she?"

"Her name is Sarah Butler."

"And?"

"And nothing. That's about all I know. She's supposed to start self-defense lessons with me today."

"You have to know more than that," Felicity complained.

"I know she doesn't feel safe. That she has an admirer who's making her uncomfortable. The cops don't feel he's a threat, but she does."

Felicity frowned. "The cops don't believe her?"

Cole shook his head. "To be fair, there's not a lot of evidence point-ing to the fact that he's dangerous."

"That's bullshit," Felicity fumed.

"They can't investigate every time a single woman receives a love letter and she doesn't return the person's admiration."

Felicity studied Cole. "I can't tell where you stand on this. Your tone says you think she might be acting too cautiously, but the fact that you have a meeting with Ryder and the others says differently."

"She's scared to death," Cole said, reasoning out loud what he'd been thinking since meeting Sarah. "On the surface, I have to agree with the cops." He held up his hand to stop the protest he knew Felicity was about to make. "But I haven't seen the letters or the gifts she says she's received. I saw firsthand how freaked she was. And I doubt she would've reached out to Ace Security for help if this wasn't serious."

"If she already called the guys, how did you get involved, and why are *you* asking to meet with them about her?"

"Logan referred her to me for self-defense."

"He didn't take her case?"

"I think it was a matter of money. She found out how much it would cost to hire them and backed off. You know how he is, he wouldn't let her just do nothing. So he referred her to me."

"And now you're referring her back to *them*," Felicity concluded.

"This isn't a usual case, I don't think. I'm meeting with Sarah this evening, and I'm going to try to get more information on the guy who thinks he's in love with her. Try to convince her to talk with Logan and the others. If nothing else, they can look into the buttmunch and let her know what they think about how dangerous he might be."

"If you're already giving this guy one of your trademark fucked-up nicknames, then I know where you stand on the issue," she said with a grin.

"Something about this case makes me extremely nervous. And you didn't see Sarah. She didn't want to meet me too long after she got off work because it would be dark. And she was gripping this cat-shaped brass-knuckles thing as if it were all that was standing between her and certain death. And I *really* want to call this guy an asshole and ten other swear words, but I'm trying to cut down on my swearing so Grace's babies don't say *fuck* or *shit* as their first words. I'm getting creative."

Felicity didn't say anything for a moment, then finally nodded. "You're a good guy, Cole."

"Uh . . . thanks?" he said, his brow furrowed.

"I mean it. You've never hesitated to wade in when shit gets crazy. Look at *my* situation. If anything, I think your heart is too big sometimes. You always want to help everyone."

"Is that bad?"

"No," she said immediately. "I just worry about you. I hope this woman appreciates you and doesn't take advantage of your generous heart."

Cole smiled at Felicity. They'd met five years ago when they'd literally bounced off each other while running in the park. They'd clicked immediately. Neither had ever felt anything romantic toward the other, but they'd decided to go into business together. It had been the best decision he'd ever made.

"Thanks. But I'm not sure you should call that preacher who married you and Ryder and Blake and Alexis just yet. I don't even know Sarah."

"But you like her," Felicity insisted.

Cole opened his mouth to deny it, but knew he couldn't. "Maybe. There's just something about her."

"Be careful," Felicity warned. "If she has a stalker, someone who thinks she should be his, you could be in danger if he thinks you guys are dating. The last thing I want is for *you* to get caught in the middle of her situation. Believe me, I know better than anyone how horrible it is for someone I love to be in danger because of my shit."

"It wasn't your shit," Cole told her. "It was Joseph Waters who kidnapped Grace's baby."

"Because he was trying to get to me," Felicity said softly.

Cole stepped toward Felicity and took her head in his hands, forcing her to look up at him. "It. Wasn't. Your. Fault."

She hesitated, but finally nodded.

"And I'll be careful," Cole continued after dropping his hands and stepping back. "Besides, this might be nothing more than an admirer taking things too far, and once he realizes that Sarah really doesn't return his affections, he'll back off."

"I hope so, for both your sakes."

"Me too."

"So . . . do I get to meet her?" Felicity asked with a grin.

Cole rolled his eyes. "That depends."

"On?"

"If you're going to behave or not."

She laughed. "I'll be good. Promise. Can I at least call Grace and tell her the scoop?"

"What scoop?"

"That you met a girl, and we should start planning your wedding for next year sometime."

Cole reached for Felicity, but she leaped out of his way, laughing.

"Kidding!" she called out as she disappeared through his office door. "Sort of. See you after my aerobics class!"

Still chuckling, Cole went back to his desk and sat. As usual, there were papers everywhere. He glanced around his office and mentally winced. The shelf along one wall was stuffed with books, and the love seat against the other wall still had a bunch of crap on it. He really needed to clean his space. It was never high on his list of things to worry about . . . but ever since Sarah had been there the week before, he'd become more and more aware of what a pigsty his office was.

Deciding that there was no time like the present to do what he could to make it look nicer, Cole stood once more.

He wasn't going to admit that he was cleaning because Sarah was supposed to come to their first lesson tonight. Nope, that wasn't why he was suddenly going out of his way to organize things. Not at all.

~

Sarah walked quickly down the sidewalk to the gym. She couldn't decide if she was walking so fast because she was nervous to be out in the open, or because of the man who was waiting for her at Rock Hard Gym.

She'd spent the last week chastising herself for thinking about Cole so much. But that hadn't stopped her from looking him up on the internet. She couldn't find much about him, because there seemed to be thousands of men named Cole Johnson, but when she'd paired his name with the name of the gym, she was able to pull up some general information.

He and Felicity Jones, now Sinclair, had opened Rock Hard Gym five or so years ago. They were known for throwing "black light" parties, where people would come dressed in white and spend the evening dancing and socializing, their clothes glowing under ultraviolet lights.

She found out he was thirty-one, only a year older than she was. He had a brother who lived in Washington State, and his parents lived in Arizona. That was all she'd been able to discover. Of course, digging for information about Cole led her to reading about his friend Felicity and her husband, Ryder, and the drama that had taken place in the not-so-distant past. That led her down a rabbit hole, and she'd spent way too much time reading about all the Anderson brothers and their wives.

To say she was intimidated was an understatement.

Her situation wasn't anything like what those women had been through. She should've probably called Cole and apologized and told him she had changed her mind and didn't need self-defense lessons, after all.

But she didn't.

He was so out of her league. He owned his own business and had a ton of good friends, and she was . . . just Sarah. Nobody special. An orphan with no close friends.

Besides, he probably thought she was overreacting anyway, just like the cops and most of her coworkers.

Earlier that day, Justine, one of Sarah's coworkers, had told her she should milk Owen's infatuation for all it was worth—insinuating she should use him to get more expensive gifts. But even if she weren't creeped out by his attention, that wasn't her. She didn't need "stuff" from someone she cared about; she just needed their love and affection.

Shaking her head, Sarah took a deep breath and opened the door to the gym—

And almost got run over by a man coming out.

He muttered, "Excuse me," under his breath and pushed past her without a backward glance.

"It's okay," Sarah said, even though she knew the man wouldn't hear her, since he was already halfway down the block.

She entered the gym, heading for the front counter, but stopped.

Standing behind the desk was none other than Felicity Sinclair herself. Sarah recognized her from the internet searches she'd done. She had short blonde hair and was wearing a tank top that showed off the multitude of tattoos on her arms. She wore a huge grin on her face as Sarah resumed her approach.

"You must be Sarah," she said, still smiling.

"Uh . . . I am. How'd you know?"

"Just a guess. Cole's waiting for you." Felicity eyed the medical scrubs she was wearing. "Did you bring something to change into?"

Sarah panicked. She'd thought she could wear the scrubs because they were loose and comfortable. Was she supposed to have brought something else? "No. Should I have?" she asked. "I can come back another day." In fact, that sounded awesome. Maybe this wasn't such a good idea, after all.

As if she could hear Sarah's inner thoughts, Felicity came around the counter and put her hand on Sarah's arm. "What you've got on is fine. Heck, you should probably come to one of the lessons wearing heels and an LBD."

"LBD?" Sarah asked.

"Little black dress. I mean, this *is* self-defense, and you won't be wearing comfortable clothes like those at every moment. You have to be ready to defend yourself no matter what you're wearing."

Sarah wanted to tell her that she pretty much wore the scrubs all the time, and that she didn't even own an LBD, but she simply nodded. Felicity was already steering her down the hall, so her escape window had closed. The other woman continued to chat about nothing in particular as she led her to where Sarah assumed Cole was waiting.

"Have fun," Felicity told her as she opened a door.

Sarah smiled at her and said, "Thanks." She walked through the door—

And froze in her tracks as she stared.

The room wasn't overly large, though it was obviously used as an aerobics room or some other sort of group-workout space. There was a mirror covering the far wall, making the room look bigger than it was. There were mats on the wooden floor . . . but it was Cole who'd immediately caught her attention.

He hadn't seen her enter and was currently doing pull-ups on a bar to her right. His back was mostly toward her, so she could stare to her heart's content.

His tattooed biceps bulged as he pulled himself up, then lowered himself down. He had on a pair of black shorts, a white tank top, and athletic socks and shoes. His body gleamed with a sheen of sweat.

He was literally a walking wet dream—and Sarah swallowed hard. She wasn't sure she could do this. The idea of learning how to protect herself, just in case, was one thing; the reality of having to get up close and personal with Cole as he trained her was something else altogether.

She could admit it.

She was officially intimidated.

Sarah turned to leave, but the movement in the mirror must've caught Cole's attention, because he dropped to the floor and turned.

"Sarah," he said with a smile as he approached.

She smiled awkwardly at him. There was no doubt Cole was handsome, but when he turned that thousand-watt smile her way, he was devastating.

"Hi," she said somewhat lamely.

"Hi," he returned. "It's good to see you."

"Uh . . . you too."

"How was work?"

"Fine. It was work."

He'd gotten close enough now to touch. He reached out a hand, and Sarah automatically raised hers to shake. His warm fingers closed around hers—and shockingly, she wondered what he'd do if she leaned in and ran her tongue up the side of his neck.

Chastising herself for the bizarre thought, Sarah tried to concentrate on what Cole was saying, and not on how delicious he looked in his workout clothes, or whether or not he had tattoos . . . everywhere.

God, this wasn't her. She wasn't like this!

Why Cole was affecting her this way, she had no idea. But she had to get herself together.

It seemed as if Cole held on to her hand longer than was appropriate, but she could have been imagining things. He dropped her hand before she could wonder too much about it, and said, "What exactly do you do?"

"I'm a CNA. Certified nursing assistant. I help patients with just about anything and everything. Repositioning them, taking blood pressure and temperature, answering their calls, explaining medical stuff that they don't understand, feeding them, cleaning the rooms and bed linens, assisting with medical procedures, dressing wounds . . . to name just a few things."

Cole nodded to her outfit. "That explains the scrubs."

Sarah shrugged. "Yeah."

"Do you like it?"

She furrowed her brows. "Do I like it?"

"Your job."

She nodded.

"You don't want to move up and become a nurse? Or a doctor?"

She appreciated the fact that he'd tacked on *doctor* to the end of his question. Most people thought of doctors as male, when that was just stupid. There were plenty of female doctors. She shook her head. "No. I like talking with people. I like spending time with them, getting to know them. Especially the ones who don't have much family visiting. So many people are lonely, and I'd like to think I make a difference in their lives in my own way."

"Nurses and doctors don't spend time with their patients?"

"They do." Sarah tried to explain. "But it's not the same. They're concentrating on symptoms and treatments. I have a bit more time to get to know the patients personally. Many times they'll tell me something they forgot to mention to the nurse or doctor, or I'm able to figure out if they're lying about how much pain they're in or if something just isn't right with them."

Sarah noted the way Cole was focused on her as she spoke. He wasn't looking around, giving her half his attention, and didn't seem to be asking questions simply to be polite. She could tell he was actually interested in what she was saying.

"But you could make more money if you were an RN, right?" he asked.

"Of course. But it's not about the money. I make plenty to live on, and that's good enough for me. I've never had aspirations to be a millionaire or anything. I just want to live a decent life, maybe go out to eat every once in a while, and just be happy. Besides, the life-insurance payments from my dads have left me comfortable enough."

The second the words were out of her mouth, Sarah wanted to call them back.

She was nervous, and talking without thinking first. Having two fathers wasn't exactly the norm, and the fact that she was spouting off personal stuff like her financial situation with a stranger wasn't smart.

But instead of immediately commenting, Cole put his hand on her purse strap that was hanging off one shoulder. "May I?" he asked.

Sarah nodded and watched as he took her purse and hung it up on a peg by the door. Then he gestured to the mats in the middle of the room. "Shall we sit while we talk? I know the floor isn't exactly the most comfortable seat in the world, but . . ."

"Of course," Sarah told him immediately. "The floor is fine." She followed him a few steps, trying really hard not to stare at his ass as they walked, and sat cross-legged on a mat across from him.

He mimicked her movements and leaned forward, resting his elbows on his knees. Every bit of nonverbal body language indicated he was completely invested in their conversation. She liked that.

"So . . . your dads?"

Sarah sighed. "I was adopted when I was six by Mike and Jackson. They taught me what it meant to have a loving family." She smiled slightly. "I aspire to have a relationship like they had one day."

"They passed?" Cole asked gently.

"Remember that nightclub bombing in Denver about four years ago?" Sarah asked.

Cole nodded, then his eyebrows shot up. "No! Shit."

"Yeah. They almost never went out, but that night was their anniversary, so they decided to celebrate. They were simply trying to enjoy themselves when that guy decided to show his disapproval for the gay lifestyle and bombed the club. Mike and Jackson were two of the ten casualties."

"I'm so sorry," Cole said gently, reaching for her hand.

Sarah fought tears. She hadn't cried about her dads' deaths in a long time. "Yeah. It sucked. Since their families weren't accepting of who they were, I inherited everything. The house is paid off, so I don't have a mortgage, and the rest of the money allows me to keep doing what I love without having to worry."

"It sounds like they loved you very much. And I can hear in your voice how much you loved *them*."

"They literally saved my life. It wasn't easy for them . . . two gay men adopting a little girl wasn't exactly normal twenty-plus years ago, but they never, not once, made me feel as if I was a burden. Though . . . there were times I still felt like the outsider, even with them. I mean, they were definitely a tight unit. Because of their sexual orientation, it felt like them against the world sometimes. Maybe it's a foster thing. They loved me, and I them, but there were times I couldn't help feeling as if I were intruding on their lives somehow."

Cole squeezed her hand. He didn't let go, and Sarah wasn't in any hurry to pull away. She had no idea why she was sharing such intimate thoughts, but something about the small connection of their hands made her feel safe enough to keep talking.

"I was scared to death of women when they first adopted me. I'd been in two previous foster homes where I was locked in closets during the day for being too loud. The women would smack me around and treat me like shit . . . at least until their husbands came home. Then they were as sweet as could be. So I was perfectly happy going to live with Mike and Jackson. I *liked* the fact they weren't married to women."

"That had to be scary for you," Cole said.

"It was. But from the second I met my dads, I felt comfortable with them. I never missed having a mother, because my dads did everything in their power to make my life happy. Mike was the one who went dress shopping with me, and took me to the spa to get pedicures. Jackson was a more typical dad, who loved to threaten my dates with a look. They were both so proud of me when I got my CNA degree." She grinned. "They were also the ones who taught me to always be nice."

Sarah knew she was talking way too much, but couldn't make herself stop. It had been a long time since she'd been able to reminisce about her dads with someone. Often people just looked uncomfortable when she brought up the fact that she'd been adopted by a gay couple, but she didn't see any judgment in Cole's gaze. Only interest.

"Yeah?" he said, encouraging her to continue.

"Yeah. Mike always said that it was easy to be mean. To talk down about someone. To make fun of them. To be an asshole. That it showed a lack of couth and compassion. Being nice is a choice. One that's sometimes hard as hell. And if you think about it, being mean often exacerbates a situation. It puts someone else on guard, and everything can escalate in a heartbeat. But simply saying *I'm sorry* or *My mistake* can calm everything down."

"That's true," Cole said.

His thumb was now brushing back and forth over the back of Sarah's hand, and she forced herself to continue talking. Rather than throwing herself against him, knocking him to his back, and kissing the hell out of him.

"I've seen firsthand how much a smile can mean to someone who's having a bad day. Or taking the time to help someone put their groceries in their car at the store. Or paying for someone's coffee or meal at a restaurant. Or just sitting down and listening to someone talk. Being nice doesn't have to cost money, and I think the fact that people are so surprised by nice gestures says a lot about society today. How messed up it is. Everyone is concerned about themselves and less about how others feel. So when I do something simple, like offer to hold someone's baby in the waiting room while they fill out the required forms, and they cry when they thank me, it's almost sad. Does that make sense?"

"Totally. And you learned this from your dads?"

"Yeah. They were always the first ones to offer to babysit for free, or to donate food and clothes to a family who lost everything in a fire, or to simply hold someone's hand when they were having a bad day. Some of my best moments at work have been when I simply sat by someone's hospital bed and held their hand while we watched television. I think that human connection is missing in today's world. We're all so busy posting shit on social media and trying to show everyone how perfect our lives are, or binge-watching shows on television, or trying to one-up our neighbors, that we forget what it's like to do something for someone else with no expectation of getting anything in return."

Falling silent, Sarah mentally winced. She'd been going on and on and probably sounded like the biggest goody two-shoes ever. But she'd been honest. It was way easier to be nice than to be a bitch.

She raised her eyes to Cole's and waited for him to say something. Anything.

He stared at her for a long moment . . . until she actually began to get nervous. She tugged at her hand, but he tightened his hold and covered their clasped hands with his free one.

"You amaze me, Sarah."

She shook her head. "I'm just me. I'm nobody special."

"You're wrong. You're so much more. You could be bitter about everything that's happened to you, but somehow you aren't. Do you know how rare that is?"

Sarah could only stare into his green eyes and shake her head.

"It is."

"One of the doctors at work told me that she thought my positive attitude was annoying."

"Fuck her."

Sarah smothered a laugh. "You haven't been around me long enough to know if I'm annoying or not."

"I guarantee I won't ever think you're annoying," Cole said in a serious tone that made goose bumps rise on Sarah's arms. "I bet you've already forgiven that asshole who killed your dads, haven't you?"

Sarah dropped her gaze from his and stared at their clasped hands resting on his knee. She shrugged. "It's not his fault his parents raised him to be intolerant of those different from him."

"Look at me," Cole ordered.

She took a deep breath and raised her eyes back to his.

"Don't ever change. You're right, the world needs more people like you in it. I'm one of those assholes who always swears at people who drive too slow or fast. I get irritated in the grocery store when someone decides to pay with an actual check instead of a debit card. And I've never offered to help someone load groceries in their car, partly because I hadn't thought about it, but also because a man like me approaching a woman in a parking lot isn't a good idea. But I—"

"A man like you?" Sarah asked, interrupting him.

He grinned. "Yeah. Big. Tattoos. Beard. Some women would scream their heads off if I got close."

Sarah chuckled. "They might scream, but not for the reason you might think." The words just popped out, and her cheeks flamed as soon as they did.

Cole smiled, and if she had been standing, Sarah knew her knees would've gone weak at the sight. "Right. Anyway, that's the kind of man I am. I see danger behind every nook and cranny. I always believe people have the worst motives in mind. But that's good too."

He paused, and Sarah asked, "It is?"

"Yeah. Because there needs to be men like me in the world to protect women like you."

Sarah swore her heart was going to beat out of her chest at his words.

He went on. "I probably would've loved your dads, simply because they made you into the woman you are today. They protected you when you needed it the most and gave you the love you deserved. They provided for you after their death, allowing you to do what you enjoy without having to worry about money.

"I'd like to get to know you better, Sarah. Outside of your self-defense lessons. I want to watch you make other people's days brighter."

"Why?"

"What do you mean, why?" he asked.

"Just that. I mean, look at you . . . then look at me. I'd bet a hundred bucks I'm not the kind of woman you normally date. Do you ask out every woman you train? It just seems . . . fast."

He stared at her for a long moment, and when he frowned, she felt as if she'd somehow disappointed him.

"No, I don't ask out every woman I train. Not even close. It's been a long time since I've asked *anyone* out. And believe me, Sarah, I'm looking at you—and I like what I see. A lot. You've got an air of innocence about you that I find fascinating. You've had a tough life, but haven't let it harden you. I respect you, and I . . . I'd like to get to know you better."

She bit her lip and took a deep breath, but didn't immediately protest, so he went on. "I want to be someone who'll stand between you and the assholes of the world. I have a feeling simply being around you will make me a better person."

Sarah shook her head. "Don't do that. Don't put me on a pedestal. I'm not some paragon walking around sprinkling glitter throughout the world."

Cole laughed. Threw his head back and laughed as if she'd said the funniest thing he'd ever heard.

Sarah tugged on her hand again, somewhat offended, but he still refused to let go.

When he got himself under control, he said, "I know you're not perfect. You're too trusting. You see the good in everyone, even when there isn't any there. You probably neglect your own health in order to do something good for someone else."

"You make me sound like an idiot," Sarah grumbled, despite being secretly kind of flattered.

"You're not an idiot. You're refreshing. And I'm not. I've got more than my share of flaws that I'm sure you'll discover sooner rather than later. But as I said, if you let me get to know you, go out on a few dates with me, I'm hoping you'll find that you like me back . . . just a little."

Sarah frowned. "I already like you, Cole, but I don't understand you. You don't know anything about me. I could totally be lying to you right now, and you just bought my lies hook, line, and sinker."

He smiled again. "You're not lying."

"How do you know?"

"Because I'm an expert at reading body language. I've been around some bad people in my life, angel. You are who you say you are. What you see is what you get."

Sarah licked her lips nervously, and his gaze immediately followed the movement.

Cole persisted. "Say you'll go out with me, Sarah."

"I thought I was here to figure out how to defend myself."

"You are. And we'll get to that. Agreeing to go out with me in no way affects whether or not I'll teach you some basic moves that will allow you to get away from someone and get to safety."

"But if I say no, things could get weird."

"Then say yes," Cole cajoled. "I swear you've got nothing to fear from me. I'll even get references if that will make you feel safer."

"It's not that. I think I feel safer with you than anyone I've ever been around . . ." She hesitated.

"But?"

"I'm afraid once you get to know me, you'll decide I'm annoying. Too much work or something. I work odd hours, weird shifts. And I looked you up online. I know about your friend and what happened to her. And about the Andersons. The last thing I want is Owen getting upset when he sees us together—because he will—and taking out any anger on your friends. If anything happened to those beautiful babies because of me, I'd die."

"Breathe, angel. Take a breath. Nothing is going to happen to them. You think Logan would allow that to happen again?"

"You can't control people, Cole," Sarah pressed. "They're unpredictable."

"Fine. Then we'll meet with Logan, Blake, Nathan, and Ryder, and make sure they know everything about this Owen guy. We'll let them investigate and figure out what will make him back off. In the meantime, we'll hang out at my place. Or here. Or your house. We won't shove our relationship down Owen's throat. We'll be discreet. How's that sound?"

Sarah could only gape at him. "How'd we go from me wanting some tips on protecting myself to having Ace Security investigating Owen and you and me hanging out at each other's houses?"

He smiled at her again, but didn't answer her question.

She took a deep breath and gave him the only answer she could. "Okay."

He beamed. "Okay," he said quietly. Then he finally let go of her hand and stood, before immediately reaching the same hand down to her again. "Time for your first lesson."

Automatically, she reached up and let him help her off the floor. She wasn't sure what she was expecting. A kiss to seal the deal. A hug. A discussion about when and where their first date would be. But so far, Cole hadn't done anything the way she expected him to.

"First lesson for today will be how to get a guy to let go of your hand if he's been holding on too long and you're uncomfortable."

Sarah knew he was referring to her feeble attempts to pull her hand out of his, and blushed. But he was right, this was something she should know. It would come in handy at the hospital too, just in case one of the patients or family members got a little too familiar, as they'd done in the past.

Concentrating on his instruction, she did her best to put her nerves about dating Cole behind her.

Chapter Four

At the end of their first lesson, Cole walked Sarah to her car. The chemistry between them during the lesson was powerful, but he'd done his best to keep things businesslike while he was teaching her the best way to get out of some easy holds. In upcoming sessions, he'd teach her how to hurt someone who was trying to prevent her from escaping.

"How do you feel about what you learned tonight?" he asked when they got to her car door.

"Pretty good. But it's just nerve-racking to think about having to use anything you taught me."

"We'll keep practicing. The more you do it, the easier it'll become. Soon it'll be second nature, and you'll simply react."

She nodded. "I appreciate you helping me."

"When are you free next?"

"For my next lesson?" she asked.

"That too."

She stared at him. "Seriously?"

"Yeah. I'd like to make you dinner one night after you get off work. I want to hear all about your shift and the interesting people you met that day."

"I can't talk about most of the stuff I do. Privacy laws and all that," she told him.

Cole grinned. "I know, angel. I was talking more about the people in general and not what ails them."

"Oh."

"And I want to arrange a time for you to come to Ace Security and sit down with the Anderson brothers too." Hiding a grin at the way she wrinkled her nose, he continued. "I know, it sucks, but the more information Logan and the others have, the more they can find out about Owen. If he's in any way a threat, they'll find out and do what they can to shut it down. You want that, right?"

"Oh yes," she breathed. "I can't imagine not having to worry about picking up my mail, wondering what he's said in a letter today. Or finding some 'gift' he's left for me. But I already contacted them. They said they were fully booked. That, and I hadn't realized exactly how expensive they'd be to hire."

"Hmm. It doesn't matter, angel. When they hear your story, I know they'll want to help."

"I don't want them to skimp on someone else's case if they take mine," she protested.

Cole shook his head. "They won't. I promise."

Sarah sighed. "Okay. If you think it's necessary. Maybe they can find something that I can use to make him back off and forget about me."

Cole wanted to say that he doubted Owen would back off. The man obviously knew Sarah was as good of a person as he was ever going to find and wanted her for himself.

Not that Cole was any different. From the second he'd met her, something about Sarah had struck a chord inside him. And now that he knew her a little better and felt their intense chemistry? Yeah, he definitely wanted to see where things could go between them. "We also need to figure out when's a good time for your next lesson."

"Sounds as if you're going to be filling up my social calendar," Sarah quipped.

"Damn straight," Cole told her with a straight face.

"I have the next two days off, then I have three twelve-hour days again. Then I get another three days off before restarting my shifts. Eventually I'll be moved to night shift, though. Then it's harder for me to do anything, because all I want to do during the day is sleep."

"We'll figure it out," Cole said confidently, not able to keep the thought of her sleeping her days away in his bed out of his mind. It was crazy how attracted he was to Sarah after mere hours. But everything he learned about her just intrigued him more.

"I didn't ask . . . and I feel horrible, now that I think about it. But is owning the gym all you do?"

Cole grinned. "Yeah, angel. It's definitely a full-time gig. But I'm happy to tell you anything you want to know about me and my life when you come over for dinner." He felt ten feet tall when she nodded.

"I'll call Logan first thing in the morning and see if he and the others have time in their schedule soon to meet with us about your situation. We'll get that out of the way first. Sound okay?"

Sarah took a big breath and let it out in a whoosh. "Yeah. But I have to get some stuff done at home first."

"What stuff?"

She shrugged. "Mow the lawn, for one. And my neighbor's too."

"They can't mow their own?"

Sarah shook her head. "No. Mrs. Grady is in her eighties, but doesn't want to move out of the house because her husband died last year and she misses him something awful. Her kids don't visit very much, and she needs help with the upkeep of her house."

"Something tells me you do more than just help in the yard," Cole said dryly.

Sarah blushed. "I like her. It's no hardship to hang out with her and let her talk while I tidy her house once a week."

Yup. Sarah Butler was an amazing person. "How about this? I'll come over tomorrow and mow both yours and Mrs. Grady's yard. I'll see if the guys can meet with us the day after that."

She gaped at him. "But you have to work."

"I have time for both the gym and you," Cole told her. "Besides, Felicity owes me for taking a week off. What do you say?"

"I . . . I wasn't fishing for you to come help me, Cole," Sarah said, flustered.

"I know. That's why I *want* to do it."

"Okay. Then thank you."

"You're welcome. If you give me your number, I'll give you a call or text when I'm on my way tomorrow."

She agreed, and they exchanged numbers. "Oh, you'll need my address, I suppose. I live in Parker, though. You probably don't want to come all the way out there just to mow a yard."

Cole was surprised. "I didn't know you lived out there," he said with a slight frown. He didn't like to think of her on the roads driving back and forth, especially in the winter, when the snow and ice made driving dangerous.

She nodded. "Yeah, that's where my dads' house is."

He wanted to keep her talking. He'd never been much of a conversationalist, but found he could listen to her talk all day.

It would have to wait, he decided; they'd been standing in the parking lot long enough. With Owen out there somewhere, maybe or maybe not watching her, it wasn't smart or safe. "It's no problem. I'll be in touch. Drive safe going home, okay?"

She got a soft look on her face.

"What? What'd I say?"

"Jackson always used to say that to me."

"Text me when you get home," Cole replied.

She looked up at him in surprise. "Really?"

"Yeah. I want to know you got home all right. Humor me?"

"Fine. But you know I've been driving for almost fifteen years now, right?"

"I do, but that doesn't mean there aren't other crazy people on the roads who haven't been driving for that long, or have been drinking, or are just bad drivers."

"Point made," she said. "Cole?"

"Yeah, angel?"

"Thanks. For everything. The lesson. For talking to Ace Security on my behalf. For offering to mow my yard for me. Just . . . all of it."

"You're more than welcome. I'll see you tomorrow."

"Bye."

Cole took a step back and watched as she climbed into her gray Mitsubishi Galant and waved before she headed out of the lot. He noticed that she waved a couple across the walkway in front of her, and let three cars go by before finally pulling out herself.

He chuckled to himself, then turned to head back to the gym. Sarah was refreshing. Comparatively, he was a selfish bastard who did what he wanted, when he wanted. And while he should maybe feel bad about hitting on her so soon, for wanting Sarah for his own, he didn't. They'd go together perfectly. He could protect her from the assholes in the world, and she could do her thing and spread kindness and joy wherever she went.

It felt kind of like they were made for each other. She needed someone to make sure no one took advantage of her kind soul, and he needed her to balance out his rough edges.

Cole had no idea if a relationship between them could last, but he wanted to try. He wanted a taste of the beauty he saw shining out through her eyes. Needed it. After the last couple of years, and the shit his friends had been through, he needed Sarah like he needed to breathe.

He had no doubt Logan would look into Owen Montrone. If there was any dirt to find, Alexis or one of the others would find it. Then Blake could pay a visit to Owen and let him know in no uncertain terms that he was to move on.

Cole wasn't a bodyguard. He didn't have any interest in getting into the security business, but when it came to Sarah, he wouldn't mind keeping close tabs on her. Very close tabs.

Smiling, he reentered the gym and headed for his office. Knowing he'd be seeing Sarah again the next day somehow made everything seem brighter. He didn't even care about the mess his office was in.

∼

Sarah pulled the curtain back a fraction and peeked out at Cole. He'd taken his shirt off and was currently finishing up mowing her front yard. He'd arrived around ten that morning and had immediately started on Mrs. Grady's lawn. It had taken him half the time it usually took her, which was irritating only because it gave her less time to admire him as he worked.

Sweat glistened on his chest, and her question about whether he had tattoos on the rest of his body had been answered when he'd whipped off his T-shirt and tied it to the handle of the lawn mower. She couldn't make out what the ink on his chest and shoulders was, but it didn't matter. His back was a blank slate, and she had a feeling he'd eventually cover that with ink too. He was too beautiful to be real.

But he *was* real. And he was here doing her a favor. All six feet three inches of him.

Knowing she was gawking, Sarah forced herself to drop the curtain and go back to what she'd been doing, namely cleaning. It was past time, and since she didn't think she had the brainpower to do anything more taxing than dust and pick up the odds and ends that had accumulated over the past month, that was what she was doing.

After she'd picked up the living room and made two trips upstairs with extra pairs of shoes, a pair of socks, a few things she'd ordered through the internet, and even a pair of sweatpants, she wandered into the kitchen. She wasn't much of a cook, but she was a hell of a baker.

Deciding that Cole would be hungry when he finished the yard, she got to work preparing a loaf of banana bread. She put it in the oven and had just started chopping some vegetables for an omelet when there was a quiet knock on the door.

Rushing to answer it, Sarah opened the door—

And simply stood there staring at Cole for a long moment.

A bead of liquid slid down his temple. Licking her lips, she imagined stepping into him and running her hands up his chiseled stomach and chest and tangling her fingers in the hair at his nape and crushing her mouth to his. She'd never kissed anyone with a mustache or beard before, and she imagined it would feel absolutely amazing against her skin.

Lost in her fantasy, she startled when he cleared his throat and smiled down at her. "I'm done," he said needlessly. "I put your lawn mower back in the garage. You should get it serviced, though. I wasn't sure it was going to last through both yards."

Blinking, Sarah forced herself to pay attention and stop gawking at the man. "Yeah, I know. It's on my list."

"Your list?"

"Yeah," she said, stepping back to give him room to enter the house. "The list of things I should do but never have the energy for on my days off."

"What else is on the list?" Cole asked.

Sarah shook her head. "I'm not telling you."

"What? Why?"

"Because. You'll probably decide it's your duty as a guy to check off all my crap jobs."

He chuckled. "I'll find out sooner or later."

She rolled her eyes. "Want to stay for brunch?"

"Yes."

His answer was immediate and without hesitation.

It had been a long time since Sarah had felt the tingles of antici-pation about spending time with a man. She hadn't been on a date in forever and had forgotten how awesome the light, bubbly feeling inside was when someone she liked seemed to like her back.

And there was no doubt that Cole Johnson liked her back. He wasn't playing games. He'd studied her from head to toe when he'd arrived before telling her how pretty she looked. Sarah would've blown him off, but she'd taken extra time with her appearance before he'd arrived.

"You didn't even ask what I was making," she teased.

"It doesn't matter. You could pour us a bowl of Frosted Flakes, and I'd still think it was the best brunch ever, simply because I got to spend time with you."

It was a cheesy line, but Sarah stupidly blushed anyway. "Well, good news, it's not cereal. I've got a loaf of banana bread in the oven, and I'm chopping up veggies for an omelet?" It came out more of a question than a statement.

"An omelet sounds delicious. Point me to a bathroom so I can clean up, and I'll help."

Sarah pointed down a hallway. "Second door on the left. But you don't have to help, you've done more than enough for one day."

Cole walked right up to her, and Sarah took a step back, only to find herself against the wall in the hallway. He didn't touch her in any way, but if Sarah took a deep breath, her breasts would brush his naked chest. She felt her nipples tighten in anticipation, but didn't dare look down to see if he could see them through her shirt.

Putting his hands on the wall on either side of her head, Cole leaned in even closer.

She could smell the scent of sweat, but surprisingly, he didn't stink. He smelled more . . . manly. Not that she really knew that much about what men smelled like, but she again had to resist the urge to throw herself into his arms.

"Mowing your grass is nothing, angel."

"And Mrs. Grady's too," she whispered.

He grinned. "Mowing both your grass and your neighbor's is nothing, angel," he sort of repeated. "I might be an asshole, but I'll never be the kind of man to sit on my ass with my feet up while my woman slaves over a stove for me."

"Throwing together an omelet isn't slaving over a stove," she protested. She didn't know why she was arguing the point. She *liked* what he said.

The smile stayed put on his face. "Find something that I can do to help. Otherwise, I'll take over and force *you* to sit."

"Okay."

"Okay."

Sarah stared up at him as he brought his hand toward her face. Using only his pinky, he brushed the stubborn curl that refused to stay out of her eyes off her forehead. Then he straightened and headed for the bathroom.

Staring at the way the discarded shirt tucked into the back waistband of his jeans twitched as he walked, it took a moment for Sarah to shake her head and walk toward the kitchen once more. A girl could definitely get used to being spoiled by Cole.

He might call himself an asshole, but he'd shown her nothing but kindness. She had no doubt he *could* be an ass; heck, that first time she'd met him, she'd sat outside his office and heard the way he'd complained and bitched about having to meet with her. But he'd been tired and overworked, so she understood.

Thirty minutes later, she sat at her small table as Cole brought their plates over. He'd put his shirt back on, and she'd almost pouted when he'd come out of the bathroom. He'd insisted on taking charge of the skillet even though she'd told him she was good. So she'd busied herself with taking the bread out of the oven and slicing it. She'd gotten them both drinks before he'd put his hands on her shoulders and turned her. He'd pointed to the table and ordered, "Sit."

Deciding to enjoy being waited on while she could, Sarah sat.

After they'd both taken a bite of the delicious, perfectly cooked omelet, she asked, "How did you become half owner of a gym?"

As they ate, he told Sarah his story. "I grew up in Castle Rock. Went to high school with the Andersons, actually. I wasn't part of the popular crowd, but I wasn't on the outskirts either. I tended to do my own thing, never was one to fall prey to peer pressure. I got okay grades, and for lack of knowing what I wanted to do with my life, I went to college up in Denver. I joined a gym up there and started working out. I found that I loved it."

Sarah was intrigued. "What appealed to you?"

Instead of responding immediately, Cole thought about his answer. She liked that about him. That he wasn't worried about filling silence in a conversation, and truly reflected on what he wanted to say.

"I loved that people who weren't in the best shape came in and were cheered on by the others. There were regulars who I didn't really know personally, but I still 'knew.' I started going in the mornings right when the gym opened, and I'd see the same people every day. We'd smile, say hi, and get on with our workout. One day, one of the older patrons didn't show up. And when he wasn't there the next day either, a few of us regulars got together and begged the employee to look up his address so someone could go check on him. It was against policy, but finally he agreed. Me and two others went to the old man's house and found him on the floor. He'd fallen, broken his hip, and couldn't get up. We called an ambulance, and they were able to get him to the hospital and fixed up."

"Oh my gosh, that's horrible!" Sarah exclaimed.

"It was . . . but it was also at that moment when I realized how much the people at the gym had become like my family. We didn't know more than each other's first names, but it was a definite bond anyway. After I graduated, I couldn't stop thinking about that, and decided I wanted to give the same to others. Then I met Felicity, and the rest is history."

"And is it everything you thought it would be?" she asked.

"Absolutely. I love feeling as if I'm helping my community. Teaching women how to be safe and more aware of their surroundings. Mentoring young men and teaching them that being disrespectful to girls and women isn't cool. Watching as both men and women work their butts off and lose weight. It's all so much *more* than I could've imagined."

"That's great," Sarah said with a smile. She hadn't ever really thought of a gym as a place to bond with other people before, but listening to Cole talk about what he did, she got it. Like he'd said, the gym patrons were a kind of family for him. Thinking about that led her to ask about his own blood family. "And you said your parents live in Arizona, right?"

"Yeah. They got sick of the cold and unpredictable winters and packed up and headed to Phoenix."

"Do you see them often?"

"Not as much as I'd like, but I hate the heat, and they hate the cold, so . . ." His voice trailed off, but he was smiling as he said it.

"And your brother?"

"Sam lives in the Seattle area. He's an aquatic biologist and spends most of his time researching and collecting specimens in the lakes and streams in the area."

"Wow. Sounds interesting."

"Not really. Unless you want to listen to him talk for hours about plankton and algae."

Sarah laughed. "I bet he says that about your job too."

Cole smiled. "Of course he does."

They grinned at each other for a long moment before resuming their meal.

Sarah couldn't remember a time when she'd been so relaxed around a guy. As she made small talk with Cole, she realized that her dads would've totally loved him. Mike would've gone gaga over his tattoos and good looks, while Jackson would've been more reserved at first, eventually coming around, especially if he'd heard Cole's comment about not sitting on his ass while his woman slaved away in the kitchen.

"What was that thought?" Cole asked, as perceptive as ever.

Sarah's gaze whipped up to his. She hadn't realized she was staring off into space. "Oh, nothing."

"Don't do that," Cole said softly. "If you don't want to tell me, that's okay, but don't blow me off."

Sarah apologized immediately. "Sorry. I was just thinking about my dads and how much they would've liked you."

Cole looked surprised, but quickly hid his reaction. "Yeah?"

"Yeah."

"I wish I'd had the chance to meet them."

Making a split-second decision, Sarah stood and held out a hand. "Come on."

Without questioning her, Cole stood and took her hand. Sarah led them down the hall to what was Jackson's office once upon a time. She'd slowly given away most of the business and accounting books that had been on the bookshelves, and even some of the knickknacks, but the pictures on the walls she hadn't touched.

This was Jackson's space. The spot where he'd spent the most time. And he'd surrounded himself with the things he'd loved most: his family.

When they stepped inside, Sarah dropped Cole's hand and gestured around. "I've always loved this room. When I was little, I'd do my homework in here while Jackson sat at his desk. Inevitably, Mike would come in and hang out with us, help me if I needed it. I'd catch Jackson staring at him with a look in his eyes so warm, I couldn't mistake it for anything *but* love."

Cole wandered around the room, looking at the portraits and other pictures that were scattered everywhere. Mike and Jackson saying their vows, both looking incredibly handsome in their tuxedos. Sarah's adoption day. The three of them in various places on different occasions.

"You remind me of Jackson," Sarah told him. "He was the protector of our family. He'd hover over me and Mike at the beach, making sure no one messed with us and that we were safe. He didn't laugh a lot, but when he did, it was as if the sun came out, bathing everything with its warmth. When they found their bodies in the rubble of the nightclub, Jackson was on top of Mike . . . as if he'd died trying to protect him from the blast."

Cole turned toward her.

"I miss him. I miss them both."

Without a word, Cole came toward her and took her in his arms. Sarah had to lift her chin so she didn't smother herself against his chest, but once settled, they fit perfectly. He didn't say anything, simply held her.

It felt amazing. Sarah was sad, but she wasn't on the verge of tears. She'd reached a point where she could think of her dads and not burst into tears. Eventually, she pulled back, but Cole only let her go far enough so she could look up at him.

"They were lucky to have you as their daughter," he said gently.

She immediately shook her head. "No. I was lucky to have them as my dads."

Cole huffed out a small laugh. "Po-tay-toe, po-tah-toe."

"Like I said, they would've liked you, Cole. Especially Jackson."

"I'm gonna take that as a compliment."

"You should."

"And I'm gonna do what I can to act in a way that would ensure they liked me for *you*."

Sarah took a deep breath. "This is weird."

"What?"

"This. You. Us."

"What's weird about it?" Cole asked.

"Seriously? How about the fact that we just met and we're standing in my dead gay father's old office hugging and being all mushy."

"*You're* being mushy," Cole rebutted. "I'm just standing here."

Sarah smiled. "You know what I mean. I'm not like this. I'm the cautious one. The one who takes two weeks to decide if I want to go out with someone. Who doesn't kiss until at least the third date, and only if the guy I'm with has behaved himself. This isn't me." She gestured to their current position with a head nod.

"You probably won't believe me, but I've never been the impulsive type. Felicity and I went over and over our business plan before we decided to take a chance on the gym. I've never had a one-night stand in my life. It's never seemed sexy to me at all. I'd rather get to know a woman before I'm intimate with her. But from the moment I caught up to you on the sidewalk, and you didn't rip me a new asshole when I more than deserved it, you intrigued me. And the more I learn about you, the more I like."

"I'm nothing special," Sarah replied, desperate to believe him but equally cautious.

"And that right there is why you *are* special," Cole countered. Then he leaned down and kissed her forehead before pulling back and asking, "Does this count as our first date?"

Sarah frowned. "What?"

"I'm only asking because I'm looking forward to our third date so I can get that kiss."

She knew she was blushing, but shook her head in exasperation. "You are such a guy."

"Glad you noticed," Cole said with a grin. Then he sobered. "Thank you for sharing your dads with me. I didn't know them, but I have a feeling they'd be proud of the woman you are today."

"Thanks."

"And because Jackson isn't here to do it, I'm gonna make sure that Owen leaves you alone, once and for all. I'm not much of an investigator, but I've got friends who are. And I *can* be intimidating. I'm more than happy to make it clear to that shitgobbler that he needs to back off. That you aren't interested."

"Shitgobbler?"

Cole nodded. "I like to get creative with my name-calling."

Sarah licked her lips, then pressed them together. She didn't have the words to say what she was feeling. She'd felt alone for so long. Without her dads to support her, to talk things out with, she'd been overwhelmed by the situation with Owen. Unsure what to do. When she'd tried to get help from the cops, they'd blown her off. The fact that Cole not only believed there was something to be concerned about, but he was going to help her deal with the situation, was almost overwhelming.

"Thank you."

"Stop thanking me," Cole said sternly. "I'm going to get this guy off your back so I've got all your attention. I'm a selfish bastard, and I don't want you wondering when and where he's going to pop out. I want you to concentrate only on me and our relationship."

She couldn't help but huff out a breath. "See? This is weird."

"Nope. This is what people who are dating do. This is our first date. We ate food together, I met your parents, we got to know each other a little better, and in a few minutes, when I take off, I'm gonna promise to call, and you'll blush and say you'd like that, and I'll text when I get back to the gym just so you don't worry."

"What if I don't want to date you?" Sarah asked, trying to keep a straight face.

Instead of laughing, Cole leaned down until his nose almost touched hers. "You do. You couldn't keep your eyes off me while I mowed your grass. I saw you peeking out from behind the curtain. Then you went out of your way to make me something to eat instead of thanking me on your doorstep and sending me away. You showed me your dad's room and the place you feel closest to him. You didn't protest when I said I was gonna have my friends look into your case. You want to date me, angel. *Almost* as much as I want to date you."

She didn't say anything, simply looked at him.

He straightened and brought a hand up, running his pinky finger down the bridge of her nose. "You gonna be okay the rest of the day?"

"Yeah."

"You gonna be able to come to Castle Rock tomorrow and meet with the guys at Ace Security?"

Sarah nodded.

"Good. Can you make a list of the gifts and letters that you remember receiving from Owen, and the approximate dates you received them?"

She frowned up at him. Before she could speak, he said, "I know it'll be hard to remember exact dates, but it's important so Logan and the others can get a full picture of what they're dealing with."

She opened her mouth to respond, but once more, he talked over her. "You've got nothing to be embarrassed about either, angel. Everyone knows that you didn't ask for this guy's attention. So don't worry about that."

She waited a beat when he stopped speaking.

"What?" he asked.

"Are you done?"

He grinned. "Yeah."

"Good. What I was *going* to say is that it won't be a problem. I took a picture of every single thing he sent me, the day he sent it. I even have it cataloged on my laptop."

Cole gaped at her. "You do?"

"Yeah. I figured that if I ever disappeared one day or my body turned up mutilated and dead, that maybe the police would look at my computer files and find it, and if it was Owen who did something to me, they'd be able to use all my notes to make their case."

"You took pictures?"

"Yeah." Sarah nodded. "Is that odd?"

"No! It's awesome. Holy shit, that's going to make Logan's day."

56

Sarah's lips quirked up. "Do you have his email? I can mail the file to him today."

"Send it to me," Cole ordered. "I'll pass it along."

For the first time, Sarah hesitated.

"What's wrong?"

She wrinkled her nose. "I just . . . I'm not sure I want you seeing all the evidence."

"Why?"

"Because. It just seems . . . weird or something."

"I thought we've been over what is and isn't weird."

"Okay—I don't want you to lose your shit," Sarah said bluntly. "I want you to like me."

"And you're afraid if I see the love letters this Owen guy has sent that I won't like you anymore?"

It sounded silly when he said it out loud, but Sarah nodded anyway.

Cole took her face in his hands and tilted her head up. "Nothing that jizzjockey says will change the way I feel about you, angel. Got it?"

She nodded.

"Good. Now I'm gonna go before I say anything else that will freak you out. I'll text you when I get to work. Send me the file you've got on the gifts and letters he's sent, and I'll get it to Logan. I'm going to shoot for a meeting around eleven tomorrow morning. That work for you?"

"Can we make it one? I need to go grocery shopping in the morning and pick up a few things for Mrs. Grady, then I have an appointment at ten in Aurora with the Adoption Exchange—the agency that Mike and Jackson went through to adopt me. The foster parents bring the kids to group meetings fairly regularly, and I try to meet with the kids every other month or so and talk to them about what it was like having two dads, and how families come in all shapes and sizes."

When Cole didn't say anything, Sarah frowned. "Cole? I can cancel if that won't work."

"It works, angel. It's just that every time you open your mouth, I realize exactly how amazing you are."

She shook her head. "No, I just . . . They advocate for gay and lesbian parents who want to adopt, and I just want to give back in some way."

One intense beat of silence as he stared at her, then Cole dropped his hands from her face, turned without a word, and swung his arm over her shoulders, guiding them both out of the room toward the front door. Once there, he hugged her briefly again, reminded her to send the file she'd made about everything Owen had sent her, and then he was hustling toward his black Acura TLX sports car.

Sarah would've been worried about his abrupt departure—if she hadn't seen the evidence of his arousal in his jeans. She'd seen Jackson do the same thing often enough, leave a room before he did anything inappropriate in front of his daughter, to know it was an alpha man's way of making sure he didn't do or say something he'd regret later.

Smiling to herself, Sarah closed her front door and danced a little jig right there in the foyer of her house. Evidence was showing that maybe, just maybe, Cole Johnson liked her. *Eek!*

Chapter Five

At twelve fifty-three, Sarah pulled into a parking space in the lot near Ace Security in downtown Castle Rock. She was cutting it close for the one o'clock appointment Cole had set up for her, but her visit to the Adoption Exchange had run long because there were several kids, after her group chat, who wanted to talk privately about her experience of being adopted by a gay couple.

She was happy to talk about the pros and cons and share her experiences. The children at the Adoption Exchange were mostly older—five and up—and they were well aware that with every year that passed, the likelihood of them being adopted shrank. Sarah knew there were a lot of gay and lesbian couples who would love to have children, and she wanted to do whatever it took to help facilitate the process.

She climbed out of her Galant and clicked the button on her key fob to lock it, then turned to rush through the lot toward Ace Security.

"Ooof!"

The sound came out involuntarily as she slammed into a hard body. Her head came up in alarm, and she tried to take a step backward at the same time. Her legs got tangled, and she teetered for a second before she started to go down.

Cole's strong arm wrapped around her waist as quick as lightning, catching her before she fell on her ass on the ground.

"Cole!" she exclaimed, grabbing on to his arm with one hand. "You startled me."

"You weren't paying attention," he admonished. "I thought we talked about this in our lesson. You have to be aware of your surroundings at all times. It's important, angel. It could be a matter of life or death. If I were that dickchomper, he'd have you in his grip before you even knew what was happening."

Sarah blushed. He was right. She'd been lost in her head, wondering if she looked okay, if Cole would like her outfit. What he'd thought about the file she'd sent him, and if the Anderson brothers would think she was overreacting just like the cops did.

"You're right," she said softly. "I'm sorry."

"Don't be sorry," Cole told her, his voice gentling. "Learn from your mistake."

She nodded. "What are you doing out here?" she asked, wrinkling her brow.

"I've been watching for you. I saw you pass by the gym and came out to meet you."

"Oh . . . thank you."

Cole's gaze traveled from her face down her body, then back up. "You look nice," he observed.

"Thanks," Sarah whispered. It wasn't often that she wasn't wearing scrubs or sweatpants, but she told herself that since she'd gone to the Adoption Exchange, and because she wanted to make a good impression on Cole's friends, she'd dressed to impress.

She wore a V-necked, black blouse that showed a hint of cleavage, but not enough to be indecent, a knee-length gray skirt, and a pair of two-inch heels. She'd paid particular attention to her shoulder-length hair, doing her best to make it look soft and flowy instead of simply throwing it up in a ponytail or bun like she usually did. She'd even put on a bit of makeup and jewelry. It was silly—she never dressed up like this, but in the back of her mind, she knew she hadn't done it because of her presentation or because she was trying to convince the men from Ace Security to help look into Owen.

She'd done it solely for Cole.

She wanted him to see her in something other than the messy scrubs she always wore to work. Wanted him to see her as more than the woman who'd come to him for help with whatever Owen was. He wasn't exactly a stalker, as she didn't think he was following her around at all times. He was more of an unwanted admirer who gave her the creeps.

Owen aside, Sarah wanted Cole to see her as a competent woman.

And with the way his eyes widened when he took her in, it looked like she'd succeeded.

"No, not nice," Cole corrected. "Beautiful."

"Let's not get crazy," Sarah said a little self-consciously. She wanted to impress Cole, but she knew that she wasn't anywhere near beautiful.

He didn't say anything in response to her remark, simply shook his head in exasperation. "What's that?" he asked instead, nodding to the plastic bag she was holding in the hand that wasn't holding on to him.

"Oh!" Sarah had forgotten all about the gift waiting for her on her front steps.

Grimly, she held it out to Cole. She hadn't thought her actions through, though, because he had to let go of *her* in order to take the bag. She watched as he peered into it.

He frowned and looked back up at her. "From Owen?" he asked.

Sarah simply nodded.

Without a word, Cole wrapped his arm back around her waist and turned her toward the sidewalk. "Come on. Logan and the others are waiting for us."

Hmm. She'd thought she'd get more of a response over Owen's gift, but she didn't say anything because Cole was walking fast, and she was having trouble keeping up. She did her best, even as she was taking two steps to his one. It wasn't until she stumbled a bit that Cole realized he was practically carrying her and slowed down.

"Shit, I'm sorry, angel. Next time, tell me I'm going too fast."

"Normally it wouldn't be a problem," she told him honestly. "I'm used to walking really fast in the hospital, but it's these stupid heels. I'm not used to *them*." Mentally smacking herself in the head for sounding completely stupid, Sarah gave Cole a weak smile.

"Right. I guess this is something I'll also have to be on the lookout for."

She frowned up at him. "What?"

"You trying to make me not feel bad for shit I do that is totally my fault. It's okay, I'm a fast learner."

"Cole, no, that's not—"

"Come on, angel. The guys are waiting."

Still confused about what Cole had said, she was silent as they continued walking toward the Ace Security office . . . but this time, Cole matched her steps, and she didn't feel as if she were being dragged alongside him. His arm stayed around her waist, and Sarah could feel his fingers resting at her hip as if they were branded there. She seemed to fit against him perfectly, and every time their legs brushed against each other as they walked, she wanted to squeal in excitement.

She hadn't had a crush on someone in a very long time, but she definitely had a big-time crush on Cole.

He held open the door to Ace Security for her, and the second she cleared it, she felt his fingers on the small of her back as he followed her in.

She couldn't help but picture his large hand touching her the same way as she lay naked on her bed. He'd lean over her, brushing a kiss on the back of her neck, his calloused fingers tickling her as he put his hand on that sensitive part of her back right before he covered her body with his own—

". . . to do this?"

She raised guilty eyes to Cole's. "What?"

He chuckled as if he knew exactly what she'd been thinking. "I said, are you ready to do this?"

Blushing, Sarah nodded. God, she had to get herself together.

The smile still on his face, Cole flattened his hand on her back and put gentle pressure there, urging her forward. They walked past the desk in the front room of the space and went through a door behind it. Instead of a hallway, the door led into a large, open room. There were several desks littered around the area, each with a man sitting behind it. All four men stood, staring at her and Cole.

Sarah took an involuntary step backward and bumped into Cole.

"Easy, angel," he murmured, before shifting his stance and taking her hand in his. He towed her toward the nearest man. "Sarah, this is Ryder. Ryder, Sarah."

Sarah untangled her fingers from Cole's and stretched out her hand. "It's good to meet you," she said politely.

"You too," Ryder said in a deep, gruff voice.

He was tall, but not overly so. He had light-brown hair and hazel eyes that looked at her with such focus, she immediately wanted to blurt out everything she'd ever done wrong.

As if he could read her mind, Ryder said, "Relax, Sarah. We don't bite."

"Unless you want us to!" one of the other men said from their right.

Sarah turned to see who she knew was Blake, standing there smiling. Now that she wasn't as freaked out, she was remembering who was who from her internet stalking of the brothers earlier.

"Shut it," Cole grumbled from next to her.

Sarah smiled and reached out to shake the man's hand. "I'm Sarah," she said politely.

"I know. I'm Blake."

"I know," she returned with a smile.

Blake grinned and nodded.

"Nathan," the tallest of the brothers said. He didn't reach for her hand, just nodded instead.

"Hi," Sarah said.

"And this is Logan," Cole said, touching her back once more.

This time, Sarah barely felt his fingers on her—she was too nervous to meet the man she'd first contacted about Owen.

He held out his hand.

Sarah shook it and took a deep breath to try to relax. Logan was big, somewhat intimidating, and from everything she'd read about him, good at his job.

"I'm sorry. I didn't realize how serious your case was when you contacted me. I also apologize for getting the facts wrong. I thought the man in question was your ex. That was my mistake."

Sarah nodded. "It's okay. I mean, there are days when I'm not sure my case is all that serious."

Logan shook his head. "Don't do that. Don't downplay it. I've seen way too many people, men and women alike, who've thought the same thing as you, that the other person wasn't a threat, that they'd never hurt them, only to end up seriously wounded or dead. Let us figure out if Owen Montrone is a threat or not. Okay?"

Feeling as if she wanted to cry, Sarah simply nodded. It felt good that Logan, a man she didn't know, believed her. For some reason, she'd kinda figured that Cole was an anomaly, that he believed her because he wanted to go out with her. But it was more than obvious from the serious looks on the brothers' faces that maybe, just maybe, she'd been right about Owen all along.

"Okay," she agreed. When she happened to glance over at Cole, he was eyeing her with a look so intense that she blushed.

Logan either ignored the look or didn't see it, because he said, "As far as this douchebag Owen Montrone goes, we've got your back. What he's doing isn't cool. No matter that he hasn't done anything but give you notes and presents. We all know that things can easily escalate from there, especially when he sees you out and about with Cole. I looked over your file yesterday, and we'd like to sit down and discuss your case with you . . . if you're willing."

Sarah immediately nodded. "I'd like that, but I also want to talk about payment first. I know Ace Security is expensive, and I do have some money. I don't want to be a charity case."

Logan's brows came down at that, and it was obvious he wasn't happy, but he said, "We'll work something out."

Sarah figured that was as good as she was going to get at the moment. She nodded.

Logan turned and headed for a large table in the back of the room, and Cole urged her to follow. He held her chair out as she sat, then scooted the chair next to her a little closer before seating himself. The other men took their seats as well, and Blake asked, "So . . . what's in the bag?"

Without a word, Cole opened it and set the cookbook in the middle of the table. It was a manual for all things cast iron, including how to care for and season the pots, and how to make everything from cakes to gourmet meals using the iconic cookware.

"It's inscribed too," Sarah told the men.

Cole scowled and opened the cover to read what was written inside.

To Sarah.

Cooking fills the body and soul.

Love, Owen

"Interesting," Logan observed.

The others were silent.

"It was on my doorstep this morning," Sarah explained. "It wasn't wrapped or anything."

"The first thing that needs to happen is that you need to get some sort of camera set up," Ryder said.

Cole nodded. "It was on my agenda already."

"But we know it's Owen," Sarah protested. "What difference would having a camera make? It won't make him stop."

"True, but it would be one more thing to use against him," Blake said.

"Start from the beginning," Logan ordered. "From the day you met Owen until today. Don't leave anything out, even if you think it's silly or unimportant. Let us decide what is and isn't relevant."

Sarah suddenly understood why Ace Security was in such demand. She had the focused attention of four pairs of eyes.

She glanced to her right and amended that thought. Five pairs of eyes. Cole was looking at her just as intently as the others. She knew he wasn't an investigator like Logan and his brothers, but if she hadn't known he was a small-business owner of a gym, she would've thought he was a member of Ace Security.

"Okay, um . . . I'm a CNA, and Owen's mother, Aubrey Montrone, was one of the patients on my floor."

"What was she in for?" Blake asked.

Sarah wanted to chastise him for interrupting her before she'd even started her story, but that wasn't who she was. Luckily, his brother wasn't as nice.

"Let her talk," Nathan said sternly. "She'll never get through the explanation if she's interrupted."

Blake looked at her, chagrined. "Sorry. Carry on."

Resisting the urge to smile, Sarah continued. "Right, so Owen was super attentive to his mom, which I thought was very sweet. He was shy too, not really looking at me much when I was in the room helping his mother. He's overweight, in his midforties, and not very attractive. I feel bad saying that, but if you saw him, you'd understand. He was wearing a pair of overalls the first time I saw him, and his beer belly was quite prominent. It literally looked like he had a beach ball hidden under his clothes. His hair was too long, and his beard looked like it hadn't been groomed or trimmed in quite a while. He didn't smell, but he wasn't exactly a poster boy for Irish Spring. Ultimately, though, while he looked a little rough, I thought he was nice enough.

"I saw them both quite a bit over the next couple of weeks. Aubrey had terminal cancer and was in the hospital with complications from that. She'd already decided not to do any more treatments because, even though it would give her a little more time, they made her really sick. She decided on quality of life rather than living longer and sicker.

"Owen was always quiet and very polite. One day, when he stepped out of the room so I could give his mom a sponge bath, she asked if I would consider going out with him. She said she knew he was older than I was, but he was a good boy, and he thought I was nice. She went on to tell me all about how helpful he was around the house, and how they'd always taken care of each other. I told her that I was flattered, but wasn't sure we really clicked. She pressed, and I finally agreed to go to lunch with him at the hospital, just to get her off my back."

Sarah took a deep breath and, not for the first time, wished she'd stuck to her guns and refused the sweet dying lady. She felt Cole's hand rest on her thigh. He gave it a short squeeze, and his touch gave her the push she needed to continue.

"So when Owen came back in the room, I figured I'd just get it over with. I told him that I was about to go on my lunch break and asked if he wanted to go to the cafeteria with me. He nodded, we went downstairs . . . and the conversation was extremely awkward. He didn't talk, so I did my best to chat about anything I could think of. He stared at me a lot, and nodded, but didn't initiate any of the topics. Eventually, toward the end of the thirty minutes, he talked for just a minute or two about his mom, how much he loved her and how much she meant to him. He bragged a little about taking such good care of her.

"Then we went back upstairs. I continued on my shift, and he went back to his mom's room. Aubrey was discharged the next day, and I thought that was that. About two weeks later, I heard through the hospital grapevine that Aubrey had passed away. I felt bad for Owen. I mean, we didn't click in any way, but he seemed nice, and very shy, and I knew he was probably devastated about losing his mom.

"I started receiving the first gifts not too long after that. At first I didn't know who they were from, and I was flattered. First was the flowers sent to work. Then candy. The first time he signed his name to one of the gifts, I was completely confused. I had to think to even remember who Owen was. Then the letters started. They also came to work at first, but then I started receiving them at home.

"That freaked me out. But not as much as the presents. They continued to come. As you probably saw from the pictures, it's not as if he went to the store and bought them. They look like something he picked up from around the house, wrapped up, and sent. The drinking glasses with the note that said he dreamed of sitting on the porch of his house and sipping tea with me as the sun went down. The stuffed animal that was missing an eye. Or the God-awful pillow that seemed like it probably came from his couch. They were weird gifts." Sarah shuddered. "I've seen him here and there a few times, but recently not as much."

"What did he do when you saw him?" Blake asked.

"This was a month or so ago, and the last time I talked to him in person. I was at a take-out Mexican place near my house to pick up dinner, and he pulled into the parking lot while I was at the counter. I wouldn't normally have confronted him, but I was frustrated and worried. I grabbed my dinner and stormed out of the restaurant. He had a big smile on his face when he saw me, and even as I told him that I was sorry but I didn't feel the same way about him as he obviously did about me, and that he should stop sending me presents and letters, he still smiled. It was as if he didn't even hear what I was saying.

"After a few minutes of him smiling creepily at me and not saying a word, I just turned around and left. I drove around for thirty minutes, making sure I wasn't being followed before I went home. Which was stupid, because he already knew where I lived since he'd been dropping off gifts and notes for a while. I haven't seen him since. And I actually hoped I'd finally gotten lucky and he'd gotten the message, but then the letters and gifts started up again not too long after that confrontation. No such luck. And now . . . that." She shrugged and gestured to the cookbook in the middle of the table.

"Do we know where Owen lives?" Ryder asked the group.

Nathan had a computer in front of him and had been concentrating on it while they'd been talking. "A search of public records shows his address as the same as his mother's here in Castle Rock. I shot Alexis an email to see what she could find, and she just replied and said that it looks like there hasn't been a payment made on the house since Aubrey Montrone passed away a few months ago, and the loan company is starting the process to foreclose."

"Does he work?" Logan asked.

Nathan shook his head. "If he does, I haven't been able to find out where. But I'm guessing the answer is no. Alexis says there have been regular payments from the disability office deposited into a joint account he shares with his mother."

"Disability?" Cole asked. "What kind?"

"No clue," Nathan said calmly.

"I'm surprised Alexis hasn't found out already," Blake said. "She's gotten scarily good at that shit after working with that retired Navy SEAL guy."

Sarah's gaze went from one man to the next as they talked. She almost felt as if they were discussing someone else's life and not her own. It was a peculiar feeling. But she couldn't deny the sense of relief. They were taking this seriously. They weren't blowing her off because the gifts and letters all seemed to be sent with love and not hate.

"When you were eating with him, besides him not really saying much, did anything else strike you as off about him?" Logan asked.

Sarah tilted her head in question. "What do you mean?"

"Don't think too hard," he urged gently. "Just tell us your initial reactions to him."

She nodded and closed her eyes, trying to remember that lunch so long ago. "I was tired, as the shift had already been tough . . . I had a lot of very needy patients . . . sometimes that happens, they seem to come in bunches. Anyway, I was kinda irritated at Aubrey for pressuring me into lunch with her son in the first place, but I didn't want to be mean. I figured we both had to eat, so why not? The first sort of weird thing was in the elevator." She paused, trying to figure out how to put her feelings into words.

None of the men rushed her. They let the silence stand as she thought. Cole hadn't said anything since she'd started talking, but his hand on her thigh let her know he was still there and still very concerned about her.

Her eyes opened, and she looked around the table. "You know how, when you get in an elevator, there are certain unwritten rules? The first person stands by the buttons. The second stands across from the first, near the wall. The third goes into the back left corner. If there's a fourth, he or she goes into the other corner. The fifth typically stands against the back wall. Now, if there are more people who get in, they stand in the middle, or against one of the walls, filling in the spaces. Then everyone faces the doors or looks at the numbers as the elevator goes up or down."

"Owen didn't do that?" Ryder asked.

"No. There were already two people in there when the car arrived, and I went to the back left corner. Owen stood in the middle of the elevator with his back to the doors and stared at me." Sarah felt silly even mentioning it.

"Interesting," Logan murmured. "What else?"

Relieved when no one said her impromptu elevator-psychology observations were stupid, she closed her eyes again. "We arrived on the bottom floor and headed to the cafeteria. Owen was walking a bit behind me, and when we got in line, he picked up a tray and followed me as I wandered around to the different stations. Then he picked up the exact same things I did for lunch. I got a banana, so he added one to his tray. I went and got a small salad, and he did the same. I ordered a ham-and-cheese flatbread, and he did too. As I said earlier, then we went and ate, and I did most of the talking."

"When he spoke, what did he say, precisely?" Blake asked.

Sarah pressed her lips together and tried to remember exact words, but eventually she shook her head. "I'm sorry, I just don't remember anything other than what I've already told you. It must not have been anything too weird or out there, because it didn't stick in my mind at all."

"It's okay," Cole said, squeezing her leg a little.

Feeling disappointed in herself, Sarah did her best to answer the rest of the questions the men had for her. Before she realized it, two hours had gone by.

"I think that's enough for today," Logan said. "Grace and Felicity are meeting for some girl time, so I need to get home to look after Nate and Ace. If we have more questions, can we contact you?" he asked Sarah.

She nodded. "Of course."

"Good. In the meantime, keep doing what you're doing. Let Cole teach you everything he knows. Be on your toes. Lock your door, try to alter your schedule if at all possible. Order a camera, or lots of cameras, for your house. Continue to take pictures and document everything you receive. Ryder, I know Sarah said the cops weren't much help, but can you talk to them anyway?"

"Of course. I'll also give a call to Rex. See if he can help in any way."

"Rex is Ryder's ex-boss . . . for lack of a better word for him," Cole told Sarah in a low voice.

She nodded.

"Good. Blake, Nathan? Got anything to add?" Logan asked.

"Nothing here," Nathan said.

"I'll have Alexis see what she can find in regard to why this guy's receiving disability checks," Blake added.

"Great. We'll be in touch," Logan said as he stood.

Sarah stood as well, and her knees felt a little weak. She wasn't sure why. She was so relieved that someone was helping her. Ace Security had connections with the police, and they were going to talk to them. They'd believed her and seemed concerned about the letters and gifts. She knew things wouldn't be resolved after one meeting, but even knowing they were continuing to investigate Owen made her feel better.

"Come on, angel," Cole said from next to her. "Did you have lunch today?"

She looked up at him and said softly, "No."

"Right, I can see your hands shaking. Come on, we'll head over to Scarpetti's. Francesca will take care of us."

"I really should just go home. I'm sure you have lots of stuff you have to do today. You already took way too much time off for this."

"The gym is covered."

"But Logan said Felicity and Grace were going to do something," she protested, not sure why she was trying so hard to let Cole off the hook. The truth of the matter was, she was starving. And she'd been wanting to try out the Italian restaurant ever since she'd heard some of the nurses at work talking about it. But she felt as if she'd taken up enough of Cole's time.

Cole didn't answer her. Instead, he gestured toward the cookbook. "You want that?"

"No!" Sarah exclaimed. She didn't want anything Owen gave her.

"Didn't think so. Hey, Blake!" he called out to the other man.

Blake looked up from his desk. "Yeah?"

"Take care of that, would ya?"

Blake looked to where Cole was gesturing and gave him a chin lift before looking back down at the computer in front of him.

"Come on, angel. Let me feed you."

Sighing, Sarah gave up. She let him take her hand and followed him to the door. At the last minute, she turned and said loudly, "Bye. Thank you for your help!"

Blake and Nathan nodded, but didn't look up.

"You couldn't help yourself, could you?" Cole asked.

Sarah looked at him. "It would've been rude to just leave without saying anything."

He smiled and shook his head, but didn't reply. He pulled her out of the building and headed for the Italian place. "Have you eaten here before?"

"No. I've wanted to, but haven't had the occasion."

"You're in for a treat then."

Cole approached the door, and Sarah pulled back on his hand when she saw the hours listed on the front. "What are you doing?" she asked.

"Getting you some food. Why?"

"They're closed," she pointed out. "You can't just walk in."

"It's fine. Francesca doesn't mind," Cole told her, opening the unlocked door.

"It's rude," Sarah hissed as they entered.

"Francesca!" Cole called out once the door shut behind them.

Sarah stared at him incredulously.

An older woman, petite and round, peeked out from a door that Sarah assumed went to the kitchen, and smiled hugely as she walked toward them. "Cole! It's been way too long since you've graced us with your presence! What's the occasion?"

"My girl's hungry. Think you can hook us up?"

"Of course!" Francesca said immediately. "As long as you're both willing to give me your thoughts on the special for tonight."

Cole beamed. "God, I've missed this place."

"Not my fault you haven't been here," Francesca told him.

Cole patted his stomach. "My mind is willing, but too much of your food is bad for my body. Wouldn't be good to have a gym owner be overweight."

The Italian woman laughed and shook her head. Then she took a step toward him and went up on tiptoe, offering her cheek. Cole kissed it, and she turned her head so he could kiss the other one. "Introduce me to your girl," she ordered.

Sarah wanted to protest, to say she wasn't Cole's "girl," but she didn't get the chance. Besides, it would be rude to contradict the older woman.

"This is Sarah. She works at the hospital."

"Bless you, child," Francesca said. "Anyone who works in the public sector has my highest gratitude and admiration."

"Thank you," Sarah said. She could usually tell when people were just saying things like that because it was expected of them, but Francesca seemed to genuinely appreciate her and others like her.

"You can't do any better than Cole here. He's a good boy."

"Francesca," Cole complained.

"Shhh," she said. "Anyone who goes out with you deserves to know what she's getting."

Cole rolled his eyes and crossed his arms, letting Francesca say what she felt she needed to say.

Sarah was surprised by the sincerity of Francesca's gaze when she looked at her.

"As I said, Cole is a good man. He looks out for this community. After Mr. Brown had a heart attack, Cole offered him and his wife complimentary memberships to his gym for life. When that little boy went missing last year? Cole organized a search party for him and stayed out there in those mountains for twenty-five hours, making sure everyone had food, water, and adequate clothing for the searches. And he was the first to congratulate me on getting my four-star rating from the *Denver Post*, telling me I was robbed for not getting a five-star one." Francesca chuckled. "I've also seen him buy a dinner to go, then give it to a homeless man down the street. If the measure of a man can be determined by how he treats those around him, Cole Johnson is one of the best."

Sarah was fascinated by the blush that turned Cole's cheeks a bright pink. But he simply leaned down and kissed Francesca once more before saying, "Sarah hasn't eaten since breakfast. Think you can help me out by getting something in her belly before she passes out on me?"

Smiling, Francesca nodded. She brought them over to a table in the back of the restaurant, near the kitchen doors. "It's not the best seat in the house, but my waitresses aren't here just yet, and since I'll be serving you, it's more convenient to have you near."

"It's perfect," Sarah told her quietly.

Cole held a chair for her and, once she was settled, took the seat next to her instead of across the square table. Francesca disappeared into the kitchen.

"Just in case you're not keeping count," Cole said once they were alone, "this is date number two."

Chapter Six

Cole held back the smile as Sarah blinked in confusion. "What?"

"This is our second date. After the third, I get a kiss," Cole told her with a straight face.

She shook her head. "Francesca forgot to say, when she was listing all your qualities, that you're insane."

That did it. Cole couldn't stop himself from smiling anymore. He laughed out loud, loving the deadpan way she'd given the rebuke. "I meant to tell you way earlier . . . good job on the self-defense lesson on Monday." It was an abrupt change of subject, but Cole had been thinking about it throughout the meeting.

It was obvious she hadn't had any kind of training before, but she'd picked up the things he'd taught her quickly and hadn't shied away from really kicking the crap out of the bag he'd held for her to practice on.

"Uh . . . thanks," Sarah said, confused by his change of subject.

"Not everyone picks up defensive moves so fast. It can take them weeks to be able to execute moves as effectively as you did."

"I didn't want to hurt you, but you told me to kick as hard as I could."

"That I did. Now . . . will you tell me what's bothering you?" He'd figured out something quickly in the short time he'd known her. In order to get her to drop her polite facade and tell him exactly what she was thinking, he had to keep her slightly off-kilter. That way, there was a chance she'd forget to say what she thought he *wanted* to hear, and instead blurt out her real thoughts.

"I have no idea how you can read me so well," she mumbled. Then she looked him in the eye and said, "You got me a meeting with Ace Security, and they're looking into my case. What could be wrong?"

"Don't do that. Not with me. I know it's in your nature to be nice, but I don't want nice Sarah. I want the *real* Sarah. Tell me to piss off when I'm being an ass . . . because Lord knows there will be plenty of times when I'll be one. Disagree with me when we're having a philosophical conversation, tell me which side of the bed you prefer to sleep on, and for God's sake, when we're watching television together, don't just watch whatever I want because you want to please me—because then we'll probably never watch anything other than football and hockey."

He'd purposely tried to shock her, especially with the bed comment, to get her to open up.

Sarah gave him a weak smile. "Jackson used to tell me that I needed to speak my mind more often."

"It sounds like he was a very smart man."

"He was." She took a deep breath and stared down at the empty plate in front of her for a long moment. Cole didn't rush her, gave her time to think. He was rewarded when she looked up at him and said softly, "I'm more grateful for the help from your friends than I can say. They did more to make me feel as if I'm not alone in dealing with all this in one short meeting than the police ever have, but . . . deep down, I'm still scared. Every time I drive up to my house, I wonder if there'll be another gift. Or if maybe today's the day he's done with the presents, and he's going to be inside my house, ready to grab me or something."

Sarah looked away from him again and bit her lip. Reacting without thought, Cole brought a hand up to her face and gently freed her lip from her teeth.

Her eyes met his in surprise. But she took a deep breath and continued. "And now I'm confused after hearing about Owen's disability
payments. I don't know if I should be relieved, like maybe he's not as
much of a threat as I'd thought. That he's got some sort of disability that
explains his behavior . . . or if I should be even *more* worried because it
could be something that makes him more dangerous. But ultimately . . .
I'm terrified that I'm going to disappear one day and no one will ever
find me. It happens more often than we know. People up and disappear
and aren't ever seen again."

Cole couldn't stand it anymore; he scooted his chair back and
reached for Sarah. He gently pulled her out of her chair and onto his
lap. Her legs hung to the side, and his arms banded around her, one
hand on her hip, the other tangled in the hair at the base of her neck,
his arm supporting her back at the same time.

"You bet your ass if you disappear, I'm going to find you. And I
think being scared is normal and probably somewhat healthy at this
point. Not that I like that you're frightened, but it'll keep you on your
toes, which is important. I also think you hide your feelings more than
most, and as a result, none of us realized exactly *how* frightened you are.
What can I do to help? To make you feel safer?"

She didn't answer for a long time. Cole saw Francesca poke her head
out of the kitchen, but when she saw them, she backed away, giving
them privacy.

"I don't know. That's the problem," Sarah said. "I've spent a few
nights in a hotel up in Denver, and I felt fairly safe there, but I can't
spend the next who knows how long blowing my money on hotels. I
live in a pretty nice neighborhood, but I don't know most of my neighbors, besides Mrs. Grady, and she wouldn't be much help with Owen.
He outweighs us both by at least a hundred pounds. Even though I've
lived there all my life, the people I used to know have moved away. And
since I work such weird hours, I haven't been able to get to know the
new people who've bought houses around me."

"Have you thought about moving? You work here in Castle Rock. What if you sold your house and got an apartment here until you found something you liked?" Cole asked.

She was quiet a moment. Then, in a small voice, she said, "You don't think they'd be upset if I sold their house?"

Cole hated how unsure the woman in his arms sounded. "Absolutely not," he said with conviction. "I know you probably have a lot of great memories of your dads in that house, but you'll never lose those. You'll carry them in your heart and head forever. I didn't know your dads, but I'd venture a guess that Jackson would probably be mad if you were only holding on to it because of them."

A minute went by, then she said, "I *have* thought about it. I love my house, but it would be easier if I didn't have to drive back and forth to Castle Rock every day. And . . . sometimes being there is hard. Makes me miss them more. And when I wake up and Owen has left me something else, it scares me to death."

"There's an apartment complex here in Castle Rock that has a monitored entrance, and no one can get past the doorman unless they're a resident or they're specifically buzzed up by security," Cole told her.

"I saw that online. But there's a waiting list a mile long."

"We can talk to Logan and see if he has any pull."

Sarah's head came up at that, and the hope he saw in her gaze would've brought Cole to his knees if he were standing.

"Really?"

"Really."

Her face fell. "But I'd feel bad if I stole an apartment from someone else."

Cole's thumb moved back and forth on her soft skin at the base of her neck, trying to soothe her. "Would it make you feel safer?"

She nodded.

"You want me to ask Logan about it?"

Sarah hesitated, but eventually gave another nod.

"I'll call him later tonight."

"Thank you."

"Do you have a real estate agent?"

"No."

"Can I help you with that too?"

"I . . . I know what I just said, but thinking about selling my dads' house still freaks me out."

"You don't have to make any decisions right now. We'll see about moving you into an apartment and making sure you're safe first. You can decide if you like living here in Castle Rock. *Then* you can decide what you want to do."

"Okay. Cole?"

"Yeah, angel?"

"You promise if I disappear, you'll try to find me?"

Cole's heart almost broke. He moved the hand at her hip and palmed the side of her face. "I promise," he said, looking into her beautiful hazel eyes. "In fact, starting tonight, we'll institute a check-in system. Whatever you're comfortable with. You can text me when you get home and when you leave. If you give me your work schedule, I'll know when you're supposed to arrive at work and when you're leaving. That way, if I don't hear from you, I'll know something could be wrong."

"You'd do that?"

"Absolutely. You can check in with me as much as you want. It won't bother me, and if you ever need anything, or you're scared, just get in touch, and I'll come check things out."

"But I live twenty miles away."

Cole couldn't stop his thumb from brushing over the edge of her mouth. Her lips parted, and he resisted taking more liberties. "I wouldn't care if you lived an hour away. You need me, I'm there."

Her hand, which was curled around the nape of his neck, tightened.

"And you should know, I'd planned on texting and calling you anyway . . . not just because of that buttmunch messing with you. I want to hear about your day. Listen to you laugh. And it's probably too soon to even offer this, but if you're ever too scared to go back to your house in Parker, you can come to my place. It's not much, just an apartment not too far from the gym, but I have a guest room. I know we're just getting to know each other, but there are no strings attached to the offer. You can hole up in my guest room and not even have to see me if you don't want to. I want you to feel safe, Sarah. And if you're with me, I can guarantee I'll make sure no one fucks with you. Okay?"

He saw the tears in her eyes, but wasn't surprised when she fought them back and simply nodded.

"Good. Trust me, angel. Logan and his brothers are taking this very seriously. If there's anything to find on Owen, they'll dig it up. And even if there's not, they'll still figure out a way to get him off your back so you're free to live your life without having to watch behind you all the time. Okay?"

"Okay. Thank you. I've been so scared. I just knew I was going to end up on one of those shows on the ID channel. You know, where the women disappear without a trace and their bodies are never found?"

Her words made Cole shiver, but he leaned forward and gently kissed Sarah's forehead. "Ready to eat?"

"Yeah."

He helped her stand, then sit again in her own seat. Francesca must've been watching and waiting for them to finish their heartfelt discussion, because the moment Sarah had scooted back up to the table, she reappeared with a tray of food in her hand.

She placed steaming plates of pasta on the table. "Here you go! This is tonight's special. I expect you to tell me if it's too spicy or not spicy enough. Give me your honest reactions, no holding back. Okay?"

"It looks and smells delicious," Sarah told her.

Francesca beamed. "Ah, you are easy to please," she said, then turned to Cole. "Since your woman is too nice to tell me if something's wrong, I expect *you* to. Got it?"

Cole smiled. "You know I will. But when have I ever complained about anything you've made?"

"Never. But there's always a first time," she said with a smile. "Enjoy!" Then she turned and hurried back into the kitchen.

They ate in silence for several minutes before Sarah looked at him. Her fork was poised over her half-eaten meal, and she had red sauce on her chin. She smiled and said, "I can't believe how good this is."

Cole leaned over with his napkin and dabbed at her chin. "Right? I swear, Francesca is a genius with food. It's been a while since I've been here, and now I remember why."

"Why? I'd eat here every day if I didn't care about my cholesterol or weight," Sarah joked.

He patted his stomach. "Because I eat too much. It wouldn't look good for the owner of Rock Hard Gym to weigh four hundred pounds."

Sarah laughed, and Cole had never heard a better sound in his life. She'd had a hell of a day . . . and an even worse couple of months. But she hadn't lost the ability to find joy in the smallest things.

"That's true. I'm totally full, but can't stop eating."

"If you can't finish, I'm happy to help you," Cole told her as he reached toward her plate with his fork.

Sarah mock-stabbed at him with her own fork. "Keep your silverware to yourself!" she admonished. "I'm gonna eat every bite of this, then bitch and moan the rest of the day about how full I am . . . but it'll be worth it."

God, she's beautiful, Cole thought as he watched her relax and joke with him. Once she let down her guard, her true inner light shone brightly. He knew he was waxing poetic, but couldn't help it.

They finished their food and had nothing but praise for Francesca. When it came time to leave, Cole pulled out his wallet, but Francesca refused to take his card.

"Your money's no good here, Cole. Put that away," she fussed.

"Are you ever going to let me pay?" he grumbled good-naturedly.

"Nope," she told him with a smile.

A waitress came out of the kitchen just then with a large plastic bag and handed it to Sarah, who took it without a word, but with a confused look on her face.

"In case you get hungry later," Francesca told her. "It's a little sampling of just about everything on the menu. Anyone who can make Cole here smile like he hasn't a care in the world is good people and always welcome in my restaurant. You come in anytime. No reservation necessary. I keep a few tables every night for my very favorite guests. You're now included in that small number."

Sarah just stared at Francesca for a moment before thanking her profusely.

As Cole expected, the older woman waved off her thanks. "Hush. I could tell the second I saw Cole that you're special. Not many people have seen past Cole's tough exterior. You've obviously not only seen beyond it, you've embraced all that he is. Don't let that food go to waste. Now, you two get. I've got customers coming soon, and I'm sure you have better things to do than stand around talking to an old woman."

With that, Francesca stood on tiptoe, and Cole leaned down so she could kiss him on the cheek. She hugged a slightly shell-shocked Sarah, then turned and headed back to the kitchen.

"What just happened?" Sarah asked as Cole took her arm and steered her out the door.

"You were just officially welcomed to the city of Castle Rock," Cole said warmly. "The only people who have an open invitation to come and eat whenever they want are Logan and his brothers, and their wives, of course."

"And you," she said.

"And me," Cole agreed. "And now you."

"Why?"

"This space used to be the Mason Architectural Firm. When Grace's parents were put in jail, the business closed, for obvious reasons.

Francesca bought it and turned it into Scarpetti's. She worked her butt off trying to get customers to give her a try, but it was rough going there for a while. Logan and his brothers ate here practically every night, since they were single and too lazy to cook for themselves. They also worked a lot of cases before they found their women. I think Francesca felt sorry for the 'poor single men' and discounted their meals almost every time. Eventually the restaurant took off, but she never forgot their support, and how loyal they were from the very beginning."

"And you?" Sarah asked as they headed for the parking lot. "How'd you get in her good graces?"

"Because I'm cute?" Cole asked with a smile.

Sarah smiled and playfully smacked his shoulder. "I'm serious."

Cole shrugged. "I'm single. I don't like to cook. I live nearby. I think she felt sorry for me too because I ate there so much. I also might've given her a free membership for life to the gym, and she comes in most mornings at five when we open to get in her daily two-mile walk."

Sarah stopped in the middle of the sidewalk—and Cole immediately looked around to see if she was reacting to a threat. When he felt her hand on his arm, his gaze swung to hers.

"You're a good man, Cole Johnson."

He shook his head. "I'm not. At least, not like you're thinking."

"Cole, you gave Francesca a free membership to your gym."

"Yeah, because I knew it would put me in her good graces, and I'd be able to get homemade Italian food whenever I wanted. It costs me nothing to let her use one of the treadmills for forty minutes every day for free. Don't put me on a pedestal, Sarah. I'm not always the nice guy you're thinking I am. I mean, I'm not a serial killer or anything, but I'm happy to take the parking space closest to the door, I cut people off on the highway, and I've never offered to help carry anyone's groceries."

She didn't look away from him as he outlined his transgressions. "It might not cost you anything, but you've given Francesca a safe place to walk every morning where she doesn't have to worry about being harassed or hit by a car or even assaulted. You aren't a woman, so you have no idea how important that is. I bet she's made friends with everyone she sees every morning, so you've also given her that too . . . the ability to meet people."

Cole shook his head and brushed a lock of her hair behind her ear. "I love that you see the world through those rose-colored glasses of yours."

Sarah frowned. "I'm not an idiot, Cole. I know there's bad in the world. I see it on a daily basis. People die in the hospital without the comfort of their children at their side. I've seen people fight over their loved ones' belongings before they've even gotten cold on their deathbed. I've seen the harm a husband can do to his wife and watched her go right back to him the second she's able to get up from her hospital bed. And I've seen women who've tried to kill their boyfriends for some imagined slight.

"I choose to be nice instead of being mean. There's way too much hate in the world. Maybe it's the same amount that was always around before the internet came to be and we could see the bad stuff the second it happened. There have always been shootings, kidnappings, and murders, but now they're all shoved down our throats every second of every day. I know I remember when someone's nice to me way longer than when they're mean. That's the world I want to live in. One where humans do nice things for each other without wanting something in return. You're a *good* man, Cole. And nothing you can say will convince me otherwise."

She took a deep breath after her little speech, as if she'd been talking as fast as possible in case he decided to interrupt her.

"Don't ever change," he told her. "You're right. And like I've said before, the world needs more people like you in it. I'm going to do my damnedest to let you live in your world of nice by standing between you and the anuspinchers whenever possible."

She chuckled at his word usage, but said, "You don't have to shield me, Cole. Just let me do my thing, and don't make fun of me for it."

"Never," he vowed. The day he mocked her for being a gentle, beautiful soul was the day he stopped deserving her. "Come on, I know you're tired. You've had a long day."

He crooked his elbow and draped her arm over it, keeping her snug against his side as they walked the rest of the way to the parking lot. When they got to her car, he placed the bag of food on the floor of her back seat. After she opened the driver's-side door, he crowded her against the metal, placing his hands on her hips.

"Text me when you get home," he ordered.

"Okay."

"Make sure you lock all your doors when you get there."

"I always do," she told him.

"And if you go out again, let me know, and text when you get home."

"I will."

"I'll make some calls about the apartment here in town."

"I appreciate it. I'm still not sure about moving, but every time I have to drive to the hospital, I'm paranoid, wondering if Owen is following me. He could easily run me off the road and snatch me before I knew what was happening. And without Mike and Jackson, the house just seems too big. Empty."

"When can you come by the gym for more lessons?" Cole asked.

Sarah shrugged. She was working for the next three days, but she had no idea what Cole's schedule was and didn't want a repeat of the day they'd met, when he'd overbooked himself.

"I can come to your house if that works out better."

She stared up at him. "You can't come all the way to Parker."

"Why not?"

"Because. It's out of your way, Cole."

"If you live there, it's not out of my way," he reassured her. "Sarah, I'm not sure if you understand what's going on here. I'm not just some guy you're working with. Or, I was until that first lesson at the gym. Then I became more."

"More, huh?" She liked that. A lot.

"Yeah. This was our second date," he reminded her. "*Date*, angel. The thing that two people do when they're interested in each other. When they want to get to know each other better. And I want to know more. I'm not stupid either. I know a good thing when I see it . . . and you could possibly be the best thing that's ever happened to me. I'm not going to let you slip through my fingers simply because you happen to live in the next city over.

"The question is—are you feeling even a tenth of what I am? Can you feel the chemistry between us? I think you can, but I could be misreading everything. You might just be thankful for my help with the situation with Owen. If that's the case, speak up now. The last thing I want to do is make you uncomfortable with my attention. That's what's happening with jerkhead, and I definitely won't be that guy. Just say the word, and I'll back off. I'll be your self-defense coach, be the liaison between you and Ace Security, help you get that apartment, and that'll be it."

"No!" Sarah exclaimed.

Cole breathed out a sigh of relief at her vehement response.

"I couldn't believe you bothered to chase me down. I mean, I know you did it because you didn't want to lose a potential customer, and you were doing Logan a favor, but you were so apologetic . . . and I have to admit that I thought you were good-looking, even if you *had* been kind of a jerk."

He smiled. "So you'll let me know when you get home?"

She nodded.

"And you'll let me take you out on another date?"

She nodded again.

He smiled gently. "And you'll let me kiss you at the end of our third date?"

She blushed, but nodded yet again. "You can kiss me now if you want," she said shyly.

God. Cole's dick immediately got hard. Oh, how he wanted to. He wanted to lick her plump lips and hold her against him as he learned her taste. But he was enjoying the buildup. The anticipation. He'd only known her for a week. He could wait. Maybe.

He leaned in and loved how her eyes slowly closed and she tilted her chin up to take whatever he wanted to give her. His lips brushed against her forehead gently, and then he kissed each closed eyelid before pulling back.

"Far be it from me to break your no-kisses-until-the-third-date rule," he said with a smile when her eyes popped open and she stared at him incredulously.

She returned the grin and hugged him tightly for a long moment. "Thanks for being a good guy," she whispered.

"Drive safe," he told her, pulling back and holding the door as she sat in the driver's seat. He wasn't going to tell her that he wasn't a good guy again. He liked that she saw him that way and vowed to never do anything that would tarnish the image she had of him. "Don't forget to text me when you get home."

"I won't."

"Later."

"Later."

Cole stood in the parking lot for a few minutes after she'd pulled out, until he couldn't see her car anymore. She might not truly understand how much her life had just changed by agreeing to go out with him . . . but she would.

Cole had a feeling Sarah was the woman he'd waited his whole life for. He'd watched his friends fall in love and get married, and he hadn't once felt jealous of them. He'd known his time would come.

And it had. In the form of a five-foot-seven angel.

Chapter Seven

The next week and a half passed without Sarah having a chance to see Cole. But that didn't mean they didn't communicate. She went from having her phone as simply a piece of safety equipment, carrying it around just in case her car broke down, to texting nonstop.

Cole sent her notes all day, every day. Sometimes he just inquired about how she was doing, and other times they got into in-depth text conversations about some random topic or another.

As Sarah drove home after a grueling shift, she thought back to the conversation they'd had during her last break that day at the hospital.

Cole: Did you talk to any of the real estate agents I recommended?

Sarah: Yeah. I have an appointment with one in a few days. She's going to come over and look at the house and let me know what she thinks.

Cole: Good.

Sarah: Thanks for the recommendation.

Cole: Of course. And I heard from the manager of that apartment complex here in town. He says they have a vacancy coming up in about two weeks, and that it's yours if you want it.

Sarah: Really? Wow!

Cole: The only thing is that it's a studio apartment.

Sarah: Oh.

Cole: Yeah. Not ideal. But I can help put the stuff that won't fit into storage for you, and it won't be forever. Once you're in, you'll have a better shot at getting a bigger place when it becomes available.

Sarah: True. I appreciate your help more than I can say.

Cole: You have the next three days off, right?

Sarah: Yes.

Cole: We haven't had a chance to get together in a while . . . are you up for another lesson?

Sarah: Yes.

Cole: Good. Because I'd already planned to have Nathan and Joel come tomorrow afternoon and help me out.

Sarah: Joel?

Cole: Bailey's little brother.

Cole: You still there?

Sarah: Yeah. I'm not sure about this.

Cole: About having them help? Trust me, angel. It'll be fun.

Sarah: If you say so.

Cole: I do. And I was thinking if you could come a little early tomorrow, around four, we could do the self-defense thing, I could take you over to the apartments so you could check out the studio, then I could bring you back to my place for dinner.

Cole: That is . . . if you don't already have plans.

Sarah: The only plan I had was to maybe try to figure out where to start on packing.

Cole: I can help you with that the day after tomorrow.

Sarah: Felicity is gonna fire you if you don't start working more. :)

Cole: Nah. She knows I'll be around less when you're not working and more when you're on shift.

Cole: Sarah? You still there?

Sarah: You changed your work schedule to match mine?

Cole: Yeah. After the last week or so when we couldn't get our sched-ules to mesh, I figured if I want to see you, that was the easiest way to accomplish it.

Sarah: I don't know what to say.

Cole: Say you'll come for a lesson tomorrow, then have dinner with me.

Sarah: I'd love to.

Cole: Good.

Sarah: Cole?

Cole: Right here.

Sarah: I think that's the nicest thing anyone has ever done for me.

Cole: Get used to it, angel. I was serious when I told you I wanted to see where this thing between us could go.

Sarah: Thank you.

Cole: I need to get going. There's some sort of altercation out at the front desk. But first, you okay? No more presents or letters?

Sarah: I'm good, and I haven't received anything since the cookbook.

Cole: Excellent. But don't let down your guard. Let me know when you leave work and when you get home.

Sarah: I will.

Cole: Be safe. I'll talk to you later.

Sarah: You too. Bye.

Cole: Bye.

Sarah had dated in the past. Men who she'd thought were nice and who'd treated her with respect. But no one had ever made her feel the way Cole did. She knew some people would think he was high-handed and bossy . . . especially for someone she'd known for such a short time.

But Sarah saw him in a different light. They'd talked on the phone for hours in the past week or so. Cole was a worrier. He worried about Felicity. He worried about societal pressures on Bailey and Nathan since they had no plans on getting married, even though they were both more than happy about their decision. He worried about his parents in

Arizona and the fact that he was so far away if they needed something. He worried about his brother. He especially worried about Logan and Grace's babies . . . little Ace and Nate.

So everything he'd done for her so far—giving her recommendations for real estate agents to help her decide if she wanted to sell her house, talking to the manager of the apartment complex in Castle Rock with the security he thought was vital, sending her reviews of the best video cameras for outside her house and lightly badgering her to make a decision already, even telling her he'd researched the Adoption Exchange and had made a donation on behalf of Rock Hard Gym—had been done because he was thinking, and worrying, about her.

So far, she hadn't seen that he was all that traditionally romantic, but she'd take someone looking out for her well-being and safety over roses and candy any day. She'd had enough of the latter two to last a lifetime.

The second Sarah pulled into her driveway, she saw the box tied with a big red bow on her front porch.

It was dark outside. She'd had to stay late and finish up some paperwork before she'd been able to leave the hospital. Then there'd been a wreck on the road, and she'd been held up for an extra fifteen minutes or so.

Hating that she still hadn't cleaned out her garage, and vowing that was the first thing she was going to tackle when she started packing up the house, she turned off her car and took a deep breath. Gathering up her purse and holding her phone in her hand, her thumb hovering over the speed dial for 911, she got out of the car and headed for the front door.

She didn't see Owen or anyone else lurking around her front porch, but that didn't mean he wasn't going to leap out of the bushes or come running around the side of her house the second her back was turned.

The box was smaller than the one that had held the dollhouse, but Sarah had learned when it came to Owen's gifts, sometimes the smaller the box, the scarier the contents. She wanted to leave it sitting outside, but knew she needed to open it and document whatever he'd sent her this time.

Feeling sick, she quickly unlocked the door and pushed the box inside with her foot. Once the door was shut behind her, and she'd locked the dead bolt and put on the safety chain, she relaxed slightly.

Then, doing the thing she hated the most, she put her purse down on the kitchen counter and started her walk-through of the house. She turned on every light she passed, checking inside the closets and under the beds to make sure she was truly alone in her home. Her greatest nightmare would be to wake up in the middle of the night to Owen climbing out from under her bed or something.

Once she was one hundred percent sure she was alone, she stood in the middle of her bedroom and shot a quick text to Cole.

Sarah: I'm home.

The three dots on the bottom of the screen letting her know Cole was responding showed up immediately.

Cole: It took longer than usual for you to get home??

Sarah: Accident.

She knew she wasn't being as chatty as she usually was, but the dread of having to open the box downstairs was hanging over her like a wet blanket.

Cole: What's wrong?

Figured he'd pick up on her feelings.

Sarah: Long day. Long drive. And a freaking box on my doorstep.

Twenty seconds later, Sarah startled badly when the phone rang in her hand. She saw it was Cole calling.

"Hi," she said after she unlocked the phone.

"Are you all right?"

Sarah sighed. She loved Cole's voice. It was deep, soothing, and just hearing it made her feel a hundred times better.

"Yeah. Just dreading finding out what he sent me this time."

"You been through the house yet?"

Cole knew her ritual. She'd told him how she'd started searching the house to make sure she was truly alone after she started receiving the presents.

"Yeah. It's empty."

"Good. You want to come earlier tomorrow?"

Damn, he was sweet. "Yeah, but I can't. I promised myself that I'd get some packing done. I've been putting it off way too long. I have a ton of stuff I have to take to Goodwill, and I really want to clear out one side of the garage so I can park in there."

She heard Cole sigh. "I wish I could come and help you, but I'm meeting with Grace and Felicity to talk marketing in the morning, then I have a couple of classes I'm teaching in the early afternoon."

"It's okay," Sarah told him.

"It's not," Cole insisted.

"Cole, I'm a big girl. I've been putting this off, and I need to get off my ass and get it done, once and for all. Besides, I have a feeling it's going to be hard, because I know I'm going to have to get rid of a lot of Mike and Jackson's stuff that I've been holding on to. I wouldn't be good company."

"You don't have to always be 'on' around me, angel. That's part of being in a relationship with someone. You see them when they're upset. Or angry. Or sad."

"I know, but . . . I don't want you to have any reason to not want to be with me. Cole, we've barely been dating."

"Sarah, that's one thing you definitely don't have to worry about. I swear I feel as if I've already come to know you better in just a few weeks than anyone I've ever dated before."

Sarah sat on the edge of her mattress and closed her eyes. She felt exactly the same way. They'd had some pretty open conversations on the phone since they'd last seen each other. They talked about a lot of the things that new couples wouldn't touch with a ten-foot pole. Gay marriage, politics, sexual harassment in the context of celebrities and public figures, the death penalty, even the legalization of marijuana.

"I feel the same," she told him after a beat.

"Feel free to come early," Cole said. "Joel and Nathan can't get here until around four, but you're always more than welcome to come before that. It'll give me time to have you all to myself for a while."

Sarah giggled at that. "All to yourself except for the million questions your staff will inevitably have for you."

"Semantics," he said with a laugh.

Sarah loved this. Loved bantering back and forth with him. She'd never been a phone kind of gal, but found that she could talk for hours with Cole and not even realize how much time had gone by.

"Feel better?" he asked quietly.

Realizing what he'd done, that he'd successfully taken her mind off the fact that she had to go downstairs and open her latest present, Sarah took a deep breath. "Actually . . . yes. Thank you."

"Don't ever thank me for that," he said gruffly. "I hate that I'm not there with you now. That I can't take care of that damn box for you. That you have to open it yourself. Maybe you can bring it with you and open it here tomorrow?"

She appreciated his concern, but said, "There's no way I can leave it unopened all night and most of the day tomorrow. I have to know what's in it."

"I could call Logan or one of the others, and they could come over there and do it for you."

"No. Don't bother them. And before you offer, the cops aren't going to come over and watch me open a present, Cole."

He sighed. "What if it's something dangerous?"

"Owen isn't going to send me a bomb," Sarah told him. She was about eighty-five percent sure of that. The fact that she wasn't one hundred percent sure was a little scary, but she refused to even go down that road.

"You don't know that," Cole said.

"Please, you're not helping," Sarah replied.

Cole was silent so long, she wondered if he was still there, but he finally said, "Okay. But I'm staying on the phone while you open it."

Sarah sighed in relief. "I'd like that."

"Whatever you need, I'll bust my ass to do it for you, angel."

"Okay. Here I go." Neither said anything as she padded back down the hallway to the stairs. She walked through the living area to the front foyer, where she'd left the box. Leaning down, she gingerly picked it up and carried it into the kitchen. The package was about the size of a shoebox, and very light. She got a pair of scissors and sliced through the tape on either side.

There was no address on it, meaning Owen had dropped it off in person rather than mailing it. Sarah hated that he knew where she lived, but she'd had months to reluctantly accept that creep factor.

"I'm going to put you on speaker," she told Cole, doing just that. Putting her cell down on the counter, she said, "I'm taking the top off."

"Easy, angel. Slow and easy," Cole told her.

Sarah held her breath as she lifted the lid and placed it to the side of the box. "It's got a ton of paper towels inside it," she said as she began taking them out one by one. The counter was littered with the paper by the time she got to the contents of the box.

"What is it?" Cole asked.

Sarah gazed down at the plastic bag inside the shoebox for a long moment. "Jewelry," she told Cole.

"Seriously?"

"Yeah." Sarah picked up the plastic bag and held it so she could examine the contents. "Earrings, bracelets, and necklaces, from what I can see. They look old. Maybe antiques? I'm not sure."

"Is that it?"

"No. There's a note."

When she didn't say anything for a long moment, Cole asked, "What does it say?"

"I'm scared to open it," Sarah admitted.

"I'm right here. It could be important," Cole said softly.

Taking a deep breath to try to bolster her courage, Sarah slowly unfolded the piece of paper. It was wrinkled and folded over and over four times. It reminded her of something a kid would do when passing a note in class. She read the words written there out loud.

Sarah,

Mom said I should give these to a girl I liked and she'd love me forever.

So I'm giving them to you so we can be together until we're dead.

See you soon.

Owen

Sarah blanched. Reading the creepy letter, knowing Owen was out there somewhere, watching, waiting, pushed her stress level that much higher.

She must've made a noise, because Cole swore long and hard. "I'm on my way."

Realizing that he was serious, and probably literally walking out the door right that second, Sarah shook her head and got herself together. She snatched up the phone and spoke into the speaker even as she was heading back up the stairs to her room.

"No! I'm okay."

"You're not okay," Cole countered. "That note was creepy as fuck, and I don't blame you for being scared."

"I know. But I'm really okay. We knew it would be from him, so that wasn't a surprise. I'm just tired of this. I don't know what his end-game is. I'm okay, Cole. I promise. I'll feel terrible if you drive all the way out here. I'm a big girl. I can handle this."

She could hear him breathing hard, and wasn't sure if it was because he was still headed for his car or if he was trying to control his obvious frustration and anger on her behalf.

Sarah knew Cole had been frustrated the last time he'd talked to Logan, when the other man had reported that Ace Security had yet to find anything in Owen's background that led them to believe he was dangerous or otherwise unstable. He had dropped out of school when he was sixteen, had worked at several fast-food restaurants over the years, and was currently a forty-four-year-old recluse . . . but that was about it. He didn't have a criminal record, and when Alexis had hacked into the juvenile records at the police station, she hadn't found anything on him there either.

"This shit has to stop," Cole said. "I'm calling Logan after I hang up with you to tell him about the latest gift and note, and see what he's been able to dig up. There has to be *something* more we can find on this guy. He has to be somewhere. He's not a wizard; he can't just conjure himself up on your doorstep, then disappear again."

His comment had Sarah trying to stifle a chuckle. It was bad timing, but the thought of Owen wearing a wizard's pointy hat and robe was funny.

"God, I love that sound, even if I have no idea what you're laughing about," Cole said after a moment. "And I also have no idea how in the world you can find anything humorous right about now."

"I can either laugh or cry. And Mike always told me the best thing to do when you feel shitty is to find the bright side of the situation."

"There's a bright side to this asshole harassing you?" Cole asked.

Sarah sat on the edge of her mattress, then fell backward and stared at the ceiling above her head. The phone was still on speaker, and she held it close to her mouth as she said, "Yeah."

"What?"

"You."

Cole didn't respond, so Sarah tried to explain.

"If Owen hadn't started his campaign of gifts for whatever reason, I wouldn't have emailed Logan. And if I hadn't emailed Logan, he wouldn't have referred me to Rock Hard Gym's self-defense classes. And I wouldn't have met *you*."

"Damn, angel," Cole said softly. "But I disagree."

"With what?" she asked, confused.

"I would've found you without that ass scaring you half to death. Somehow, someway. I have to believe that. I've never felt this way about a woman before. Never found myself thinking about her nonstop. Wondering how her day was going. If she was thinking about me. How she was feeling. If she was happy, sad, worried, hungry, or any of a hundred other emotions. We would've found each other, angel. I know it."

It was one of the nicest things anyone had ever said to her. "I've thought about you too."

"Good. You get something to eat tonight?"

Sarah's eyes went to the clock. After a full twelve-hour shift, the accident making her get home later than normal, talking with Cole, and dealing with her latest gift, she realized she was exhausted. "No. But I'm not hungry," she tacked on quickly, knowing he'd insist on her getting up and getting something. "Besides, I finished off the rest of Francesca's leftovers for lunch today. I swear, if I ate that way all the time, Owen wouldn't be able to drag me off anywhere because I'd be too heavy."

"First, you're dating a guy who owns a gym. Which means you have free access to work out whenever you want. Second, when we progress a little further in our relationship, I can guarantee you a *great* workout anytime you want, which doesn't include going to the gym at all, if you know what I mean. And third, I don't give a shit how much you weigh. I just want you to be happy. And if that means eating Francesca's food every day for the rest of your life, and you gaining a million pounds, so be it."

Sarah rolled over on her side and squeezed her thighs together. She was still stuck back on number two and barely heard the rest of what he'd said.

"Text me tomorrow," he ordered gently.

"But when I leave here, I'm going straight to the gym, and I'll see you there," Sarah reminded him.

"Don't care. Hearing from you has been the highlight of my days the last week and a half. Text me when you get up. When you're sad from going through your dads' stuff. When you stop to eat lunch. When you leave to head down here."

"I thought you were going to be busy?" Sarah asked.

"I'll never be too busy for you. Just text. Okay?"

"Okay," she agreed without hesitation. She'd never complain about Cole wanting to hear from her, because the alternative was that he didn't give a shit.

"Sleep well," he said softly.

"I will. I'm exhausted."

"I'll see you tomorrow."

"Bye, Cole."

"Bye, angel."

Sarah clicked off the phone and rolled back over so she was once again looking up at the ceiling. She stayed that way for a while, then sat up and headed for the bathroom. She changed and brushed her teeth, then climbed back into her bed. Leaning over, she grabbed her vibrator from the drawer in her nightstand. She hoped it still worked, as it had been a while since she'd been in the mood to use it.

Clicking it on, she was rewarded with a strong buzz. Smiling, she scooted under the covers and closed her eyes. She pictured Cole in her mind, lifting weights, his muscles bulging as he smiled at her.

She shoved her sleep shorts down to her knees and put her feet flat on the mattress. Then she brought the buzzing vibrator down between her legs and let herself fantasize about Cole. How he'd feel under her hands. Between her legs. If his beard would be scratchy against her inner thighs. She knew without a doubt Cole would be a generous lover, that he'd do whatever it took to make sure she was satisfied. She couldn't wait to get her hands on his body as well. To feel his muscles for herself. To lick every inch of his tattooed skin.

Before she knew it, she was soaked, and the vibrations against her clit had done their job. Her thighs shook, and her ass lifted off the bed as she came. The orgasm hit her hard and fast . . . and was satisfying enough. But even as she wiped off the toy and placed it back in the drawer, she had a feeling it was nothing compared to how she'd soar when she was with Cole.

Maybe assuming that he could make her come harder and longer than she could with her vibrator was wishful thinking, but she doubted it. Cole was more observant than anyone she'd ever been with. And she had a feeling that would carry over into the bedroom as well.

If Cole Johnson was terrible in bed, it would be a shame. He had a body built for sex, and she hoped like hell he knew how to use it accordingly.

Chapter Eight

Cole was thrilled when he was able to pawn off his second CrossFit class of the day on one of the newer employees. Brittany was outgoing and enthusiastic and happily said she'd take over the class for him.

The morning had been taken up talking with Grace and Felicity about what new activities they could offer that weren't available at any of the other local gyms and organizing another "black light" night. They hadn't done one in a while, and the community seemed to really enjoy them. It was another chance for locals to hang out in a relaxed atmosphere and chill.

But Cole couldn't keep his mind off Sarah. She'd texted him like he'd asked, and every time his phone vibrated, she'd made him smile. He wasn't able to talk to her like he wanted, but he still took the time to send her short responses so she knew he'd received each text and appreciated it.

He hated that she lived all the way out in Parker. It wasn't exactly Timbuktu, but it felt like it. He wanted her here in Castle Rock. Partly because it would be safer in the apartment complex. Owen wouldn't be able to leave her any more gifts because he wouldn't have access to her front door. But most important, living there would bring her closer to Cole.

He had tried to figure out what it was about Sarah that drew him like a moth to a flame, but quickly gave up analyzing his feelings. He liked her. Plain and simple. She was pretty. Considerate. And had a core of inner strength he didn't think Sarah even knew she had.

And she had no idea of her own worth. But that was okay. He'd teach her how special she was.

Around two thirty, Cole headed outside toward the parking lot at the end of the downtown area. Sarah had texted him almost twenty-five minutes earlier and said she was on her way. About four minutes after he'd leaned against the brick wall of the building on one side of the lot, he saw her Galant pull in. He was at her door by the time she'd turned off the engine.

He reached down and helped her out and, without thinking about it, brushed a short kiss on her lips. "Hey, angel."

She blushed, but smiled up at him. "Hi."

"It's really good to see you."

"You too."

Cole ran his eyes down her body, then back up. She was wearing a pair of jeans and a simple T-shirt. Her outfit was perfect for what he had planned for their lesson today, and more important, she looked comfortable in her own skin. He loved that. He'd dated women who felt they always had to look as if they'd just walked off a runway or something. He liked Sarah's comfortable, laid-back look much better. That wasn't to say he wasn't looking forward to seeing Sarah all dolled up for him—he was—but for now, what she was wearing was perfect.

As if she could tell he was thinking about her outfit, she asked, gesturing to herself, "Is this okay? I usually don't wear scrubs on my day off, but I wasn't sure what I should wear."

"It's perfect. You have everything you need?"

She nodded and hitched her purse onto her shoulder as she stepped out of the way of her door.

Cole shut it, and when they started walking back toward the gym, he put his hand on the small of her back. He hadn't missed the way she leaned into him anytime he did so, and he'd never complain about the opportunity to put his hands on her.

"How'd the rest of the morning go?" he asked. "Did you get the garage cleaned out enough so you could put your car in there?"

She beamed. "I did. And honestly, it wasn't as hard as I thought it would be. Most of the boxes in there were full of crap from when I was little. I'm guessing Mike didn't want to throw it away—he was always the more sentimental of my dads. Clothes, stuffed animals, toys."

"Where is it now?"

"I made a sign with the word *free* on it and stuck it all on the curb. Guarantee by the time I get home tonight, most of it will be gone. Anything that might be left, I'll take to the Adoption Exchange. I'm sure they can use it."

"That's awesome."

"Yeah." Her face fell. "But tomorrow I have to tackle the rest of the house. I know there's a bunch of stuff up in the attic, but it'll just have to wait. I hadn't realized exactly how much crap we'd accumulated. I guess that's not surprising, considering how long we all lived there."

"Are you okay with this?" Cole asked as they neared the gym.

"Surprisingly, yes. I'm a little sad, I can't deny it, but I'm also excited to start over, if that makes sense. To purge all the stuff and minimize a little bit. I've been in that big house by myself for so long, I think it'll be nice to have a smaller place that won't be as hard to keep clean or tidy."

A sudden vision of him and Sarah standing shoulder to shoulder as they cooked in the kitchen in his apartment came to mind. Right after that, he saw them dancing and fooling around in his living room. And on the heels of *that* was the carnal mental image of the two of them in his bed, making love among his mussed sheets.

And that thought brought back the memories of the night before . . . when he'd lain there fantasizing about her and jerking off.

"Cole?"

Her voice brought him out of his ruminations. "Yeah, angel?"

"Where were you? You seemed a million miles away," she observed.

Cole smiled at her. "Just thinking. And yeah, I can imagine that it would be freeing not to have to worry about the upkeep of your house anymore. You'll always have the memories you made in that house. I love my apartment. It's got three bedrooms and is plenty roomy. I don't have to take care of the lawn, and it's even relatively quiet. I've got good neighbors."

She made a face. "I hadn't even thought about that. I hope the people who live near that studio are quiet."

"We can ask later today when we go over there," he reassured her.

He followed her into the gym, and smiled when she greeted an older woman who was leaving and waved at a toddler on her dad's hip as they headed for the childcare center. He and Felicity had recently set it up to accommodate parents so they could work out without having to go through the hassle of getting a babysitter.

Cole waited patiently as she went over and said hello to Felicity, who was standing behind the front desk. Sarah had been there only minutes, but he swore the atmosphere in the lobby was already ten times happier because she was spreading her unique brand of niceness.

"Sorry," she said sheepishly when she got back to him. "Felicity texted me this morning and said she would be here, and that she was looking forward to seeing me again, so I had to go say something. I don't even know how she got my number."

"I gave it to her," Cole told her.

"You did?" Sarah asked as they entered his office.

Cole wanted nothing more than to drag her over to the love seat and ravish her, but he controlled himself. "Yeah. I thought it was important that all the guys and their women have your number."

"Why?" she asked.

Cole stopped and eyed the door, making sure it was closed. The last thing he wanted was everyone in the waiting area to hear his conversation. He'd learned his lesson after his fuckup with Sarah.

"Because you're a part of our tribe. I want you to get to know Grace, Bailey, Alexis, and Felicity better. I want you to know bone-deep that you can count on their men to be by your side if you need them, just as you can rely on *me* to be there."

"Why?" Sarah whispered again.

"Because I plan on you being around for a very long time. Because they're important to me, and so are you. Because they're like my family. Because I heard what you said the other day. If you disappear, we're going to notice and do something about it."

She smiled at him. "Thanks."

"You're welcome." They talked a bit more about how their week had gone and what they'd done. Sarah told him some amusing stories about a few of her patients, the things she could share, and Cole recounted tales about the things some of the gym patrons did to try to catch the eye of the opposite sex.

Before they knew it, Felicity was knocking on the door, letting them know that Nathan and Joel had arrived.

"You ready?" Cole asked.

"Yes. Is it wrong that I'm excited about this?"

"Nope," Cole told her with a smile.

"But I'm also nervous."

"Perfectly normal," he reassured her. He held out his hand, and she took hold. "Come on. You can leave your purse here. It'll be safe, I'll lock the door."

She nodded, and they headed for the door.

They went to the same room they'd used during her first lesson, and Cole immediately went and shook Nathan's hand.

"Thanks for coming," he told him.

"No problem. Joel was excited to come."

Cole turned to the little boy. "Hey, Joel. How are you?"

"Good. Do I get to throw you again today?"

Cole laughed. "You think you can?"

Joel's chest puffed out. "Yes!"

"Think you can help teach my friend Sarah how to do it too?"

Joel turned his gaze to Sarah and eyed her up and down. "She's kinda small," he observed.

"So are you," Cole said immediately.

"True. But I'm a guy."

Cole resisted the urge to laugh. Joel might be male, but he was shorter than Sarah, and she definitely outweighed him. But he wanted Sarah to understand that in self-defense, size didn't matter. It was all about learning how to leverage your body and getting away from whoever was trying to hurt or detain you.

"It doesn't matter if you're a guy or a girl," Cole told Joel. "As I've told you many times, it's how you use your body mass, not how big or small you are, that matters."

Joel nodded.

"It's nice to meet you," Sarah told Joel. "I'm kinda nervous about today, so I'd appreciate any help and pointers you can give me."

At that, Joel's chest puffed out again, and he nodded seriously. He walked over to her and patted her arm. "I'll help you. It's not that scary. If Nathan or Cole grab you from behind, just remember that it's them and not a bad guy, and don't really try to knee them in the nuts. Okay?"

Cole saw Sarah hide a smile behind one of her hands before she cleared her expression and nodded soberly. "Good tip. Thanks."

Then Joel took Sarah by the hand and dragged her over to the wall to see the dummies they'd practice hitting later.

Nathan wandered over to Cole's side and put his hands in his pockets. "I've never seen Joel take to someone so quickly before."

Cole didn't take his eyes from the woman and little boy across the room. "She seems to have that effect on everyone she meets."

"I like her," Nathan told him.

Cole dragged his gaze from Sarah to look at his friend, and Nathan continued speaking. "She seems to have a good head on her shoulders.

She isn't just depending on others to keep her safe. She's wanting to learn what she can do to help herself. And when the cops stonewalled her, she didn't give up, contacting Ace Security. She have family?"

Cole shook his head. "Her fathers were killed in that nightclub bombing up in Denver a few years ago."

"Shit," Nathan said. "That sucks."

Cole nodded.

"And she doesn't live here in town, does she?"

"No. In Parker. But I think this thing with Owen has convinced her once and for all to sell the house she grew up in and get an apartment down here. We have a meeting after this with the manager of those apartments on the other side of town, the ones that have the doorman and all the security."

"Good. Something about this case isn't right."

Cole narrowed his eyes at his friend. "In what way?"

"That's just it. I don't know. It's not presenting like any other stalking case we've had. Owen doesn't seem dangerous. He seems like a little kid with a crush. Even the presents he's left her are weird. He hasn't tried to talk to her or hurt her. Isn't tailing her everywhere. He hasn't caused any damage to her property. It's just . . . off."

Cole took a deep breath and nodded. "I'm glad it's not just me. I've been uneasy from day one. But I can't blame the cops for not being able to help her. This Owen guy hasn't broken any laws. He hasn't threatened her in any way. But that doesn't mean he isn't dangerous. That he doesn't have something planned."

"I know. As soon as Alexis finds out more about his disability claim, I'm going to look into his finances a little deeper. Maybe look at his mother's too. Blake is hunting down information on his father, to see if he's still around or what's up with him. There are just a lot of question marks in this case, and that makes me nervous."

"Same, bro. Same," Cole told him.

"Are we gonna start sometime today or what?" Joel called out from across the room.

"Keep your pants on!" Nathan yelled back. "Are you that eager for me to kick your butt?"

Cole chuckled as Joel smiled huge and took off running for Nathan, as if he were going to football-tackle him. Luckily, Nathan was ready, and he caught the little boy around the waist and hoisted him high in the air. They were both laughing by the time he put Joel back on his feet.

Cole gave the duo a wide berth and went to where Sarah was watching and smiling. "You ready for this?" he asked quietly.

She nodded. "Yes. I'm nervous, as I told Joel, but also excited. Ever since I was adopted, I let Mike and Jackson fight my battles for me— not that there have been that many," she was quick to add when she saw Cole's frown. "But learning what to do when someone puts their hands on me in a bad way makes me feel as if I'm truly taking control of my life. Is that weird?"

"Not at all," Cole reassured her. "Come on, let's get this started."

～

An hour later, Sarah knew she was going to be sore in places she didn't even know she had muscles, but she felt hyped up. Cole had taught her how to slip out of someone's hold if they grabbed her from behind, and what to do if they took hold of her arm too. She'd learned all the vulnerable spots to aim for with her elbows, knees, and even her fingers.

The main point Cole got across was that she would never win in a one-on-one fight with someone bigger and stronger than she was. Her goal was to make as much noise as she could and use her moves to get away from whoever was trying to overpower her.

It was a switch in thinking for her. She'd always worried about what she would do if Owen decided to snatch her off the street or from her car or something, but now she was more confident in the plan to bring attention to her situation and run like hell, if at all possible.

"That was fun!" Joel said with a huge smile as they made their way back to the front of the gym. "The look on Cole's face when you threw him over your shoulder was awesome!"

Sarah smiled at the little boy. She knew Cole had deliberately allowed her to grab him in the perfect spots, and had even given a little hop when she'd bent over to try to throw him. There was no way she'd be able to do that in real life, but hearing the laughter burst from Joel's mouth had been the icing on the cake.

"It was, wasn't it?" she asked. "Although I hope you aren't practicing that stuff on kids at your school."

Joel shook his head seriously. "No. Nathan says the stuff I'm learning should only be used in extreme situations. That I should use my brains instead of my fists when I can. That's how we outsmarted Donovan. He was bigger and meaner, but me and Nathan took him down with our smarts. Right?"

Nathan looked down at the boy at his side and ruffled his hair. "Yup."

Sarah had read the news stories about the gang member, and what had happened to him when he'd broken into Bailey's house and tried to kidnap her little brother. It sounded awful, but Joel obviously hadn't suffered any major mental anguish from the event.

"You ready to go pick up your sister?" Nathan asked him.

"Yup. Can I show her the thing with you grabbing me around the neck from behind?" he asked, jumping up and down as they walked.

"Yup."

"Righto!" Joel yelled and ran ahead to get the door.

Sarah was still smiling when Nathan turned to her. "You did good today. Keep practicing, and it'll become second nature. But what Joel said was right. Sometimes even when you know all the right things to do, things don't work out the way you plan. That's when you have to use your head. There's no way Cole or me or any of my brothers could tell you exactly what you should do in any given situation. There are always variables that we can't predict or analyze ahead of time. You have to play it by ear. Lie, cheat, steal . . . whatever it takes to keep yourself alive. Got it?"

Sarah knew her eyes were huge in her face, but she held Nathan's gaze and nodded.

"Good," he said, then nodded at her and Cole and made his way to Joel and the front door.

Sarah let out the breath she'd been holding in a whoosh.

"He's right," Cole said softly, walking her toward his office. "I can teach you every move in the book, and you could be an expert at them, but if someone catches you unawares, you might not have a chance to use them. But no matter what, you do *not* give up. You've got me and the others now; always know deep in your soul that we're coming for you. Got it?"

They were at his office door now, and he turned her back to the wall and stood in front of her.

Sarah looked up at him. "Do you think he's going to do something?" she asked quietly.

Cole didn't say anything for a long moment, merely pressed his lips together. Finally, he said, "Yeah, angel. I do. I'm not saying that to scare you. I think you know as well as I do that he's not right in the head. I don't know what he's planning or when he's planning on doing it, but yeah . . . I think eventually, he's going to need to act on this infatuation he seems to have with you."

Sarah was glad Cole wasn't sugarcoating her situation. Hearing someone say the very thing she was thinking was actually a relief. The cops had told her to be careful and had sent her on her way with a pat on the head. Her coworkers had thought his gifts were cute and thoughtful. Even Mrs. Grady had commented that *she* hadn't received flowers in forever.

Cole was the first person to come right out and say that he thought Owen's "little crush" wasn't normal.

"Me too," she whispered.

"I'm going to do everything in my power to keep you safe, but I can't be with you twenty-four/seven, as much as that kills me," Cole told her. "You're an adult with your own life, and you can't stop living it because you're afraid."

Sarah nodded.

"With that said, you do need to make sure you're not taking unnecessary risks, and you need to do whatever you can to be careful and smart. I think moving into the apartments here in town is a great first step. You'll feel much safer without having to worry about what gift might be on your doorstep when you get home . . . as will I."

Sarah reached out and grabbed Cole's arm. His skin was warm, and she had the momentary urge to lay her head on his chest, snuggle in, and beg him to take her to his apartment and watch over her for the rest of her life. She resisted.

But she did have the thought that with Cole by her side, no one would dare mess with her. If he'd already been her boyfriend when she'd met the Montrones, Owen wouldn't have gotten so obsessed with her.

"What is it?" Cole asked when she didn't say anything.

Shaking her head, she forced herself to stop thinking about what she wished had happened in the past, focusing on the man standing in front of her now. "Promise that you'll find me if he does kidnap me?"

Cole frowned and grabbed her elbow in his hand. He pushed open his office door and tugged her inside. He sat her on the love seat and knelt in front of her.

Sarah swallowed hard and looked into his eyes as he spoke.

"I promise," he vowed. "I'll have everyone I can think of working to find you. All the guys at Ace Security will help; Alexis will use her hacker skills to see what she can find. Hell, she'll contact the retired Navy SEAL guy she knows and have him do his thing too. Even Ryder's old team down in Colorado Springs will get in on the act. We would find you. You'd just have to hold on and be strong until we could get there. Hear me?"

She nodded, more scared than ever. She didn't feel strong. Not like Grace and the others. If Owen hurt her—

She cut off the thought. "I'll do what I can to get away," she whispered.

Cole reached up, put his hands on either side of her face, and waited until she focused on him. "Good. But if it doesn't work out, don't panic. Just know I'm coming for you, and you'll be all right."

"Okay," Sarah said.

"Okay?" he asked with an arch of a brow.

"Okay," she responded a little stronger.

"There's my girl," Cole said. Then he brought her head down and kissed her forehead before standing. "Enough talk of Creepy McCreepsters. Want to go see that apartment?"

"Yes." She reached up and took hold of Cole's hand once more. He grabbed her purse and passed it to her, and they walked out of his office hand in hand.

Twenty-five minutes later, Sarah stood in the middle of the studio apartment that was for rent and turned in a full circle. It wasn't huge, but then again, she was the only one who'd be living there. She could see the kitchen, living area, and the space where a bed would go all from her spot. There was a small closet, and a bathroom with a functional sink and shower. There wasn't a bathtub, but there was a place for a stacked washer and dryer, and it even had a dishwasher.

But the best part about the apartment was the security someone would have to go through to get up to the third floor, where she was located. The side doors were always locked from the inside. All occupants had to go through the front entrance, where there was a code to get inside the building. Then, if someone didn't have a resident ID, they would have to stop at the security desk and verify what apartment they were going to visit. There were cameras everywhere—in the elevators, stairwells, and hallways. Every apartment in the building had a chain lock, a dead bolt, and a lock on the doorknob itself.

Sarah had never felt safer.

The only problem was, there were other people applying for the apartment she was now standing in. She still felt bad about the idea of Cole or his friends calling in a favor and denying someone else the safe haven the building and apartment provided. They might need it more than she did.

"What do you think? Is it too small?" Cole asked.

Sarah shook her head.

"Are you sure?" Cole frowned, and his eyes roamed the space. "It's smaller than I thought it would be."

"It's just me," Sarah told him. "I don't need a lot of room."

His gaze found hers, and it looked like he was hesitating to speak. "What?" she asked.

"I want to say something, but I have a feeling it's too soon."

Now she was *really* curious. "It's okay. Say it."

"Fine . . . but remember, you asked for it. It's not just you who will be in here. I'm planning on spending as much time with you as you'll let me, just as I want you at my place as much as I can get you there. I'm not opposed to a queen-size bed, which will fit in here without any issues, because I like to snuggle when I sleep. But a king-size bed won't fit, not without totally overwhelming the space. And you'll need a big TV, and a comfortable couch. Once you get all that furniture in here, it might be cramped. And I like to cook. I'm not that great at it, but it's fun to try. The kitchen is functional, but I've seen the layouts of the two- and three-bedroom places here, and the kitchens are much bigger."

He didn't take his eyes from hers as he told her all his thoughts.

Sarah's pulse hammered in her throat, and she felt hot all of a sudden. Cole was a *snuggler*? *God.* The image of him spooning behind her, one arm around her waist, his leg thrown over hers, flashed through her mind.

She wanted that.

She wanted *him*.

Screw the fact that she hadn't been with anyone in years.

For a moment, she forgot about Owen Montrone and his fascination with her.

She could only think about them making dinner together, then falling into bed, making love. Snuggling as they watched whatever football game happened to be on television.

"What's going through that mind of yours?" Cole asked. He hadn't touched her. Hadn't come closer, but the look in his eyes was intense.

"I want to take the apartment." She knew he wasn't trying to talk her out of moving to Castle Rock, and she understood the space issue. "Maybe I can stay here when you're working, or during the day when I'm on night shift, but be at your place other times. My bed *is* a queen, so that should work. And one thing Jackson insisted on was a big TV so he could watch his sports, so I've got that covered. You're right that the kitchen isn't huge, but I think we could still both fit in there. I wasn't going to move the huge sectional from my house—I was going to sell it—but I've still got a smaller one that is super comfortable and should be okay in here. I don't want to wait for another apartment to open up, because Owen is freaking me out, but also because it'll mean I can't see *you* more often if I wait." She held her breath, hoping she hadn't said too much.

Cole reached out and put his hand on her nape, and she thought for sure he was going to kiss her, but instead he just stood there. His thumb brushed against the side of her neck, sending goose bumps up and down her arms. "I can guarantee you're going to see me more often," he finally said. "Ready for dinner?"

Sarah blinked. His change in topic was abrupt and somewhat disappointing after everything they'd just said. "Yeah."

He must've read the confusion in her gaze, because his jaw ticked twice more before he said, "There's nothing I want more than to boost your ass up on the counter behind us and show you exactly how much your words meant to me. But you don't kiss until after the third date, and the sooner I can feed you, the sooner our third date will be over, and the sooner I can finally have your mouth under mine."

"Then, by all means, let's go," Sarah told him.

Shaking his head, Cole let go of her neck and twined his fingers with hers. "I'll have Logan talk to the manager here about the apartment."

"If someone needs it more than me, I don't want to cheat to get it," Sarah said.

Without stopping, Cole reassured her by saying, "The last I heard, there were only two others on the list for this apartment. One's a college kid whose parents have an address here in town, but I'm assuming they have other plans for his bedroom or something. The other's a woman who let it slip to the manager when she was filling out her application that she needed a secure place to set up her boyfriend so her husband wouldn't find out about them."

"Seriously?"

"Yup."

"You swear there isn't an abused girl or guy who needs to live here to be safe?"

He stopped at that and wrapped his arms around her. Sarah reveled in how good it felt to be held by him. She rested her cheek on his shoulder and simply held on, just as he did with her.

"Sarah . . . *you're* the abused girl who needs to live here to be safe," he said simply.

She wanted to argue. She wasn't abused . . . not really. But she kept her mouth shut. She couldn't deny that she would feel one hundred times safer living here than in the big old house she'd grown up in. She loved Mike and Jackson, but Cole was right. She had the memories of them in her head. She didn't need their house to remember how much she loved them and how much they'd loved her.

"Come on," he urged, pulling away. "I need to feed you."

Smiling, Sarah happily let him lead her out of the apartment and into the hall. She watched as he carefully shut the door and made sure it was locked, before putting his hand on the small of her back and steering her toward the elevators.

Her life was changing faster than she'd ever imagined it would, but she couldn't say she was unhappy about it.

Chapter Nine

It turned out Sarah didn't get to kiss Cole that night. Or the next one. Or the next. He'd gotten a call from one of his employees that a fight had broken out inside the gym between two of the patrons, and he'd had to go talk with the cops.

Sarah had gone home, and had texted Cole when she'd arrived. Between her work schedule and his, they hadn't been able to get together for the next week either. But their phone calls and texts continued.

Even though they hadn't been on their third official date or kissed, Sarah had never felt closer to someone in her entire life. They talked on the phone whenever possible, and he was always there, supporting her, when she had second thoughts about selling her house.

The Realtor had said she thought the house would sell fast, and that she'd make quite a profit, but even though Sarah was excited about moving to Castle Rock and being closer to both work and Cole, it was still a hard decision she frequently struggled with.

That evening after work, she'd been restless and decided to work on packing up the rest of Jackson's office. She had to get the remaining knickknacks and personal items packed up so the house could be shown and pictures could be taken.

It wasn't until she was halfway done with the job that she realized she couldn't find several books her dad had loved to read. At that point, she was frustrated, exhausted, and missing Jackson and Mike desperately. She felt so defeated, filled with the biggest urge yet to just scrap the entire plan to move.

Without a second thought for the time, she reached for her phone and dialed Cole.

"What's wrong?"

"I can't do it. I can't move!"

He must've heard the note of panic in her voice, because he immediately gentled his tone. "Take a deep breath, angel. Good. Now tell me what's wrong."

"I can't find some of the books Jackson liked to read. I must've given them away the last time I went through the office and brought a load to Goodwill! What if I gave away something else important?"

"How long have you been packing tonight?"

"Since I got home."

"Sarah, it's twelve thirty. You've been at it for at least five hours."

"Holy shit . . . I had no idea. Oh! Cole, I'm so sorry. I didn't mean to wake you up!"

"You don't *ever* have to worry about that," he said firmly. "If you want to talk to me, I want you to call no matter what time it is or what you think I'm doing. I will always choose talking to you over sleeping, or working, or anything else. Got it?"

"Why are you so good to me?" she murmured. "I'm a mess. I'm an adult, and it's been years since Jackson and Mike were killed. Why is the thought of selling bothering me so much?"

"It's normal," Cole said. "You're about to make a big change, and up until now, you haven't had to face losing the only home you've ever known. Cut yourself some slack."

"You're right."

"I know."

Sarah laughed softly. "I hate that I gave away his favorite books," she said sadly.

"Tell me what they were, and I'll replace them. We can read them together and discuss them."

"Cole . . . that's . . . I think that's the nicest thing anyone's ever offered to do for me."

"I keep telling you that I'm not the nice one in this relationship," he teased.

"Whatever."

"Angel, it's late. You have to get up in less than four hours. Go to bed. The boxes will be there later. In fact, how about I come up and help you? You've got one more day of work, then you're off for a few days, right?"

"Yeah."

"Right. So I'll come over the day after tomorrow, and we can spend the day together. I'll help you pack up some more stuff, and we'll haul it to Goodwill. Then we can come back to Castle Rock, and you can fill out the background-check form for the apartment. You can't move in until that's done. Logan's also been bugging me about getting you back to Ace Security so they can discuss with you what they've found out about Owen. Then maybe we can *finally* have that third date I've been looking forward to more than you'll ever know."

There was a lot there, but the only thing Sarah could really think about was spending the day with Cole and maybe, hopefully, *finally* being able to see if the reality lived up to her fantasies when it came to kissing him.

Putting the stack of books she'd been staring at to the side, she stood up, wincing at how badly her back hurt. She'd been working longer than she'd realized.

"Okay."

"Okay? That's it?"

"I'm not sure you're ready for what I'm really thinking," she blurted.

"Try me," Cole urged.

If she hadn't been as tired as she was, Sarah knew she probably would've declined and simply said good night. But she was exhausted. And worried. And so sad after going through her dads' stuff. So she said exactly what she was thinking.

"I'm worried that I haven't received anything from Owen in a week, and I don't know what he's planning. I'm stressed out about selling the house and all the stuff I have to do in order to get it ready. I'm excited about the new apartment, but I still can't shake the feeling that I'm stealing it from someone else who might need it more.

"And last, but not least, I miss you. I know we've talked and texted every day since last week, when we last saw each other, but it's not the same. It's crazy because we haven't known each other that long, but you're the first person I think about when I wake up and the last person at night. I'm frustrated that our schedules haven't meshed, and I'm nervous that you're gonna decide going out with me is too much hassle. Between my weird work schedule, the fact that I don't live in the same town as you, and with the weirdness with Owen, I'm not exactly the best girlfriend material."

Sarah was almost panting by the time she finished, and she immediately wanted to take back everything she'd just said, but it was too late.

"If it wasn't quarter to one in the morning, and you didn't have to get up in three and a half hours, I'd be on my way to you right now," Cole said in a deep tone. "Sarah, I'm one hundred percent committed to this relationship. Yeah, it hasn't been typical, but if we feel the way we do without being able to see each other much, what do you think it'll be like when we *do*? You fascinate me. I love the loyalty you have to your job. The fact that you're reluctant to give up the only home you've ever known is not a negative in my eyes. But I also want to help you make a *new* home. One where we can make new memories. I'll do everything in my power to make sure Jackson and Mike are never forgotten.

"Owen will eventually get a clue and leave you alone, even if it takes Ace Security getting up in his face to make him realize his infatuation with you is futile. And you're overlooking the fact that I'm not exactly the best boyfriend material either. Some people judge me because of my tattoos, and I don't give a shit. I'm too abrupt and downright rude sometimes. I work too much and too hard, and my best friend is a woman.

"But together, you and me just make sense. You're the light, and I'm the darkness. You're everything good, and I'm walking the fine line of being an asshole all the time. We balance each other out. I can't wait to see where our relationship goes . . . and you should know, angel, that I'm hoping it goes all the way."

Sarah inhaled at that.

Cole obviously heard her, because he said, "Yeah. That should tell you that I'm in this just as deep as you are. One more day, and we'll get to spend some time together."

"I can't wait."

"Me either. Now go upstairs and get some sleep, angel. You're gonna be dead on your feet tomorrow."

"What about you? You're going to be tired too."

"Yeah, but all I have to do is show up and unlock the door to the gym. I don't have to be friendly to anyone. They *expect* me to be frowny faced and grumpy."

Sarah chuckled.

"God, I love that sound. Sarah?"

"Yeah?"

"I miss you too. I'll see you soon. Good night."

"Good night, Cole."

She clicked off the phone and closed her eyes, holding her cell to her chest for a long moment.

Cole looked nothing like the man she'd always dreamed she'd end up with. But the thing was, it didn't matter. He might not think he was a good man, but he was one of the best men she'd met in a really long time.

Sighing happily, she forced herself to her feet and headed up the stairs to the bathroom before going to bed. She thought she'd lie awake for hours thinking about Cole and their conversation, but almost the second her head hit the pillow, she was asleep.

∽

Two days later, Cole pulled into Sarah's driveway at seven thirty in the morning. It was too early to be showing up unannounced, but he wasn't willing to wait any longer to see her.

Glad to see her car wasn't in the driveway, that she was able to park in the garage, he jogged up to the front door, eager to see her in person. Knowing if he knocked, he'd probably scare her to death, Cole took out his phone and shot off a quick text.

Cole: Morning! You up?

Sarah: Barely.

Cole: Good. Come open the door for me.

After he hit "Send" on the phone, he rang the doorbell.

It took several minutes for him to hear her on the other side of the door, but when she opened it, she took his breath away.

Cole stared at her for a long moment, struck speechless. Her hair was in disarray, as if she'd literally just climbed out of bed. And imagining her climbing out of bed made him think about being *in* that bed with her. She'd pulled a thin robe on, and her legs were bare. The sight of her pink toenails made his stomach clench. It seemed intimate, and the color was perfect for her.

As he stared, she grabbed hold of the lapels of her robe and clutched them together as she looked at him with concern in her eyes. "Is everything all right?" she asked.

Even her voice turned him on. It was husky and cracked.

Without thought, Cole took a step forward. She gave him room to enter the house, and he absently shut the door and locked it without taking his eyes from hers.

"Cole?"

He didn't give her a chance to say anything else. One hand went to her nape to hold her still, and the other arm curled around her, his hand splaying wide on her lower back as he pulled her into his body. Her hands landed on his chest, and she stared at him with wide eyes.

Cole's head lowered, and satisfaction filled him when her eyes immediately shut and she raised her chin to meet him halfway.

The second his lips touched hers, Cole knew there would never be another woman in his life who meant as much as Sarah.

It felt as if electricity shot from her lips straight to his heart. He may have even grunted a little bit, but he didn't pull away. He wanted more. Needed more.

He felt her fingers curl against his chest, and his dick went hard. Not caring that she would feel his arousal against her belly, he put more pressure on her back, and she went up on tiptoe to get closer to him.

Her lips immediately parted, but as eager as he'd been to taste her a second ago, now he wanted to take his time. Tease her. Make her as desperate for him as he was for her. He licked her lower lip, loving the whimper that came from her throat. Then he nipped her gently, prolonging the anticipation.

But when she reciprocated and nibbled on *his* lower lip, Cole lost it.

He pushed her backward until the wall in the foyer supported them both. He tugged on her hair, forcing her head back a little more—then he devoured her.

His tongue swept her mouth as if he owned it. Owned *her*. But instead of being passive against his onslaught, Sarah gave as good as she got. Their tongues twined together, their teeth clinked, and he felt her hands move down and slip under his shirt. The feel of her cold fingers against his smoldering flesh just made him harder.

Slanting his head to get better access to her mouth, Cole lost himself in the kiss. It was everything he'd imagined it would be and more. So much more. Sarah didn't back off, she wasn't shy when it came to kissing, and the passion she'd somehow kept hidden rushed to the forefront with a ferocity that surprised and delighted him.

Knowing he was seconds away from ripping the robe from her body and laying her down on the cold tile floor at their feet, Cole forced himself to end the kiss. He stared down at her, and felt his cock twitch when she licked her lips. Her eyes were still closed, and she sighed in satisfaction.

He couldn't take his gaze from her now-rosy lips, the blush on her cheeks, and, when she opened her eyes, the pupils that were dilated with lust.

"Good morning," he said softly.

"Hi," she said.

"I woke up early, and the first thing I thought about was seeing you."

"I'm glad."

"I had planned on that third date today," he told her sheepishly. "Then taking the kiss that I've dreamed about for weeks. But seeing you . . . I couldn't wait."

"Breaking my personal dating rules for you feels right," she told him.

"Yeah?" he asked with a smile.

"Yeah. Because I feel as if we've broken all my rules anyway . . . might as well go whole hog."

Not able to help himself, Cole leaned down and kissed her again. This time it was a short and heartfelt meeting of lips instead of the intense, almost-desperate kiss of before. When he pulled back this time, he closed his eyes and simply lived in the moment for a second.

Cole wasn't an idiot. He knew what he was and what he wasn't. He was a good friend, a competent businessman. He could see through someone's bullshit a mile away. But he'd never thought of himself as a good bet as a woman's partner. But with Sarah, the doubts in his head faded away. He knew that with her by his side, he would be a better man. A better friend. The kind of man a woman could rely on, no matter what she needed. He'd be there for her.

For Sarah.

"Cole?" she asked gently.

He felt her fingers stroking his chest, and he took a deep breath. They were still plastered together from hips to stomach, and he knew she had to feel his erection against her. But she wasn't freaking out. Wasn't pulling away. She gave him the space he needed to gather his thoughts.

His eyes opened and he blurted, "I will not let you down."

Sarah frowned at him. "What?"

There was so much he wanted to say. He wanted to plead with her to not give up on them. That he was probably going to screw something up, but he'd never mean to. That he'd bend over backward to make sure she was safe, happy, and healthy. That he wouldn't be a douche and walk away if she got sick or hurt. That he wouldn't cheat on her, ever.

But the words got stuck in his throat. It was his turn to panic. He felt as if so much was at stake, and he didn't want to do anything that would spook her or make her have second thoughts.

"I . . . I'm too outspoken." The words poured out of him. Once started, he couldn't stop. "I've never given money to a homeless person in my life. I live in an apartment because I have no desire to do yard work whatsoever. I don't know the names of my neighbors because I've never tried to get to know them. One time, when a couple of Boy Scouts knocked on my door, I pretended I wasn't home so I didn't have to buy any popcorn from them. And I only gave Francesca a free membership to the gym so I could get free food. I'm selfish and an asshole."

Cole felt sick. He didn't want Sarah to know any of this shit, but he also didn't want her to find out later how fucked up he was and leave him. "I probably don't tip enough, and I always speed. I tend to see the worst in people, especially after what happened to Felicity. Most kids scare me to death, and I'm ashamed of the number of nights I've had ice cream for dinner."

He opened his mouth to continue, but Sarah put her hand over his lips, effectively shutting him up.

"You aren't going to convince me that you aren't a good person, Cole. So you might as well stop."

He mumbled under her hand, and she smiled before taking it away. "What?"

"I just don't want to fall in love with you, then have you realize you've gotten the short end of the stick and leave me for someone better. Nicer."

Cole held his breath after his admission. He'd laid himself bare for Sarah, and he hoped like hell she wouldn't destroy him.

And that was the thing . . . usually, he didn't give a shit what people thought of him. He didn't care if they thought he was too tattooed, too mean, too whatever. But Sarah's opinion had the power to break him.

"I steal those little shampoos and conditioners from hotels," she replied. "Once I flew first class and stuck the little salt shaker that came on the lunch tray in my bag. I ran over a squirrel one day on my way to work and didn't stop. I forgot one of my coworkers was retiring and didn't bring a present for her, so I pretended to get sick halfway through my shift so I could leave early and wouldn't have to go to her party. There are lots of things at work that people think are gross that I'll do without blinking, but whenever a patient asks me to cut their toenails, I always have to beg one of my fellow CNAs to do it because it makes me want to puke."

Cole blinked down at Sarah. She was smiling up at him as she listed what she obviously thought were bad things she'd done.

"We aren't perfect, Cole. I don't expect you to be a Stepford boyfriend. I like you the way you are. A little rough around the edges. It makes me feel safe. Like I don't have to worry about someone taking advantage of my propensity to be nice, because you'll be there watching over my shoulder. I just need you to be *you*. I'm going to make mistakes, just as you are."

"My mistakes will be more than forgetting someone's retirement party," he said dryly.

"As long as you never hit me, never call me horrible names, never lock me in a closet, and never cheat on me . . . I'll forgive you."

"Fuck. I don't deserve you."

"That's the thing. I think we deserve each other."

Cole gathered her up in his arms and squeezed his eyes shut. He buried his face into her hair and vowed, "I'll never raise my hand to you. I'll never call you anything other than *angel* and other loving names. I'll never lock you in a closet, unless I push you in there at a crowded party to have my way with you." He pulled back and stared deep into her eyes. "And I'll never, *ever* cheat on you."

"Okay."

And that was that.

Cole wasn't sure what he'd expected. For her to agree he was a bad person and push him out of her house? To be appalled at the things he'd shared? But he should've known better. That wasn't Sarah. She saw the good in everyone—it was just how she was wired. And something that often scared the shit out of him. But from here on out, she'd have *him* to make sure no one fucked with her.

He had a feeling her dads had seen the same goodness in her when she was just a child, and had done everything in their power to preserve it, to protect her from the shit that life could dole out.

"Did I wake you up?" he asked, trying to move on from their very emotional conversation.

She shook her head. "I was awake. Just being lazy and lying in bed trying to get up the energy to start moving."

"Why don't you go up and shower and get dressed? I'll make us something to eat, then we can tackle the office and whatever else you want packed and sorted."

Sarah stared at him for a beat, then nodded. "Okay. And if I forget to thank you later . . . thank you for being here to help me today."

Cole knew there was no way she'd forget to thank him later, but he went with it. "You're welcome, angel. And if you need any help up there in the shower, just yell."

She blushed, but rolled her eyes.

He loved that he could tease her. He'd never felt so comfortable around another woman. Cole leaned down and kissed her forehead, then took a step back. He immediately missed the feel of her in his arms, but knew they couldn't just stand around all day plastered together. He had to help her box up her stuff and decide what could be donated and what she wanted to keep. Not a lot of her stuff would fit in the new apartment, but the rest could be put into storage until she was ready to move to a bigger place.

Of course, the thought wouldn't leave his head that when she was ready, she could move into *his* apartment. Or, once a bigger apartment became available in her complex, they could move into it together.

It was too soon to even be thinking about living together, but he couldn't stop thinking about it. He would love to wake up with her in his arms every day.

She smiled at him and smoothed a lock of hair behind her ear. Then she turned and headed for the stairs without another word. Cole stood there watching her ass and legs until he couldn't see her anymore before shaking himself and heading for the kitchen to see what she had that he could throw together for breakfast.

He knew down to the bottom of his soul that he was getting the better end of the deal when it came to this relationship, but he'd given her a chance to back off, and she hadn't taken it.

Sarah Butler was his. Period.

Chapter Ten

Sarah nervously twined her fingers together at the same table at Ace Security that she'd sat behind a few weeks earlier. The morning had gone well, even though she'd been packing up her life to move on to something new and somewhat scary. Cole had kept her from getting too emotional, and he'd actually made the process fun. She got to tell him all the funny stories she could remember about Mike and Jackson, and it had been cathartic.

The trip to sign the background-check paperwork at the apartment complex had been quick and easy, and the manager had been very nice. He'd also told her that a three-bedroom apartment would be available in the not-so-distant future. The family currently living there was moving to Tennessee. She told him she'd have to think about it, but later, Cole had encouraged her to take it when the time came.

Three bedrooms seemed too big, and having a larger monthly payment was daunting after not having one for so long, but there'd been something in Cole's eyes that made her not reject the idea outright.

And even now, hours later, Sarah swore she could still feel his lips on hers. When he'd surprised her and kissed her that morning, it had felt right. Everything inside her had tingled, and she'd felt as if she'd come home when she was in his arms. So she couldn't help but think about sharing the bigger apartment with Cole. Which was crazy. Moving in with him so soon seemed insane. But she couldn't shake the idea. It was a conversation to have at a later date.

At the moment, she was nervous as hell to hear what Logan and his team had found on Owen.

"How are you today, Sarah?" Logan asked.

"I'm good. I have three days off before I go back to work, and Cole helped me make a dent in the stuff in my house, so it should be able to go on the market soon. The timing is good, because as soon as the background check goes through on the new apartment here in town, I can move in." She mentally groaned. She hadn't meant to overshare, but there was something about Logan that made her really jumpy.

He grinned as if he could read her mind. "That's all good news."

She nodded. "Yeah. I'm hoping that whatever you guys have to tell me will be the cherry on top of the good-news sundae I'm having today." She wanted to take the words back the second they were out. No wonder everyone thought she was always so freaking nice. She said stupid stuff like that all the time.

And by the way the smile disappeared off Logan's face as soon as she spoke, she knew things weren't going to go the way she'd hoped.

"Unfortunately, we haven't been able to find out as much as we'd like," Logan said, then looked at Blake.

"Right. So, Alexis was able to get copies of his evaluations from the fast-food places he's worked at, and they basically said nothing. He was an okay employee, but not great. He wasn't super reliable and missed a lot of work because of his mother. One manager wrote that because he didn't drive, he was late a lot."

"If he doesn't drive, how can he be leaving all the shit at her house?" Cole asked.

Blake shrugged. "Alexis checked the DMV records and found he doesn't have a driver's license, but that doesn't mean he doesn't drive, now that his mother has passed."

"Can't we put a 'be on the lookout' for his car and get the cops to nab him for driving without a license?" Cole asked.

"It's not that simple," Logan said. "There has to be a reason for a BOLO. And not having a driver's license isn't enough. You'd be shocked at the number of people driving around with a revoked or suspended license, or even no license at all."

"Shit," Cole muttered. "What else?"

"Right, so he wasn't the greatest worker, but he wasn't the worst either. He didn't get fired from any of his jobs, he always quit." Blake looked at Sarah. "Have you installed those cameras at your house like we suggested last time?"

She bit her lip and shook her head. "No. I figured since I was moving, it would be a waste of time."

Logan sighed, and Ryder pressed his lips together as if he was disappointed.

"I thought you'd ordered them," Cole said quietly.

"I was going to, but between work and packing, I kept forgetting. That's a crappy excuse, and I know it. I should've, okay? I admit it. I'm so sorry." She felt as if she'd let everyone down and been incredibly stupid at the same time. She was the one who'd come to them for help. She was the one who didn't feel safe. And here she was, acting just like one of those airheaded women in a horror movie who hid behind a shed filled with axes and knives.

"It's okay," Logan told her. "What's done is done. When did you say you're moving into that apartment?"

Cole answered before she could. "Next week, or as soon as the manager finishes her background check."

"I'll make sure that gets fast-tracked," Ryder said.

Logan nodded.

Blake continued. "Alexis tracked down Aubrey's death certificate, and the coroner listed organ failure as her ultimate cause of death, but leukemia was listed as a contributing factor."

Sarah nodded. She'd known that. The older woman hadn't been doing well when she'd been in the hospital. It had been only a matter of time until she passed away.

"The mortgage hasn't been paid since she died," Nathan said, joining the conversation. "I stopped by the neighborhood the other day with Joel. He had to sell at least a dozen of these stupid coupon books for a school fund-raiser, and I figured that neighborhood was as good as any to canvass."

"And a good opportunity for you to check out the house in the process," Blake said.

"But wasn't it dangerous for Joel to be around Owen?" Sarah asked, chewing her lip.

"First, Owen has no idea who I am, or Joel," Nathan said. "He would have no reason to suspect something. Second, I'd never do *anything* to put that boy in danger. I told him all about why I wanted to go there, and he was super excited to be in on an 'op,' as he called it. And third, it's a moot point, as no one was home when we knocked."

"What'd you see?" Ryder asked. "I know you checked the place out."

"Of course we did. It doesn't look like the lawn has been mowed in months. The curtains were shut on the window in the front of the house, but we wandered around to the back to knock on that door, and we could see right in through a large window on the back porch. The place was a mess. Dirty dishes stacked up in the sink with dried food on them. Trash piled everywhere. I don't know if that's where Owen's been living or not, but it was a pigsty."

Sarah couldn't help the twinge of pity that struck her.

"What was that thought?" Cole asked from next to her. He was always so in tune to what she was feeling.

"It's just that . . . Owen was so worried about his mom. And when I had that short conversation with her while Owen was out of the room, she was worried about him right back. She said something about how she'd always taken care of him, and she didn't know what he'd do when she was gone."

The men all nodded, as if the messy house made perfect sense. But Owen was an adult. There was no reason why he couldn't clean the house. But then again, he also hadn't paid the mortgage since his mother had died either.

None of it made sense, and things that didn't make sense made her very nervous.

"Which brings us to the most important thing Alexis found in her research," Blake said. "The disability money that Owen receives every month is because he's developmentally disabled."

The words made Sarah blink in surprise. She shook her head. "No, he's not. He was completely normal when we had lunch."

"A lot of times, people who have low IQs, like Owen does, can hide their disability. They seem to be just like everyone else, but they ultimately don't think the same way."

"What's his IQ?" Ryder asked.

"It wasn't listed in the disability paperwork," Blake told the group. "But I did some research. In the United States alone, there are between six and seven million people who have some sort of mental retardation. Most people have IQs between eighty and one hundred and twenty, with one hundred being the average. A score of sixty-nine or lower is what a person has to have in order to be diagnosed with mental retardation—or as developmentally disabled, which is the more politically correct term. To put that in perspective, a score in the sixty-to-seventy range is the scholastic equivalent to a third grader.

"Here's the thing: people who are developmentally disabled can be limited in the basic skills necessary to cope with everyday life. Things like self-care and social skills, among other things. They might not be able to follow directions or behave appropriately in social situations."

"So . . . Owen's standing with his back to the elevator door may have been because he simply didn't understand or know the unwritten rules of being in an elevator or personal space," Sarah said.

Blake nodded. "Exactly."

"Then the presents he's leaving really aren't dangerous. He just doesn't know that what he's doing is scaring me."

"Maybe, maybe not," Blake said, shaking his head. "You're right in that he might not quite understand how you feel about his gifts, but that doesn't mean he's not dangerous."

Sarah shivered, and even Cole's hand on her leg didn't make her feel better.

"There have been numerous documented cases of men with low IQs committing heinous crimes. Billy Wayne White was found guilty of shooting a sixty-five-year-old furniture-store owner without provocation, just because he wanted money. Also, in the seventies, Johnny Paul Penry raped and killed a woman who he'd delivered an appliance to a few weeks before the crime."

"Why do killers always have three names?" Sarah whispered to no one in particular.

"Most people have three names," Ryder said with a smile. "It just so happens that the media likes to use all three when they report on horrific crimes."

"The point I'm making is that both of these guys had low IQs. Just because someone has the mental capacity of a child doesn't mean they aren't dangerous," Blake said. "And I read that a lot of people who are developmentally disabled still know they're the least smart person in their group . . . whatever that group is. So they do their best to hide it. They can go about their daily activities just fine, and others might think they're a bit odd but don't understand the extent of their disability."

"Wow, you really did research this," Sarah said quietly.

Blake leaned forward, his brown eyes piercing in their intensity, and Sarah couldn't look away. "Cole might not have the name Anderson, but he's as much my brother as the other three men around this table. And you're important to him—therefore, you're important to us. We've all learned never to underestimate those who might want to do our women harm. So yeah, Sarah, I researched this."

She was speechless. A lump grew in her throat, and she had to swallow several times to keep herself from bursting into tears. She'd felt alone for most of her life. Yes, Mike and Jackson had adopted her and made her feel like part of a family for the first time, but being a foster child usually meant always feeling a bit like an outsider.

Cole wrapped his hand around the back of her head and drew her toward him. He kissed her temple and kept his lips on her for a long moment.

"So . . . ," Logan said, breaking the emotionally charged silence. "We know that Owen is developmentally disabled and that he has a crush on Sarah. His mother passed away, and she was presumably his primary caregiver. We don't know what his IQ is or if he's an actual danger to Sarah or not. And—the biggie—we have no idea where he is now. Has he been living in the house, or does he have a place somewhere else? Ryder, has your friend Rex been able to find out anything on any other possible family members Owen and Aubrey might've had?"

"No. Nothing. There was no will," Ryder said. "Which means that everything automatically goes to her nearest living relative, which is Owen. And this makes sense, knowing what we know now, but he never contacted a lawyer to get the ball rolling. Her accounts haven't been touched either. There's money to pay the mortgage, but I'm guessing Owen simply doesn't have the mental capacity to know how to do it."

There was another long silence around the table.

"Then where is he living?" Sarah asked. She actually felt sorry for the man. "It must've been so scary for him to have his mom die. Especially if he's got the mental capacity of a third grader."

"Yeah, this is a tricky situation for sure," Nathan said. "We need to find him. That's the most important thing. Once we do, we can make sure he's assessed and gets the help he needs."

Sarah looked over at Cole. He had been quiet for most of the conversation, but she could tell he wasn't happy. His jaw was ticking as if he were clenching his teeth, and he wore a deep frown.

"Cole? What's wrong?"

"I'm just worried that knowing about his mental retardation will make everyone let their guard down. The fact that he's in the wind isn't good. Especially if he can't think like an adult. What's his endgame? Just give you presents for the rest of his life? I don't buy it."

"It's possible *he* doesn't know what his endgame is," Nathan said. "There have been times when Joel's tried to manipulate his sister or me but can't follow through because he hasn't thought of the consequences to his actions."

"That doesn't make me feel better," Cole muttered.

"Right," Logan said decisively. "The plan is for Sarah to finish packing up her house. To get the things in storage that she wants to keep and to stage her house so it can sell quickly. She'll move into the apartment here in Castle Rock, so she's safe, and we'll continue to do what we can to find Owen. We'll contact the police department again with our findings and—"

"But won't you get in trouble?" Sarah interrupted.

"In trouble?" Logan asked, furrowing his brow.

"Yeah. I mean, you probably weren't supposed to hack into the records and find out about his disability. If you admit that to the cops, you could be in trouble."

All five men smiled.

Sarah looked from one to another in confusion. "What?"

"You're right, she *is* nice," Ryder said with a smirk.

"I know," Cole said.

"Seriously, I'm not wrong," Sarah insisted.

"I appreciate your concern, but I've got a few friends on the force. They aren't going to ask how I know what I know. They've learned over the years not to," Logan told her.

"Oh."

"Can I continue?" he asked with a smile.

"Yeah. Sorry."

"Anyway, we'll get with the cops and maybe even a representative from the state mental-health organization. It sounds like Owen would probably benefit from living in a group home or something that specializes in helping people like him navigate life."

Sarah liked the sound of that. The last place the mentally handicapped needed to be was in prison. They couldn't help that they were born the way they were.

Suddenly everything about Aubrey's cancer seemed even sadder. She had to have known when she died that Owen would be on his own. Sarah was upset that the woman hadn't done more before her health had declined to make sure her son would be looked after.

"Sarah, you need to keep doing what you're doing. Be safe, text Cole when you leave and when you get home. Park as close to the doors at the hospital as possible. If you get any more gifts, take pictures, and let us and Cole know as soon as possible. It's only a matter of time before we find Owen. We just have to adjust our thinking a bit. Think like a kid. If he's scared or hungry, where would he go? Once we figure that out, we'll be able to get him some help."

"Thank you," Sarah said. The meeting today had done a lot to ease her fears. She didn't like that no one could find Owen, but knowing that he probably wasn't a serial killer lying in wait to get his hands on her and make her his own little sex slave made her feel a little better.

"Just because he's got a diminished mental capacity doesn't make him not dangerous," Blake reminded her, as if he could read her mind. "There are several men just like Owen sitting on death row around the country for committing heinous murders."

"Gosh, thanks for that image," Sarah muttered.

"We're doing what we can to keep you safe, but you have to continue to do your part too," Logan said. "You contacted us in the first place because you were uneasy and scared. Nothing has changed since then. Understand? Just because we know a little more about Owen doesn't mean the reasons you were uneasy have gone away."

Sarah nodded. She got that. She did. But a part of her was still a teensy bit relieved at knowing Owen wasn't thinking as a normal adult might.

"I'll watch her," Cole said.

The other men all nodded.

She should've been upset at his high-handedness. But she couldn't be. If Cole watched her, that meant he'd be around. And she liked the thought of that.

"We'll let you both know if we find out any other pertinent information, or if we find him," Logan said as he stood.

"Thanks," Sarah said.

"Felicity mentioned something about a girls' get-together soon," Ryder told the others, but he had his eye on Sarah.

She frowned. Why was he staring at her?

"You said you're off for the next three days. Is that including today, or is it the next three?" Ryder asked.

"Um . . . including today," she told him.

Ryder looked at Cole, and Sarah followed his gaze just in time to see Cole shake his head at his friend. By the time she looked back at Ryder, he was smirking. "So tonight's out. But what about tomorrow?"

Sarah just stared at him.

"Sarah? Are you busy tomorrow night?"

"Me?" she asked, confused.

Ryder and the others chuckled. "Yeah, you. You want to do a girls' night with Grace, Alexis, Bailey, and Felicity?"

She could only continue to frown at Ryder.

"Yeah, she does," Cole told his friend. "She'll be with me, so just shoot me the details, and I'll make sure she's there."

"Cool. We're all gonna wait 'em out at Logan's, since he'll be on baby duty. When they've had enough, we'll go and collect them."

"Sounds good."

Sarah's head felt like it was on a swivel as she looked from one man to the next.

Cole wrapped his arm around her waist and led her toward the door. "See you tomorrow!" he called out.

She stumbled a bit as she turned and waved to the other men. Cole grinned but didn't slow down. It wasn't until they were standing outside and were headed for his car that she found her voice. "What just happened?" she asked.

"Ryder invited you to hang out with the other women tomorrow night. They like to try to get together at least once a month, but most of the time it's more often than that. They usually go to the bar down there"—he pointed across the street to the Rock 'N' Roll bar—"but because Grace is still nervous to have her kids out of her sight for too long, Bailey is pregnant, Alexis is a lightweight, and Felicity gets a hankering for her man when she gets drunk, the nights usually only last until around ten o'clock or so."

Sarah stopped in her tracks in the middle of the sidewalk, and Cole was forced to stop with her. "They want *me* to go with them?"

Cole's face softened. "Yeah, angel."

"Why?"

"Because. They like you. You're one of them now."

"How do they figure?"

Cole studied her and took a deep breath. "I don't want to freak you out, but I'm just going to come right out and say this. You're with me, Sarah. We're dating. I talk about almost nothing other than you at work—and Felicity is more than aware that I don't talk about women I date and it's been forever since I've even taken someone out. She's one of my best friends, and she wants to get to know you. And since she's best friends with Grace, *she* wants to get to know you too. And since Alexis and Bailey are sisters-in-law—well, not officially, but they might as well be—they want to know you better as well. When Felicity heard you'd be in town today, and had the next couple days off, *and* that I planned to find a way to keep you here in Castle Rock with me for as much of those three days as possible, she called up the others and planned the girls' night out."

"Oh."

Cole smiled. "That's all you're gonna say?"

"I think so, yeah."

"All right then. How about we get something to eat?"

Sarah nodded, still thinking about what Cole had just said. She'd never had girlfriends. She didn't really know how to relate to other women. In middle and high school, they'd thought she was too much of a goody two-shoes to hang out with. So she'd studied hard, made her dads happy, and got straight *A*s. When she was getting her CNA degree, she was too busy working and studying to worry much about drinking or hanging out with others her age. She'd gotten her job . . . and then her dads were killed, and emotionally, she'd just been trying to keep her head above water ever since.

Cole held the door until she got situated in the passenger side of his car, then walked around to the driver's side. Once he sat, she remembered something else he'd said to Ryder.

"So . . . I'll be with you?"

Cole turned hopeful eyes her way. "I want you to stay the night with me at my place tonight." He spoke faster, as if she'd agree if he got the words out quickly. "I've got an extra bedroom, so I'm not presuming anything. I just want to spend as much time together as possible, get to know each other better, and make sure you're safe. Until Owen is found, I'm extremely uneasy with you gallivanting around by yourself, even though you're an adult and have been on your own for years, and even though I've been giving you self-defense lessons. You said Owen outweighs you by at least a hundred pounds, so he could easily take you by surprise and overpower you. I'm trying not to be an overbearing boyfriend, but I can't help it. That's who I am. I worry about everyone. Ask Felicity. I was the biggest pest when her stalker was after her."

When he stopped to take a breath, Sarah put her hand on his thigh, shutting him up. She hadn't ever seen him so nervous before. It was cute as hell—and made her fall for him even more. "I'll stay with you," she said softly. "On one condition."

"Anything," Cole said, his eyes half closing as he sighed in relief.

"I don't know what to wear tomorrow night. Will you help me and maybe take me shopping? It's not like I've got anything with me, and most of my clothes, other than scrubs and jeans, are packed in boxes in my house."

Cole reached out, tagged her behind the neck, and pulled her across the console toward him. "There's no one in this world who could get me to step foot in a department store with her . . . other than you. Yes, I'll take you shopping, angel. I'll take you wherever you want to go."

They were face-to-face, and Sarah couldn't take her eyes off Cole's lips. "Thanks," she whispered.

"Before we go to bed, we can throw your stuff in the washer. I know it's not ideal to wear the same thing two days in a row, but I think that's preferable to you wearing my clothes. Although I'm not opposed to giving you one of my shirts to wear to bed."

The idea of wearing one of his huge T-shirts and nothing else made Sarah shift restlessly in her seat.

"I should've thought about telling you to pack a bag, but I didn't want you to say no," Cole admitted. "I'm sorry. I know girls like to have their stuff with them."

"As long as you can find me an unused toothbrush and have shampoo, I'm good," she told him.

"I've got you covered there."

"Okay."

Cole closed his eyes for a second before staring deeply into hers once again. "I won't let you down," he vowed.

Sarah nodded. She didn't know if he was talking about tonight, tomorrow, or some unknown time in the future, but it didn't really matter. She believed him.

Then his head dropped, and she met him halfway. She'd only kissed him once before, and when her lips met his, it was as if they were the only two people in the world. The kiss was short but passionate, and when he finally pulled back, they were both breathing hard. Cole squeezed her neck affectionately, then reluctantly let go.

"I was gonna find a nice restaurant to take you to, but I think I'd rather take you home. To *my* home."

"Are you gonna feed me?"

"Yes."

"Then take me home, Cole."

She understood the satisfied smile that formed on his face because she felt the same way inside. She was beginning to think that anywhere Cole was would be home for her. It was a scary thought, as it was so soon in their relationship, but everything within her trusted him. If her dads were still alive, she knew they'd trust him too.

After he pulled out of the parking lot, he reached over and grabbed her hand. He twined his fingers with hers, and they stayed that way for the rest of the ride.

Chapter Eleven

It was ten o'clock and dark outside. Cole was sitting on the couch with Sarah in his arms, and they were simply talking. They hadn't turned on the television all night, instead using their time to get to know each other, just as he'd wanted. As it turned out, they already knew quite a bit. Their frequent phone calls and text conversations had laid an excellent foundation.

But the longer Cole sat there, Sarah soft and pliant in his arms, the harder it was to hide the effect she had on him. And the last thing he wanted was to make her uncomfortable. She'd agreed to spend the night, which was huge.

Not wanting his rock-hard erection to accidentally brush against her, Cole shifted.

"I'm sorry, am I squishing you?" Sarah asked.

Cole chuckled. "As if. No, you're fine."

She looked back at him, then said, "For our third date, this one was pretty amazing."

He couldn't read her mood. "I warned you that I'm not the best cook. Main dishes are hard, but I can grill a mean steak, and breakfasts are my jam."

She grinned and her lids fell. Cole noticed how long her eyelashes were for the first time. He was more a tits-and-ass man, but sitting there, his face inches from hers, he decided that he was an idiot for not noticing how beautiful a woman's lashes were.

When she looked back up at him, he wasn't prepared for the lust he saw in her gaze.

Then she moved before he could anticipate her actions.

She straddled his lap and scooted forward, pressing her pussy against his cock as if she'd done it every day of their lives.

Shocked, Cole could just stare up at her and pray she didn't freak out when she felt how aroused he was.

Instead, she shimmied against him for a moment, then wrapped her arms around his neck.

"Here's the thing," she started. "Jackson had the sex talk with me when I was twelve. He told me that men were pigs and they'd take advantage of me if I let them. Later that night, Mike came to my room and had a very *different* sex talk. He told me I should make any boy I liked wait for it. Said if the boy was good, if he wanted me for me, he'd wait."

Cole barely dared to breathe. Hearing Sarah talk about sex at all was hotter than he would've ever dreamed.

"It turns out they were both right. Of course, Jackson was just trying to make me not like boys, since I was his little girl, and Mike was always the more romantic of the pair. There *have* been guys who've taken advantage of my niceness. I'd forgotten what my dads had told me. That's where my three-date rule came in for kissing. I figured if someone liked me, *really* liked me, they'd wait until I was ready before moving forward. And if I imposed a three-date kissing rule, it would separate the men from the boys."

Cole winced. *Shit.* He hadn't been able to wait. He'd fallen on her like a horny teenager the second he'd seen her that morning. His hands fell to the cushion at his sides, afraid to touch her in case she was pissed at him.

She leaned forward, and Cole held back the moan that threatened to escape when her tits brushed against his chest. They were both fully dressed, but that didn't stop his imagination from kicking into overdrive. He imagined how her nipples would feel as they dragged across his chest. It would tickle, and the plump mounds would feel both soft and hard as she gave him her weight.

"If I told you that things were moving too fast and I needed to slow down, what would you do?" she asked.

Cole looked into her eyes and refused to even think about how he could feel the heat from between her legs on his cock. How he wanted to fuck her exactly like this . . . with her in his lap, naked, tits bouncing as she rode him. "I'd wait until you were ready."

"Even if it was months?" she pressed.

"You're worth the wait," he choked out.

"Lucky for you, I don't want to wait," she said calmly.

Cole's mouth opened, but nothing came out.

Sarah leaned back and reached for the hem of her shirt. Before he knew what she was up to, she'd whipped it up and over her head.

Without thought, his hands moved from where they were desperately clutching the cushion to clasp her hips once more. His fingers dug in as she pressed herself even harder against his dick and wiggled a little for good measure.

"You're a good man, Cole," she said softly. "I've never felt this way about anyone before. I have no doubt that if we were about to have sex, and I told you I'd changed my mind, you would immediately pull back. I've had that three-date rule in place because no man has ever made me yearn to be with him for longer than that. But I think I knew from the first time I saw you that you would be different."

"I was an ass," Cole choked out.

"You were busy and stressed," she protested. "And you came after me. Took the time to reassure me. To apologize. You have no idea how rare that is. I want you. If we didn't have things to do this morning, I would've let you take me right there in my foyer."

Cole licked his lips and dropped his eyes to her chest. *God.* Her tits were encased in a plain cotton bra, but he'd never seen anything sexier. She wasn't stick thin; her stomach had a pooch, and her boobs were definitely lush—and all he saw was perfection. Cole was surrounded by rock-hard, muscular bodies all day long. Sarah's beat them all, hands down.

His fingers itched to pull down the cups of her bra and feast on her succulent tits. But he had to make sure. *She* had to be sure.

"If we do this," he warned, knowing his voice sounded too husky and a bit harsh, but not caring even a little, "you're mine. Don't give yourself to me unless you're sure. It would kill me."

And that was the truth. He wasn't telling her because he was a possessive guy—okay, he was, but that wasn't why. He was warning her because it would literally kill him if he had her, then had to watch her walk away.

He knew, down to the marrow of his bones, that she was it for him. His match. The other half of his soul. Whatever sappy romantic term poets liked to call true love. He was there. And if she gave herself to him and then left, it would destroy him.

"I'm sure," she said softly.

Cole knew he should ask her again. Make her understand exactly what she was doing. That they weren't about to merely have sex. That she was making a commitment. That she was agreeing to let him protect her. To provide for her. To stand up for her and stand *with* her on causes she believed in. To be the asshole when needed so she could always be the nice soul she was born to be.

But with her sitting on his dick, pressing against him, her luscious tits against his chest, he didn't have the willpower. "Mine," he growled.

Instead of arguing, Sarah smiled. "Mine," she repeated.

And Cole moved.

He shoved one hand down the back of her jeans to palm her ass as best he could, and the other went to her back, pulling her against him.

He fell on her like a starving jackal who hadn't had a meal in weeks. Their teeth clacked together as they devoured each other. Cole felt his dick get even harder as Sarah's hips undulated, as if she were desperate to get him inside her. He couldn't help but smile. His angel was all goodness and light, but in bed, he knew she was going to be a wildcat . . . demanding and insisting on getting what she wanted.

He tore his mouth from hers, and she moaned, but when he pushed her backward and dipped his head, she acquiesced immediately, throwing her head back and arching to give him room. Cole kept his hand on her ass, pressing her against his crotch, even as he brought his other hand up and yanked the cup of her bra down, exposing her pert, rosy nipple. He latched on to it and sucked. Hard.

She let out a combination shriek and moan at his action, but Cole didn't stop or let up on the intensity of his sucking. If he could've inhaled her at that moment, he would've. He was out of control, and he couldn't have stopped if his life depended on it.

As Sarah writhed in his grip, he alternated sucking, biting, and licking her nipples. Both bra cups were pulled down now, pushing her tits up almost obscenely. Her hands were thrust into his hair, and she was pulling him closer, asking for more.

Cole hadn't ever been this hard before. Nor this close to release without sex. He knew if he didn't get a handle on the situation, he'd come in his pants before he'd even gotten hers undone.

Taking a deep breath, and ignoring the way Sarah tugged on his hair, trying to get him to suck on her some more, Cole held her away from him.

He couldn't help but let his eyes roam over the vision on his lap. Her chest was flushed from desire, and her nipples were rosy red from the scruff of his beard and his teeth. She was breathing harshly, fast-and-hard pants, and her hips moved against his dick impatiently. She was fucking beautiful. And all his.

"Fuck, you're gorgeous," he said in awe.

Her cheeks flushed, and she bit her lip. "I love your tattoos," she said in response. "I don't think I've told you that yet."

Cole chuckled. He loved that he could rattle her. "You haven't seen all of them," he teased. Yeah, she'd seen his chest when he'd mowed her lawn that first week, but she hadn't seen what was hiding behind his zipper.

He'd gotten drunk one night in his early twenties and thought it would be hilarious to get a compass inked right above his dick. Knowing what a colossal mistake he'd made, he'd tried to fix it by adding geometric designs all around the damn thing. He thought the final result was pretty badass, but there was always the chance Sarah would think it was stupid.

Her hands immediately went to the hem of his shirt.

Grinning, Cole helped her pull his shirt over his head. Then, knowing he was seconds away from opening his pants, and hers, and shoving himself as deep inside her as he could get, he stood.

Sarah let out the cutest little screech, then immediately hooked her ankles together at his ass and draped her arms over his shoulders. With every step he took toward his bedroom, her pussy rubbed against his cock. It was the best kind of pain.

He walked straight to his unmade bed and leaned over, dropping her on the mattress. As she scooted herself to the middle, he followed, not wanting to lose contact with her body for one second. As if they were sharing the same brain, her fingers went to the button on his jeans at the same time he went for hers.

He stood up to shove his jeans off, the separation from her almost physically painful. He watched as she shimmied her jeans and panties over her hips until she could kick them off absently.

Taking a breath to savor the moment, Cole stared down at the woman he loved, seeing her naked for the first time.

Yeah, he loved her. With everything he was.

He would kill to keep her safe, if necessary. She was going to be the most spoiled woman in the history of the world, because all she had to do was ask for something, and it'd be hers.

Her thighs were pale and full. Her hips wide. Her tits were perfectly proportioned for her frame, nipples still hard, beckoning to him.

"So fucking beautiful," he said before putting his knees back on the mattress and crawling to her.

~

Sarah couldn't believe she'd been so forward downstairs. But she knew Cole was seconds from being a gentleman and leaving her on the couch while he went to his own room. She didn't want him going to bed without her. So she'd done the only thing she could think of at the time . . . she'd sat on him.

But the second she'd straddled his lap, her brain had short-circuited. His dick felt huge, and she couldn't help put push herself against him. One thing led to another . . . and here they were.

In his bed.

Naked.

And she'd never wanted anything more in her life.

Cole was big. All over. But the way he towered over her only seemed to make her feel that much more protected and cared for. She'd felt how big and hard he was when she'd sat on his lap. His thighs were like bricks, but it was his dick that she was most interested in at the moment.

When he'd taken off his shirt, she already knew his tattoos carried over from his arms, down his chest and to his stomach. But the second he took off his jeans, she couldn't tear her gaze from his cock.

She vaguely noticed he was tattooed down there too, but her eyes wouldn't leave his dick long enough to check out the ink.

His cock was thick. Much thicker than anything she'd taken inside her in the past. She felt moisture flood her pussy at the sight, as if her body was readying itself for him. She remembered the way he'd gone at her breasts as if he couldn't wait a second more to get his mouth on them. And the way he'd palmed her ass. And how he'd taken control of their kiss and directed her head exactly where he'd wanted it.

Everything about Cole turned her on—and she wanted him inside her. Now.

Her legs fell open, and he immediately took advantage, kneeling between her thighs, forcing them apart even more. She should've been nervous. It had been a long time since anyone other than her doctor had seen her there, but the reverent look on Cole's face made her feel sexy instead.

His cock head was dripping precome. Some landed on her thigh, so hot it almost seemed to scorch her.

"Cole," she moaned, running her hands up and down his arms, vaguely admiring the way his tattoos moved and flexed as his muscles bunched.

He leaned over her, and she felt his dick brush against her pussy lips for a second before he moved, then it rested hot and heavy against her stomach. She sucked in deep gulps of air and felt him shift up and down with her breathing.

"Are you on the pill?" he said huskily into her ear.

Blinking up at him, Sarah realized that she hadn't thought once about birth control. Or protecting herself against any kind of sexually transmitted disease. But almost the second the thought of protection crossed her mind, she dismissed it. She was in Cole's world right this second, and she knew without even thinking about it that he'd never do anything to put her at risk.

"No."

He nodded, as if he'd expected that answer. "Knowing I could make you pregnant right now is the biggest fucking turn-on," he said in that same low, rumbly voice. "But I need to make sure you're safe first."

"Safe . . ."

"From that asshole who thinks he's in love with you," he clarified.

Sarah practically melted at the protective vibes he was giving out. She nodded.

"I'll wear a condom in the meantime, because the last thing you need to be worried about is a child growing in your belly when we don't know where he is or what he's planning. But, be forewarned, angel, the second Owen is out of the picture, once and for all, I'm taking you bare. As much as you'll let me. When we wake up in the morning, in the shower, at the table after breakfast, lunch breaks, and definitely at night before we sleep." Then, briefly, uncertainty crept into his eyes. "You okay with that?"

"Yeah." She literally couldn't say anything else. The thought of him making love with her bare, of filling her up with come, was sexy rather than daunting. As she'd told him, she wasn't on birth control now, but she could easily start.

Though . . . once she started thinking about having a child with Cole, she couldn't put it out of her mind. She had a feeling he wouldn't freak out if she became pregnant.

Without another word, Cole leaned over and opened a drawer next to his bed. His cock smeared precome all along her belly as he moved. Sarah smoothed a hand down his front and wrapped it around him just as he grabbed a brand-new box of condoms. He hissed out a breath and sat up on his knees over her.

Sarah couldn't take her attention from him. He was so beautiful. Hard and soft at the same time. His dick pulsed as blood pumped into his erection. As she stroked him, he got even harder right in front of her eyes.

Cole gently nudged her hand out of the way, and she watched as he rolled the condom over his cock. When he was covered, he scooted backward and dropped to his elbows.

Frowning, as she'd thought she was finally about to have Cole inside her, Sarah threw her head back as he once again devoured her breasts with his mouth. It felt good, but she wanted more. "Cole," she protested.

He lifted his head. "Yeah, angel?"

"Fuck me," she pleaded.

His lips quirked up in a grin. "I will. But I want to taste you first."

"Oh God, yes . . . please."

He scooted farther down her body with a sexy smile and, with the same enthusiasm and intensity he'd used on her nipples, began to lick and suck on her pussy.

Sarah groaned, and her hands immediately went to his head. She alternated between holding on for dear life and trying to press him harder against her. Cole latched on to her clit and nibbled. He went at her as if he were a starving man. She'd never imagined someone could be this enthusiastic about going down on a woman. She'd already wondered if Cole was the kind of man who'd do this for her. If he would enjoy it. And she was giddy to realize the answer was yes on both counts.

She looked down and saw his eyes were up, watching her face as he ate her out. His beard was covered in her juices, and, as she stared back, he covered her clit with his mouth, closed his eyes as if he were in ecstasy, and devoured her. Within seconds, Sarah was approaching orgasm. She couldn't stop it if she tried.

"Oh shoot, Cole!" she cried, right before he threw her over the edge. Then he kept her there by pressing two fingers inside her tight sheath and stroking her in a place she'd heard of but had never experienced before.

Shrieking in earnest now, she shoved her hips up, almost dislodging him, and shook violently as she had her first G-spot orgasm.

Cole pushed up to his knees and held her thighs open while she was still panting and shaking. Looking into her eyes, he licked his lips, as if savoring her flavor there, and then began to slowly penetrate her still-spasming body.

"Fuck, angel. You're incredible," he breathed.

She wanted to disagree. To tell him that, no, *he* was the one who was incredible, but she couldn't talk. All she could do was feel and hold on to Cole so she didn't shatter into a thousand pieces.

He was big. Stretching muscles that hadn't ever accommodated anything close to his size. But instead of just shoving himself inside her, he took his time. Pressing inside an inch, holding himself still, then pulling back out. Then he'd do it again, gaining another half inch before retreating once more.

Before he'd worked all of himself inside her, Sarah was begging. "Please, Cole. I need you. All the way in. More!"

"Easy, angel. I refuse to hurt you," he murmured. "You're so tight. God, you feel amazing." A vein in the side of his neck was pulsing with the effort it took for him to go slow, and his biceps felt like rocks under her hands. He was suffering. For her.

The next time he started to slowly push inside, Sarah planted her feet on the mattress and shoved her hips up as hard as she could.

They both gasped as he bottomed out inside her. She could feel his balls against her ass, and his pubis rubbed against her clit. He was that far inside her body.

Groaning, Cole reached down and grabbed hold of her ass, pressing her harder against him.

"You. Are. Mine," he bit out, staring down into her wide eyes.

She could only nod. The small bite of pain at her rash action was fading away into pleasure.

"I mean it, Sarah. This pussy is mine. These tits are mine. Every orgasm, every moan, every sigh. They're *mine*. I tried to warn you.

Tried to make sure you knew what you were getting into, but it's too late now."

His words were over-the-top possessive. Even crazy. But Sarah didn't care. They were like a balm to her soul. She'd never belonged to anyone before.

"If I'm yours, then you're mine too," she said fiercely, wrapping her legs around him and latching her ankles together at his ass. "No one gets your dick but me."

"I'm yours," he said gruffly as he began to slowly thrust in and out of her.

Sarah let her legs drop as she arched her back and groaned. He felt so good. So big. His cock was making nerve endings she didn't know she had sit up and take notice. She was so wet from the orgasm he'd given her earlier that the noises his dick made as he pushed in and out of her body were almost embarrassing.

But she soon forgot all about that as he sped up his thrusts.

"This okay?" he panted.

"Oh yeah," she reassured him. "Harder."

"I won't hurt you." He almost seemed like he was talking to himself rather than trying to reassure her.

He felt amazing inside her. But it wasn't enough. She'd never be the kind of woman who could get off with mere intercourse. She needed more. Not sure if she should tell him, show him, or just forget about it this first time, she didn't realize Cole had been studying her while she was lost in thought.

"What do you need?" he asked.

"What?" she asked breathlessly.

"What do you need to get off again?" he clarified.

Feeling shy, but knowing she wanted to make sure their sex life was as amazing as it could be, she blurted, "My clit. I need direct stimulation."

Cole didn't hesitate. Didn't tell her to do what she needed to do. He simply shifted above her and reached one hand down to strum her clit while he resumed fucking her. "Like this?"

Sarah's eyes just about rolled back in her head. His thumb working her clit, at the same rhythm that he penetrated her, was heaven.

"Yesssss," she hissed.

She caught his smile before he got serious about the whole love-making thing. His hips began pistoning back and forth steadily, as if he were some sort of machine. At the same time, he varied the pressure and speed of his thumb on her clit. The combination drove her crazy. Within a minute, she was writhing under him again. Pulling away from the intensity of his touch, then pressing up into him, wanting more. It was confusing as hell, and she'd never felt anything like it in her life.

"Come on my cock, angel," he said when she got close. Her thighs trembled, her ass clenched, and she felt the orgasm coming on like a freight train. The second she flew over the edge, she cried out in ecstasy. She felt Cole grab hold of her hips—and if she'd thought he was fucking her before, she was wrong.

Now he was fucking her.

His cock powered through her clenched inner muscles, prolonging her climax. He slammed in and out, his pelvis smacking into hers with every thrust. He was grunting, and she could see sweat snaking down his temple.

He was beautiful.

She wasn't sure she'd ever seen anything so gorgeous in all her life.

Then he came.

And *that*—that was the most beautiful thing she'd ever seen.

His jaw clenched, his eyes closed, his breathing stopped, and he threw his head back. He pushed his cock once more inside her as far as he could get, and exploded.

She actually felt his dick twitch inside her as come shot out of his tip, presumably filling the condom. It took several seconds, but he eventually let out the breath he'd been holding, and every muscle in his body sagged, as if he were a balloon that had suddenly deflated.

Without a word, he fell to his elbows over her, careful not to squish her, and buried his face in her hair on his pillow. They stayed like that for a few minutes, both breathing hard, trying to recover from being turned inside out.

Sarah had no idea if sex with Cole would be like that every time; she kinda hoped it wouldn't. It was intense and almost scary . . . but oh so good.

She could feel him slowly softening inside her, and when his cock finally popped out of her body, they both sighed in disappointment. Then Cole did something surprising. He scooted down until his head was level with her chest and rested his cheek on her boob. His hand came up and rested on her throat, not threatening in any way, just resting there, its weight comforting.

The exhalations from his nose wafted over her nipple, bringing it to attention, but he didn't move.

"Did you mean it?" he asked after a while, and Sarah had never heard him sound so uncertain.

But she didn't have to ask what he meant. She was his, just as she hoped like hell he was hers. "I meant it," she reassured him.

Cole nodded. "You won't regret it. I swear."

"I know I won't. But you might." She had to say it. She wasn't exactly the best bet. She was too nice, kind of a loner, had no family to speak of. But he immediately shook his head.

"Never," he vowed.

They fell asleep that way. With Cole wrapped around her, using her chest as a pillow. The sheets would be a mess when they woke up, but Sarah didn't care. Nothing could burst her bubble of happiness. Nothing.

Chapter Twelve

Sarah's "bubble of happiness" lasted until about seven the next evening.

The day had been amazing. Cole had woken her up and led her to the shower. He'd made love to her there, and it had been just as intense and thrilling as the night before.

Then they'd had breakfast and gone to the mall to find her something to wear. Since neither of them had remembered to throw her clothes into the washer, she'd ended up going commando under her jeans and wearing one of his T-shirts tied in a knot at her hip. Sarah felt as if everyone who saw them knew exactly what they'd done the night before—and that morning—but surprisingly found that she didn't care.

Cole had talked her into buying a little black dress for her girls' night that evening, and she'd found a few cute tops on sale that she'd also decided to purchase. She hadn't counted on Cole refusing to let her pay for her things, though. She'd argued, but he'd simply stared at her with the certain look she was beginning to realize meant he wasn't going to back down, and said, "You agreed."

So she'd backed off and let him buy the clothes, but made a mental vow to only shop for clothes in the future when he wasn't with her. Then they'd gone back to his apartment, and one thing led to another . . . She'd found they could make love playfully, without the intensity of the night before, and it was just as satisfying.

But now Cole had pulled up to the Rock 'N' Roll bar, where she was meeting the other women for their girls' night out—and she was nervous.

"Stop stressing," Cole told her, and tucked a stray lock of brown hair behind her ear.

"I can't help it. What if they don't like me? What if they think I'm weird? If they don't approve of me, then that'll make things awkward between you and your friends. I don't—"

"Relax," Cole ordered. "They're going to love you. Hell, they *already* love you. Have some drinks. Loosen up. Just be yourself. It'll be fine."

Sarah took a deep breath. Cole was right. She'd already met Felicity, who hadn't treated her with anything other than kindness.

Cole leaned forward, and Sarah felt his breath tickle the hair near her ear before he whispered, "I can't wait to help you out of this dress. In fact, maybe I'll take you while you're still wearing it. Bent over in front of me."

She shivered.

"You think you'd like that?" Cole asked.

Sarah turned to look him in the eyes. "I think I'd like anything you did to me."

He licked his lips, and she was happy to see his pupils dilate with her words. That gave her the courage to continue. "If you like sober Sarah, wait until you meet tipsy, takes-what-she-wants Sarah."

"Fuuuuck," Cole muttered.

Sarah chuckled, kissed him hard and fast on the lips, then opened her door. "I'll text you later when we're ready."

She saw him adjust his hard-on in his pants and nod. "We'll all be at Logan's, so we can be here within minutes when you guys are ready to go."

Sarah nodded and went to shut the door.

"Sarah?"

She paused and leaned back down. "Yeah?"

"They're going to love you because you're considerate, kind, and there's no way they could *not* love you."

"Thanks," she whispered.

"Now go, before I snatch you back inside this car and take you back to my apartment and ravage you."

"Sir, yes, sir," she quipped, then slammed the door and waved before she took a deep breath and headed for the door to the bar.

~

An hour and four alcoholic drinks later, Sarah was having the time of her life.

She was very definitely tipsy, bordering on drunk, but she couldn't remember when she'd had more fun.

Grace was somewhat quiet, like she was, but the others made up for their reticence. Bailey wasn't drinking because of her pregnancy, but it didn't matter—she didn't need alcohol to be just as hilarious as the others.

"So there I was, trying to get the scoop on the gang, and I had to keep doing shots of tequila," Alexis said, waving her hands around as she told her story. "It was so gross. Then Damian put his hand right up the waitress's skirt, right there at the table!"

Everyone groaned in disgust.

"Right? I mean, I like a good fingering as much as the next girl, but not by *him*, and not in the middle of a busy bar!"

Everyone roared with laughter at Alexis's off-the-cuff remark.

Felicity rested her chin on her hand and stared at her. "So, Sarah . . . tell us all about you."

"Me? There's nothing to tell," Sarah said.

"Bullshit!" Bailey exclaimed. "One day Cole is single and free as a bird, and the next he's all like, 'I'm busy. I have to go home and sit my ass on my couch and talk to Sarah.'"

Sarah covered her mouth with her hand and giggled.

"Right?" Felicity agreed. "I go off to Chicago to visit my mom's grave, and when I get back, my workaholic partner is allowing our employees to actually do their *jobs* so he doesn't have to be there twenty-four/seven. What's your story?"

"He was a jerk when we met," Sarah admitted.

All four of the other women leaned toward her, hungry for the details about their friend.

"He didn't know I could hear him, and he was kinda mean. But he apologized. And I guess we grew on each other." Sarah knew her explanation was weak, but she wasn't sure how to explain her relationship with Cole and how it had happened so fast.

"She's got a stalker," Alexis blurted.

"Seriously?" Grace asked.

"Yup," Alexis answered before Sarah could. "He leaves her creepy presents and love letters. But he's not like Donovan," she told Bailey. "He's got the mental capacity of, like, a ten-year-old."

The others were suitably shocked, and Sarah simply sipped her latest mixed drink as Alexis filled in the others on her situation.

"So what are you doing about it?" Felicity asked.

Sarah shrugged. "I'm selling my house, renting an apartment here in town that has twenty-four-hour security, I'm sleeping with Cole, and Ace Security said they were gonna do what they could to take care of it for me."

Silence met her statement.

"That's it?" Felicity asked after a moment.

Sarah stared at her in confusion. "Uh . . . yeah? Should I be doing something else?"

"How about getting a gun? And a knife? And thinking up a plan just in case this guy gets you?"

"Cole's been teaching me self-defense," Sarah said quietly.

"Look, I don't want to scare you, but that might not be enough. Trust me, I know," Felicity said, her words slurring slightly because of the amount of alcohol she'd drunk.

"Leese," Grace warned.

"What? No!" Felicity exclaimed. "I like her. She's nice. *Nice!* You saw her earlier when she went up to the bar to get drinks. That skank ho cut her off and flashed her tits at the bartender, and Sarah didn't even get pissed. She just waited her turn. Who waits their turn at a *bar*? No one! That's who. You shove your money under the bartender's nose so he'll wait on you. Then when that other chick looked down her nose at her, she didn't say anything. Not one word! The last thing I want is some crazy guy who thinks he's in love getting his hands on her. She needs to arm herself! Be ready to go all whoop-ass on him if she has to."

Sarah put a hand on Felicity's tattoo-covered arm to try to calm her down. "Felicity, it's okay."

"It's not!" the other woman insisted. "It's scary as hell, and I don't want you to go through that. When Joseph took me, I wasn't as prepared as I should've been. He could've shot me in the head! And if his even-crazier father hadn't shown up when he did, I would've been dead. And it wasn't just me. He took Nate!"

"Leese!" Grace said more forcefully, but Felicity ignored her. She turned and grabbed hold of Sarah's arm, her fingers digging into her skin. "Because of me, he almost ruined my best friend's life by taking her baby. What if this Owen guy tries to get to you through Cole? Or burns our gym down? Or tries to kidnap one of the babies again? You have to be ready. You have to have a plan!"

Sarah wasn't sure if Felicity was being a bitch on purpose—until she saw the tears in her eyes. This badass woman was extremely distraught over what Owen might do to Sarah and maybe even to others.

Sarah started to panic. Felicity was right. She couldn't handle it if Owen did something to someone else because of her. "Oh my God," she whispered and turned to Grace. "I don't want your babies to be taken." Then she looked at Alexis. "And you were already almost buried alive once, it can't happen again." She stared over at Bailey. "And you and Joel . . . you almost died of ass-fix-ee-tion . . . or whatever . . ." She waved her hand in the air as she butchered the word. Then she poked Felicity in the shoulder. "And I don't want you to be shot in the head!"

"Everyone, just calm down," Bailey, the only sober one, demanded. "No one is getting kidnapped, buried, smothered, *or* shot."

"You don't know that!" Sarah said in a high-pitched, stressed-out voice. "Today it's nice presents and love notes. Tomorrow Owen could hate me and all my friends. And you guys are my friends. I haven't even *had* friends before! I don't want to lose you!"

"You aren't going to lose us," Bailey started, before Alexis got up off her chair and came over to where Sarah was sitting at the bar-height table. She threw her arm around her and leaned heavily into her side.

"You're one of us," Alexis said seriously, even though her words were slurred. "Grace only had Felicity for a friend because her awful parents were super awful. I was too rich to have friends. Bailey was a former gang leader's girlfriend, and everyone was scared of her, and Felicity didn't allow herself to have friends other than Grace and Cole because she was scared of her stalker. We're like the anti-friend friends. And since you're with Cole, and he's Felicity's best friend, and she's *Grace's* best friend, and Grace is my sister-in-law, and Bailey is common-law married to my man's brother . . . you're now one of us!"

Sarah couldn't even follow Alexis's drunken reasoning, but it didn't matter. All that mattered was that she was being invited into the inner circle of this amazing group of women. "I accept!" she blurted.

Everyone cheered except for Bailey. She rolled her eyes, but smiled and held up her water glass as Alexis proposed a toast.

"To Sarah! The nice one!"

"To Sarah!" everyone echoed.

Sarah's eyes filled with tears.

"No crying!" Grace ordered, pointing her finger at Sarah. "If you cry, I'll cry. And if I cry, Logan will be worried, and he won't make love to me in my slutty new black dress!"

Felicity laughed. "As if!" she exclaimed, obviously having gotten herself under control. "There's no chance in hell he won't attack you the second you walk through the door."

"Our guys love our LBDs," Alexis added.

"And when we get tipsy!" Grace added.

"Tipsy?" Bailey muttered. "Try trashed."

"Don't be a hater," Alexis said as she stumbled back around the table to her chair and hoisted herself onto it. "Just because you've got a bun in the oven and can't imbibe with us doesn't mean you have to rain on our parade."

Bailey laughed and ran a hand over her still-almost-flat stomach. "I'm not being a hater at all. I'm actually enjoying this."

Sarah put her hand over Bailey's and asked in concern, "Are you still gonna get some when you get home even though you aren't drunk?"

There was silence for a moment—before all four women burst into laughter.

Sarah blinked. "What's so funny?" she asked when everyone had calmed down a bit.

"You are," Grace said.

"Why?"

"Let's just say the Anderson brothers are . . . *enthusiastic* when it comes to their wives and taking them to bed," Bailey said with a small smile.

"If they make it to a bed," Felicity added.

"Or even in the house," Grace said.

Sarah looked from one woman to another and saw they all had smirks on their faces.

"But you've all been married awhile," Sarah said, her brain officially fuzzy.

"And?" Alexis asked.

"I just thought . . . uh . . . that . . . you know." She'd gotten the impression earlier that night that the other women enjoyed girls' night out because their husbands liked to have sex with them when they were drunk. They'd had a short conversation about how all the guys were looking forward to being summoned when they were ready to go home because that meant they'd get to "take advantage" of their wives. And somehow, as she'd consumed more and more alcohol, that had gotten twisted in her brain to mean they only got some when they were drunk.

"Does Cole only fuck you when you're drunk?" Alexis asked.

"Ummm, no," Sarah said.

"Holy shit, have you and him not done it yet?" Felicity asked, her brows shooting upward.

"No! We did. We have. Last night. And this morning . . ." She hesitated, then added, "And this afternoon."

Everyone guffawed as if she were the funniest stand-up comic they'd ever heard in their lives. "Oh, just shut up," she said with a wrinkle of her brow.

Bailey had pity on Sarah, and explained, "Girl, Cole might not be an Anderson, but he's cut from the same cloth. Once our men find something they like, they're one hundred percent in. From their commitment to their job, to making us pregnant"—she again rubbed her belly—"or pleasing their woman. We just like dressing up and having some drinks because it's fun. And the anticipation of knowing how horny we get just gets the guys revved up even more. You'll see when Cole comes to pick you up."

"I'm not on the pill," Sarah blurted.

"Giiiiiirl," Alexis said, shaking her head. "You better do something about that if you don't want kids."

"I want them," Sarah said. She took another small sip of the fruity cocktail. She liked the idea of having friends. And it was nice to be able to talk about sex and other girly stuff. "I definitely want kids," she said succinctly.

"But?" Alexis pressed.

"No *but*. I want them. Like six or more. A houseful. But I want to adopt some. Older kids who feel as if no one wants them. Like me," Sarah said.

"If you aren't on the pill, you're gonna get 'em sooner rather than later," Alexis warned.

Sarah smiled dreamily. "I know. Cole hinted that he wanted them. Said the idea of getting me pregnant was a turn-on. He also said he didn't want to use condoms anymore once Owen was caught . . . and he didn't tell me to go on birth control or anything, so . . . I just assumed maybe that meant he wanted them right away. I think I'll like the process of making them."

"Cole's my best friend, and I want what's best for him," Felicity commented. "But things with you have been pretty fast."

"I know they've been fast, but honestly, things just seemed to click between us from the start . . . well, after he apologized for being rude to me before he met me. But I can talk to him about anything. He's the first person I think of when I get up in the morning, and the last person before I go to sleep."

"But . . . babies?" Felicity pushed.

Sarah shrugged. "My first real memory is of sitting on a swing, watching a man and a woman playing with their kid in a sandbox. I remember thinking how weird it was that adults were playing with a child. I didn't understand that they were her mom and dad."

"How old were you?" Felicity asked.

"Maybe four or five. The point is that I've never connected to people very well. I think maybe it's because I didn't have anyone *to* connect to when I was little. I liked my dads, and eventually loved them. But with Cole . . . I connected with him right away. I know I can't rescue every foster kid out there, but maybe I can help a few learn how to form friendships and connect with others earlier than I did. And I can't imagine anyone being a better father than Cole."

There was silence for a moment after she finished, and she awkwardly said, "That . . . and I'm pretty sure I love Cole."

"You love him?" Alexis asked gently.

"Yes. I know it's crazy. I haven't even known him that long. But he looks at me as if I'm the most beautiful woman in the world, when we all know that's *so* not true. He listens when I talk, and when he takes me in his arms, I feel as if nothing and no one can hurt me."

Felicity put her hand on Sarah's arm. "He loves you too," she said bluntly.

Sarah blinked.

"He does," she insisted. "All I've heard in the last few weeks is stuff about you. How brave you are. How smart. How great you are at your job. He can't stop talking, thinking, or worrying about you."

Alexis leaned across the table and took Sarah's hand in hers. "When I was lying in the trunk of that car and was being taken who knows where, one thing kept going through my head."

"What?" Sarah asked.

"That Blake would find me. Somehow. Someway. He'd find me. I think when you have that bone-deep conviction in your soul that your man will move heaven and earth to keep you safe, that's how you know he's the man you were meant to fall in love with."

"Cole promised that if Owen got ahold of me, he'd never stop looking for me until I was back home," Sarah said.

"And do you believe him?" Alexis asked, her eyes boring into Sarah's.

"Yes," she said.

"No," Alexis said, shaking her head. "Do. You. *Believe.* Him? Like, if you were lying on the ground being stabbed, or raped, or someone was burying you one shovelful at a time—"

"Alexis!" Grace interrupted. "Gross!"

Alexis waved her friend's words off and kept staring at Sarah with an intensity that would've been scary if Sarah weren't already drunk. "No matter what happens to you, or how long it takes, do you believe that he'd never stop looking for you? Do you believe that he'd still love you no matter what? If you had scars all over your body or if you were defiled?"

Sarah didn't immediately answer. She thought about the look on Cole's face as he asked her to be sure before he took her to his room. She remembered the force in his tone as he'd said "Mine" before he'd made love to her.

Then she licked her lips and nodded. "Yes."

Alexis smiled then and sat back. She picked up her glass and took a long swallow. "Good."

Sarah was glad when the focus of the conversation turned from her and her relationship with Cole to Grace and the twins. Nate and Ace were apparently growing like weeds and, now that they'd begun to walk, were getting into anything and everything.

She was mellow from the alcohol and from the feeling of finally being accepted into a group of women who seemed to truly like her for her. Not because she was a good CNA or because they wanted her business or just because she was with Cole.

An hour later, Felicity put her phone down on the table with a thunk and grinned at the group.

"What's that smile for?" Grace asked her friend.

"I hope everyone's had enough," Felicity said.

"Why?" Bailey asked.

"Because I'm betting the guys will be here to pick us up in about seven and a half minutes."

Surprised, Sarah squinted at the numbers on her watch. "It's not that late."

"I'm thinking I've had enough to drink, and as much as I love you girls, I need some one-on-one time with my man," Felicity said.

"What'd you do?" Alexis asked.

"I texted Ryder and told him that everyone was talking about babies, and maybe it was time we stopped just talking about them ourselves and did something about it," Felicity told them.

"You didn't!" Grace exclaimed.

"Right on!" Alexis said.

"It's about time," Bailey said with a grin.

"Since he's at Logan's with all the guys, I'm sure he told them. And I'm guessing when *Cole* hears that we're all talking about getting knocked up, he'll be here along with the others in about"—she looked at the nonexistent watch on her wrist—"seven more minutes."

"Oh God. I need to go!" Sarah exclaimed, suddenly panicked, her eyes wide. "Cole's gonna think I'm *insane* for wanting babies this early in our relationship!"

She hopped off her chair and stumbled, almost going to the floor, but Bailey reached out and grabbed her arm before she could flee.

"Stop panicking," she ordered.

Sarah shook her head. "I can't!"

The next thing she knew, she was surrounded by Grace, Alexis, Bailey, and Felicity.

"You were the one who said he brought up babies first," Felicity reminded her. "And I know my friend. This isn't going to faze him."

"It is!" Sarah exclaimed.

"He's gonna come busting through that door, ready to impregnate you here and now," Felicity told her with confidence. "Trust me."

Sarah swallowed hard.

"I'll bet you," Felicity said. "Anything you want. But you better not bet anything you aren't willing to lose."

"He's going to be upset, Felicity," Sarah argued.

"He's not. And if I'm right, you have to go with me to get a tattoo. You can pick what you want, but you have to go through with it."

"And if he's upset and weirded out that we've all been talking about having babies?" Sarah asked.

"Then I'll take care of everything associated with your move to your new apartment. I'll pack up whatever you haven't boxed already, arrange for a truck to get it here to Castle Rock, get the storage unit for whatever won't fit in your apartment, and unpack all your shit for you."

Sarah thought about it for two seconds. "Deal." She wasn't looking forward to moving at all. Tomorrow afternoon, she had to get started on the stuff in the attic. She had no idea what was up there, and she had a feeling she was going to be extra depressed if she'd lost Cole once and for all after being too loose-lipped with her new friends.

"Start thinking about what you want for your tattoo," Felicity said with a smirk.

Sarah opened her mouth to retort that *Felicity* should start figuring out where to get a bunch of boxes . . . when there was a commotion at the door of the bar.

The women around her turned, still flanking Sarah on either side.

Sarah barely heard Felicity's chuckle and soft "Told you so" before she also turned—and Cole was in front of her.

His eyes were gleaming, and she'd never seen him look quite so . . . unsettled before.

"Cole? Are you okay?"

Instead of answering, he asked, "Were you in on that conversation?"

"Um . . . the one about babies?"

"Yeah, Sarah. The one about babies."

She couldn't read his mood and tentatively said, "Yes?"

"You want to have kids with me?" he asked next.

"I love you, so yeah."

She immediately could've kicked herself for blurting out that tidbit. Darn alcohol.

Without another word, he took a step toward Sarah, bent slightly, and threw her over his shoulder.

She screeched and grabbed the side of his shirt. "Cole!" she protested.

He didn't respond, merely turned and headed for the door of the bar.

"See you later!" Blake called out.

"Drive safe!" Nathan said.

"Don't do anything I wouldn't do!" Ryder added.

Logan wasn't there, but Sarah remembered Grace saying that Ryder would take her home, since her husband couldn't leave the babies to come and pick her up.

"Cole! Put me down!" Sarah told him, propping herself as best she could by putting her hands flat on his back and arching up. She had no fear of falling—the arm around her thighs was tight . . . and this was Cole. He wouldn't drop her. No way.

He strode out of the bar toward his sports car. The world was spinning, so Sarah simply relaxed and let Cole take her where she wanted to go anyway. He tucked her into the passenger seat, still without speaking, and before she could blink, he was pulling out of the parking lot.

"Cole?" she said, but he held up a hand to stop her.

Sarah waited for him to say something, but he didn't. He merely put his hand back on the steering wheel and stared straight ahead. She honestly had no idea if he was pissed at her, or upset, or any of a hundred other emotions. She could see his jaw ticking, and he clenched the wheel until his knuckles turned white.

Despite what she'd bet Felicity, she'd hoped that Cole would be excited about her wanting kids with him. And she'd thought he was at first—the whole "throwing her over his shoulder like a Viking carrying off a virgin bride" thing was kind of hot. But now that he wasn't talking to her and looked like he was two seconds from losing his mind, she couldn't be sure.

The alcohol in her system was making her somewhat emotional, close to weepy, and she couldn't think straight. Biting her lip, Sarah kept quiet. She couldn't tear her eyes from Cole, though. If this was going to be the last time she got to stare at him to her heart's content, she wasn't going to give it up.

He pulled into the parking area of his apartment complex and jerked the car into park. He turned to her then and said, "Do. Not. Move."

So Sarah sat stock-still as he walked around the front of his car to her side. He opened the door and reached for her. This time, instead of putting her over his shoulder, he cradled her like a husband would as he carried her over the threshold of their new house. Sarah snuggled into him, loving how he felt and smelled. She laid her head on his shoulder and closed her eyes as the world spun.

She didn't open them when he placed her on her feet in front of his door either. She wrapped her arms around his chest and felt him unlocking the door behind her. He shuffled them inside and, after locking the door, simply dropped his keys.

The noise they made as they hit the floor surprised her, and Sarah's eyes popped open. She tilted her head back and stared up at Cole in trepidation, wondering what he was going to say.

Cole took her shoulders in his hands and slowly backed her up. Sarah didn't take her eyes from his, trusting that he wouldn't let her trip.

"How drunk are you?" he asked.

Sarah tilted her head and lifted a hand, showing him a small space between her thumb and pointer finger.

"How much did you drink?"

"Four mixed drinks. Wait . . . maybe five. I don't remember."

"Shit. I'm an asshole . . . but this is happening."

"What?" Sarah asked.

Cole stopped and turned her so she was facing the living room. He put a hand on her back and pushed until she was draped over the back of the sofa. His hands moved to her dress and jerked it up over her hips.

Sarah turned her head and stared back at him. Cole was gazing at her ass with a look so hot, so intense, she felt her body dampen. "Cole . . ."

"I warned you last night that if you gave yourself to me, that was it. There was no going back."

Sarah nodded, but was distracted when his hands went to the button and zipper of his jeans.

"I wasn't lying. You're mine, angel. I know you're drunk, but the idea that you'd let me put a baby in your belly is too much. And then you had to go and admit that you loved me . . . maybe I could've resisted if you hadn't said that." His cock sprang out of his jeans, looking angry and hard as a pike. It bobbed in front of him like a flag blowing in the wind.

One hand went to her back, and the other landed between her legs. He moved the gusset of her panties to the side and smiled. "Soaked," he murmured to himself before plunging a finger all the way inside her body.

Sarah moaned, and her head dropped.

"Hold on, angel. This is gonna be hard and fast." It was the only warning she got before Cole shifted, lifting her up so her feet no longer touched the floor. Her hands flew out and grabbed hold of the back of the couch at the same time she felt him enter her.

He thrust inside her with one hard push, and they both moaned at the sensation. The elastic of her panties was uncomfortable as it dug into her crotch, but she didn't complain. Couldn't complain.

Cole was fucking her. Hard. And she loved it.

"Yes . . . Cole!"

"Love you, Sarah. So fucking much," he grunted, and the words seeped into her soul and settled there like fairy dust.

She couldn't move. Could only lie there and take what Cole was giving her. But it was oh so glorious. When his hand snuck under her belly and his fingers began to strum her clit as he pounded in and out of her, she went wild. Thrashing on the back of the couch, begging him to fuck her harder, she hooked her feet around his calves as best she could in her position.

Within seconds, she was on the verge of coming.

Neither spoke, but the moment she began twitching, he planted himself inside her and grunted as he came with her.

It could've been hours or seconds, but eventually she came down from the high his hands and body had given her.

The room spun with the effects of the alcohol and his lovemaking.

Still without a word, Cole eased himself out of her, immediately turned Sarah, and picked her up. His pants were still around his hips, and his half-hard dick was still hanging out as he walked her to his room. He stripped her out of the little black dress, shoes, bra, and panties, and then took off his own clothes.

Sarah had already climbed under the sheet, and he joined her there moments later. He positioned her above him, took his cock in his hand once more and, gently this time, eased her down as he sank back into her body.

Sighing in contentment, Sarah slumped over and lay boneless atop him.

"I'm too tired to move," she complained.

"It's okay. Just sleep."

"But you . . . you're inside me."

"Yup."

"Don't you . . . Is this normal?" she asked.

"I have a feeling this is my new normal," Cole said with a small chuckle. "I'm always half-hard around you, and there's nowhere my dick wants to be more than inside you, where it's wet and warm."

Suddenly the wet feeling between her legs fully sank in. Sarah's head came up. "You didn't use a condom," she told Cole.

"Nope." He didn't sound stressed or concerned.

"I could get pregnant," she informed him.

"Yup."

Too tired and tipsy to worry about it right now, Sarah lay back down. Cole kissed the side of her head. "Sleep, angel."

"Mmm." It was the last thing she remembered.

❧

Cole held Sarah as she slept on top of him. His cock still hadn't gotten flaccid, and he was loving the feel of being inside her body. He hadn't lied about that. He could've made love to her for hours, but she was drunk. And tired. He probably shouldn't have fucked her over the back of his couch, but he couldn't stop himself.

She loved him.

She wanted babies with him.

So he'd done his best to give her what she wanted. What *he* wanted.

He wanted to see her round with his child.

Wanted to tie her to him so deeply, she'd never leave.

If she wanted to adopt, he was okay with that, but first they'd have a little boy or girl with her eyes and chin.

The urge to fill her up again was overwhelming, but he'd never take her when she was unconscious or asleep. His dick would just have to wait until she woke up.

A feeling of rightness settled over him.

The best thing that ever happened to him was snuggled in his arms like she never wanted to leave. And he was perfectly okay with that.

As the night progressed, Cole made plans. Plans for Sarah to meet his brother. And his parents. They'd all love her. They needed to do their traveling now, before she was too far along in her pregnancy.

And Cole had no doubt he could've already knocked her up, considering the amount of testosterone coursing through his veins.

Smiling, he palmed her ass and pressed her closer to him. Sarah shifted in her sleep and tightened her hold on him. Life was good.

No, it was fucking great.

Chapter Thirteen

When Sarah woke up the next morning, it took a moment to remember where she was, why her head hurt so badly, and what had happened with Cole. She pried open one eye and saw that she was alone in his bed. She might've been upset that he'd left her by herself if she hadn't needed a minute or two to regain her equilibrium.

She remembered everything that had happened the night before. What she'd told the group and how she'd admitted that she wouldn't mind if she got pregnant right away. Cole hadn't been mad that she'd wanted kids. In fact, he'd been so turned on, he'd fucked her the second they'd gotten into his apartment.

And not only that . . . Sarah moved her legs and felt the dampness between them.

He'd done it without a condom.

The thought that she could be pregnant should be freaking her out. Especially in light of the fact that the issue with Owen hadn't been resolved. But instead, it felt . . . right.

Closing her eyes, Sarah stretched. A full-body stretch. Her arms above her head, her back arched. Smiling, she opened her eyes . . .

And froze.

Cole was standing in the doorway, staring at her and smiling back. He had no shirt on and was wearing a pair of sweatpants that looked like they were barely hanging on to his hips. The V muscles and his abs were as prominent as ever. It was no wonder he'd been able to so easily haul her around last night. He was so damn muscular it was almost comical.

"Hi," she said shyly.

"Hi," he returned. "How do you feel?"

She shrugged and tugged the sheet up, making sure she was covered. "I'm okay. My head hurts a little, but not too bad."

"You remember last night?"

She considered lying, but nodded instead.

Cole pushed off the doorjamb and came toward her. He sat on the edge of the bed and brushed a lock of hair behind her ear.

Sarah had the feeling her hair was probably completely out of control. She fidgeted when he didn't say anything and merely stared down at her with an unreadable look on his face.

"I have to get a tattoo," she blurted.

He frowned. "What?"

"I lost a bet with Felicity."

"What kind of bet?"

"After she sent that text, I panicked and thought that she'd ruined everything we were building. She said that you would show up any second, and I didn't believe her. She said if you weren't upset and freaked about the babies thing, that I had to go get a tattoo with her."

"And if I was?" Cole asked with a smile.

"She had to box my stuff up, move it all, and unpack everything in my new apartment."

His smile grew. "She's sneaky, that Felicity. That was a sucker bet because she knows me too well. I've already planned on getting you moved, and she knew it."

"You have? She did?"

"Yeah. On your next break from work, I've arranged for a local moving company to pack anything that you haven't gotten to yet and move you down here."

"When were you going to tell me?" Sarah asked, scooting up so her back was against the headboard.

Cole winced. "Today?"

She chuckled. "Nice save."

"And you should know, I'd move you in here with me in a heartbeat, but I want you to be safe, and that other complex has better security. So you'll be seeing me at your new place a lot, angel. And the second a bigger apartment opens up, I'm doing what I can to get it for us. Especially now."

"Now?"

He leaned forward, practically touching his nose with hers. "I took you without a condom last night."

Sarah swallowed hard and nodded.

"And I want to do that again this morning. And before you head home today . . . If you aren't already pregnant, it's only a matter of time, because now that I've had you bare and filled you with my come, I want to do it again. And again. And again. I'm addicted to your pussy already, and you want kids. We need to get started on that so we aren't sixty when we have our last child."

Sarah's heart was beating impossibly hard in her chest. Her head spun with the speed at which Cole was moving. But she couldn't deny that she wanted it all with him. He'd be an amazing father. He'd be strict, but fair. Protective, but not smothering.

This was insane. Wasn't it?

"Okay," she whispered.

"Are you really okay with this or just saying that because you're freaked out?" he asked astutely.

"A little of both? I love you, Cole, but I can't help but think this is too fast."

He closed his eyes briefly at her pronouncement, but nodded. "And that's why you're getting that apartment. So you can make sure this thing between us is working."

Sarah frowned. "But you just said you were trying to get me pregnant."

Cole smiled sheepishly. "I am. *I* have no doubt that things between us are going to work out, Sarah. I'm just giving you a bit of room so you can come to the same conclusion."

"Oh."

He leaned in and kissed her forehead. "Now, get up. Shower. Then come out to the kitchen. I've made us breakfast."

Sarah was surprised. He'd just said he wanted to make love to her again . . . now he was telling her to shower. The man was confusing.

As if he could read her mind, Cole said, "Shower, some pills for your headache, some food for energy, then I want to eat you out again. Then watch as you ride my cock until I fill that hot little pussy."

Her stomach clenched at the thought.

He smiled. "Yeah, angel. Things between us are going to work out." Leaning forward, Cole rested his forehead on hers. "I love you, angel. More than I've ever loved anyone or anything in my life. You're mine, just as I'm yours. I'll protect, care for, and love you and our children until the end of my days."

Sarah smiled. "Just remember who said it first," she told him.

He laughed and stood. At the door, he turned and said, "I can't wait to see what you decide for your tattoo . . . but do me a favor?"

"What?" she asked when he didn't finish his sentence.

"Put it somewhere I can see only when you're naked. The thought of you with ink on your skin turns me on so much, I'm afraid I'd jump you every time I saw it . . . no matter where we were or who we're with."

Sarah laughed as he left the room. She'd have to come up with something amazing. Something that would take Cole's breath away every time he saw it. Hopefully Felicity would give her some time to think before she dragged her to the tattoo place.

~

"Do you want me to come in with you?" Cole asked as they stood by his car. He'd followed her all the way back to Parker. Sarah had tried to talk him out of it, but he'd insisted.

She'd pulled her car into the garage, and they were saying goodbye next to his.

It had been an amazing day. One Sarah didn't want to end. But she had to get back to work tomorrow, and Cole had stuff to do for the gym. She also needed to get more of the house boxed up before her shifts started again. Especially if Cole was going to have movers come and start hauling her stuff away. She needed to organize. Figure out what she wanted in storage and what she couldn't live without for the next few months.

But it still felt weird to be leaving him. They'd spent the last two days or so together, and, if she was being honest with herself, she didn't want to part. She was feeling clingy, and that so wasn't like her. It was almost as if she were six years old again and didn't want to let Mike or Jackson out of her sight in case someone from the state came to take her away.

She knew a good thing when she had it, and she definitely had a good thing in Cole. They laughed together, the sex was amazing, but more than that, she was comfortable around him. She didn't feel as if she had to entertain him, was just as happy sitting in a room with him, not talking, as she was having an in-depth conversation about health care in the United States.

"*Want?* Yes. But we both have stuff we have to do," she told him with a smile.

Cole didn't smile. He stared at her with a look so smoldering, Sarah had the feeling she would spontaneously combust if he didn't look away. "Come 'ere," he said, reaching for her.

Sarah willingly leaned toward him, not surprised when her arms broke out in goose bumps when his lips met hers. The kiss was somewhat bittersweet because she knew it would be at least three more days until she'd get to see him again. She had three days of twelve-hour shifts, so she'd work herself to the bone, then come home each night and collapse into bed.

But at the end of those three days, she was going to see Cole again, move into her new apartment, and start her new life.

Cole kept his hand on the back of her neck when he pulled away. His thumb brushed back and forth, and that alone was enough to make her nipples tighten.

"Don't look at me like that," Cole admonished.

"Like what?" Sarah asked.

"Like I'm an ice-cream cone that you want to lick," he said immediately.

Sarah chuckled. "Come to think of it, I never did get to . . . lick," she said coyly.

Cole groaned. "Shit, angel, now I won't be able to think about anything other than you on your knees, those luscious lips wrapped around my cock."

She squirmed against him. "Thank you," she blurted.

Cole frowned. "For what?"

"For being so amazing. I know I'm not exactly the catch of the century. I've got some baggage, and things are uncertain with Owen. I live too far away, and I've been told more times than I can count that I need to not be such a pushover when it comes to people being rude to me. I just—"

"Stop," Cole ordered.

Sarah pressed her lips together.

"Fuck the people who've told you that. You're a breath of fresh air. If there were more people like you than me, the world would be a better place. Don't ever change. Be who you are, and screw what everyone else thinks. I saw the look on that woman's face when you offered to unload the groceries in her cart when her baby was screaming its head off. She wasn't so sure about *me*, but after one look at your friendly and welcoming smile, the relief on her face was instant. And when I had to go to the gym today for a bit, you didn't complain. Then I swear to God I thought that woman was going to propose to you."

Sarah blushed. "She was crying, Cole. Was I supposed to ignore her?"

"No. Fuck no. But that didn't stop everyone else from ignoring her. You went right up and asked what was wrong and if you could help."

"It's not cool that those girls were making fun of her."

"It's not. And they aren't welcome in Rock Hard Gym ever again. *No one* gets body shamed in my gym. I don't care if someone is eight hundred pounds or eighty. My point is, I probably wouldn't even have noticed her if you hadn't been there. So please don't ever change. I need you in my life. I need you to slow me down and point out the beauty in the world. All I've looked for is the bad. Being around you is already making me look at the world in a different way.

"And about the other shit you just said? Everyone has baggage, angel, and I love you regardless. In less than a week, you aren't going to live so far away. In fact, all you'll have to do is roll over, and I'll be there next to you. And we're going to figure out this situation with Owen. It sounds like he needs to be in some sort of group home where they can supervise him, and if that's the case, Ace Security will make sure he gets the help he needs. Okay?"

"Okay," Sarah agreed. What else could she say? Cole made everything seem as if it was going to work out without any issues. She hoped so.

"Okay," Cole repeated. Then he kissed her once more, a short and hard kiss that was hardly satisfactory, but probably safer considering they couldn't keep their hands off each other.

"Call or text me in the morning when you leave for the hospital," he told her.

"It's going to be early," she warned.

"I'll be up. Besides, even if I weren't, hearing from you is a hell of a way to start my day."

Sarah licked her lips, and Cole groaned. He gave her neck a small squeeze, then stood back. "Go on. Before I haul your sweet ass inside and have my wicked way with you."

She had a feeling he wasn't kidding. Sarah wouldn't have minded that, but she knew he had work to do. Keeping her eyes on his, she nodded and walked backward toward the garage—she'd found no gifts from Owen on her stoop when she'd pulled in, thank God. She unlocked the garage door and turned to wave at Cole.

He grinned at her, lifting one finger from his steering wheel, and backed out of her driveway. She watched until she couldn't see his car anymore, then finally entered her house.

It seemed extraordinarily large and empty. She knew it was because she'd just spent the most amazing couple of days with Cole. He was larger than life and seemed to fill all the lonely cracks inside her. For the first time, Sarah realized that the house she grew up in, the house where she'd first learned what true love was from her dads, didn't feel like home anymore. Simply because Cole wasn't there with her.

"It's time," she whispered as she looked around. There were boxes stacked haphazardly around the living room and kitchen. The Realtor was calling a company to come in and professionally stage the house once everything was out. It cost a bit more, but it was worth it so she didn't have to worry about moving more than once. She could box up all her stuff now and have it done.

Knowing she had a lot of work ahead of her, especially if she was going to tackle the boxes in the attic, Sarah took a deep breath. Stuffing her phone in her back pocket, she headed for her bedroom. She was almost done in there, had a bit of sorting to do in the master bedroom, then she'd see how much crap there was in the attic. She'd pretty much already planned to open all the boxes up there, quickly check what was in them, then probably donate most of the contents. If she hadn't used that stuff in years, there was no need to keep it.

Feeling good about the task ahead of her, excited that with every box she packed up and sorted, she was closer to moving to Castle Rock and starting her new life with Cole, Sarah couldn't help but think about all the places she was sore where she'd never been sore before.

Cole was an energetic lover. He'd done things to her, and with her, that she'd never experienced. And he hadn't been kidding when he'd said that he was addicted to her. Every chance he got, he was inside her. Sometimes fucking her hard, sometimes slow, but every single time, he made sure she orgasmed before he did, planting himself as deep inside her as possible.

Sarah stood in the entrance to her bedroom and put a hand on her stomach. She could be pregnant right this second. She wouldn't be surprised. She had no doubt Cole's little swimmers were incredibly potent.

Closing her eyes, she smiled. Maybe things wouldn't work out. Maybe Cole would decide that she wasn't the woman he wanted, after all, but for this moment, today, she was his, and he was hers. Deciding to worry about the future another day, she dropped her hand, opened her eyes, and headed for the nearest half-empty box. The sooner she got everything packed up, the sooner she could start her new life with Cole.

∼

It was later than she'd hoped before Sarah was ready to start on the mess in the attic. She had gotten distracted in Mike and Jackson's room. She'd found some papers she hadn't ever seen before. They were hidden in a shoebox high on a shelf in the closet. Since Mike had loved shoes and had owned what seemed like a million pairs, she'd simply thought the box held one more. But the second she pulled the box off the shelf, she knew it didn't contain shoes.

She'd ended up sitting on the floor of the master closet, crying and trying to read between her tears. The box held mementos her dads had kept of her. The letter saying they'd been approved to be foster parents.

The first Father's Day cards she'd given them. Her report cards from elementary school. Even the paperwork from the school when she'd gotten detention for fighting with another girl.

Sarah remembered that day clearly. The spoiled little brat had made fun of her for having two dads instead of a mom, and had wanted to know if she was going to be a lesbian because her dads were gay. Sarah had hit her. Curled her fingers into a fist and hit her in the mouth. She'd been ten. It had hurt, and she'd had to write an apology letter to the little girl, which wasn't fair since she hadn't been the one in the wrong, but her dads had sat her down and told her that there would always be people who were mean-spirited and ugly inside, and it was harder to stand up and be the better person.

That had been the first and last time she'd ever hit anyone.

The box had pictures too. Of her when she was little, of her and Mike, of her and Jackson.

But the most precious thing she'd found was a letter her dads had written to the man she'd eventually marry.

As far as she could tell, they'd written it when she was in high school sometime and had probably planned to read it at her wedding rehearsal or something.

To the man who wants to marry our Sarah,
You are not good enough for our daughter.
But then again, no one is.
However, for some reason, she loves you, and
you love her back.
Sarah has always been special. She sees the
best in everyone and never the worst. It's both her
best quality as well as the scariest.
As her dads, we've tried to encourage her to
spread love in the world instead of hate. There's

too much hate already. We've lived it our entire lives.

Protect her from that hate. Be her shield as we've tried to be.

In return, you will never know love as pure and unconditional as Sarah's.

We wish you a long and beautiful life together . . . but if you so much as hurt one hair on her head, or make her cry with careless words or deeds, or in any way make her think she's not good enough for you, there will be nowhere you can hide from us.

Be good to our baby girl.

Love her.

Keep her safe.

Give her babies of her own.

Let her bright light shine.

She's an angel in disguise, and we are blessed to call her our daughter.

Just as you are blessed to have her as your wife.

~Mike & Jackson Butler

She'd cried for several minutes. Her dads would've loved Cole. Mike would've swooned over his protectiveness, and Jackson would've just nodded his head in approval.

But she couldn't get over the last part of their letter.

Angel in disguise . . . and Cole called her *angel.*

Give her babies . . . and Cole was doing his best to do that exact thing already.

Lifting her head to look upward, she whispered, "Thank you."

Then she folded the letter, placed it reverently back on top of the other memorabilia in the shoebox, and closed the lid. This was one of her most prized possessions, and she hoped like hell she'd get the chance to share Mike and Jackson's letter with Cole at some point. It was too early in their relationship, but if things went as she hoped, she'd read it to him the night before they got married.

Yes, she wanted to marry Cole. Wanted to become Sarah Butler-Johnson. She hoped he wouldn't have a problem with her hyphenating her name. She wanted to honor the men who'd taken her in, loved her, and given her a home and a family.

Her mind was on the letter, Cole, babies, and dreading finding out how much stuff there was going to be in the attic as she reached up and grabbed the cord that would pull the stairs down out of the ceiling.

She'd only been up in the attic a few times, not liking how hot and cramped it felt up there. She pulled the stairs down and started to climb. They were rickety and definitely didn't feel safe, but Sarah reassured herself that once this was done, she'd never have to go up into the attic again.

She was thinking that there was no way Cole would ever let her go up and down a ladder like this if he were around, especially not if she were pregnant, when her head reached the top of the ladder and she could see into the attic for the first time.

When a man's face suddenly appeared in front of hers, Sarah let out a screech and instinctively took a step backward.

Of course, since she was on a ladder, her foot landed on nothing but air. Her arms flailed, and a scream tore from her throat as she fell.

Everything happened so fast. Sarah couldn't stop herself from succumbing to gravity, until her foot got caught in a rung of the ladder, slowing down her fall, but wrenching her ankle painfully in the process.

She landed hard on her ass, then her head bounced on the hardwood floor with a chilling crack.

As she lay there, dazed, and in an extreme amount of pain, she watched as Owen Montrone clambered down the ladder that led into her attic. He looked concerned, but also excited.

And that was what scared her the most.

Blackness began creeping in from the sides of her eyes, and Sarah knew she was going to pass out. Right before things went dark, Owen leaned over her on the floor and patted her chest like a kid might pat a dog.

"It's okay. Owen will take care of you, and you will take care of him."

The large man bending over her was the last thing Sarah saw before she blacked out.

Chapter Fourteen

Cole was concerned.

It was ten o'clock in the morning, and he hadn't heard from Sarah.

They'd agreed that she would contact him before she left for work, but he hadn't heard a word from her.

He knew it couldn't be because she was mad at him for something; they'd left on very good terms. The days they'd spent together had been perfect. Besides, she wasn't the kind of woman to just leave him hanging like this. If she said she'd call or text, she'd call or text. It wasn't in her makeup to ghost him.

He'd already called the hospital, but the person he'd finally been connected to wasn't allowed to give out any information on patients or employees.

Cole was done sitting around and waiting for her to respond. Something was wrong. Very wrong. He knew it deep in his gut.

Sarah was in trouble, and she needed him.

He remembered the promise he'd made to her, that if something happened and she disappeared, he'd never stop looking for her. He felt sick to his stomach. When he'd made the promise, he hadn't thought they'd ever actually end up in that kind of situation.

But they were there now.

He knew it. Felt it.

It didn't matter if the cops told him Sarah was an adult and allowed to go somewhere without telling him.

She was in trouble—and he wouldn't stop until he found her.

Felicity hadn't gotten into work yet—she'd been picking up the slack for him the last couple of days while he'd spent time with Sarah. He knew Logan and Blake were scheduled to be in Colorado Springs this morning, protecting an older man from his greedy daughter who was taking him to court, trying to prove he was incompetent and couldn't care for himself.

But Nathan and Ryder should be arriving at work around now. He knew because Felicity had told him her schedule the night before. And if Felicity was coming to the gym, Ryder was going to the Ace Security offices.

He left without telling the college student manning the desk where he was going. He didn't care if he missed a meeting or if he was supposed to teach a class, Sarah was more important.

He burst into the Ace Security offices as if the hounds of hell were after him. Nathan and Ryder were sitting in the large open space behind the front desk. Cole blurted out the only thing he'd been thinking for the last few hours.

"Sarah's missing—and that asshole Owen took her."

∿

Three hours later, Cole paced back and forth while the Anderson brothers did what they did best—try to figure out what the hell was going on. Ryder had called one of his Mountain Mercenary friends, and he'd taken over at the courthouse for Logan and Blake so they could race back up to Castle Rock to help find Sarah. Cole had never been so grateful for his friends in all his life. They hadn't blown him off or told him he was being paranoid. They'd sprung into action and done what they could to figure out what had happened to Sarah.

"Her car isn't at the hospital or at her house," Ryder said. "The cops in Parker did a drive-by and welfare check. No one answered the door, and they didn't see her car in the garage. There was no sign of a break-in, and the house was locked up tight. They looked in the windows but didn't see any sign of her."

"She didn't clock in this morning either," Nathan mumbled.

"I talked to her boss, and she didn't call in sick or send an email saying that she wouldn't be there today," Logan added.

The more they talked, the faster Cole paced.

"We need to get to her house and see what we can see," Blake said impatiently. "It's likely that whatever happened, happened there."

"Why?" Nathan asked. "She could've been ambushed on her way to the hospital. It's over twenty miles from her house to Castle Rock. Something could've happened between there and here."

Blake shook his head. "No. Cole said that she's been texting him before she leaves her house and when she gets to the hospital. If something happened on the way to work, he still would've gotten that first text."

"She could've forgotten," Logan said.

"She wouldn't forget," Ryder said firmly. "She knows better. Look, she was the one who came to *us* with this case. She was uneasy with Owen even when she didn't know why. Even when the cops didn't believe there was any threat, she still felt it. And after spending the last two days with Cole, I honestly don't think she would've just 'forgotten' to text him before she left for work this morning."

Cole agreed. But he kept his mouth shut and let his friends talk things out.

"Fine. I agree. Cole, when did you drop her off yesterday?" Logan asked.

"Three o'clock or so," he told him.

"So sometime between, say, three thirty yesterday and five thirty this morning, something happened," the oldest Anderson brother concluded.

He wasn't saying anything Cole hadn't already thought, but hearing it put so succinctly made him want to puke.

Fourteen hours. She could've been missing for fourteen hours before he'd realized something was wrong. And now it had been almost twenty-four. There was no telling what Owen was doing with her. Developmentally disabled or not, the man thought he was in love with Sarah and could be doing anything to her right now.

Yup, he was going to puke.

Striding quickly to the bathroom, Cole leaned over the trash can and dry heaved. He hadn't eaten anything that morning, too worried when he hadn't heard from Sarah.

He felt a hand on his back and turned his head to see Felicity standing there. She'd heard what was going on when she arrived at the gym and had immediately come to the Ace Security offices. She hadn't said much and was doing her best to deal with the phones while the rest of the group figured out what their next steps should be.

"This is the men's room," he said, not really knowing what he was saying. "Last I checked, you don't have the right equipment to be here."

"Shut up," his best friend told him. "They're going to find her."

He nodded and went to the sink to splash his face with cold water.

"They are," she insisted.

Cole propped his hands on the sides of the sink and stared at himself in the mirror. All his life, people had told him how good-looking he was. Women slipped him phone numbers, and the woman who did most of his tattoos had made it clear she was more than happy to take him into the back room and blow him. He'd worked his ass off to keep his body healthy and fit. He'd been recruited to be a professional bodybuilder more than once.

All his life, when people saw him, they saw his outer trappings.

But not Sarah.

The first time her eyes met his, he knew she saw past his looks. It was as if she'd looked into his soul. And she loved him. *Him.*

He'd be damned if he'd stand around for one more minute speculating about what happened to her. He needed to get to Parker and make sure she wasn't lying hurt on her floor, unable to get up or get to a phone. If she wasn't at her house, he needed to figure out where the fuck she was, what Owen had done with her, and bring her home.

Another thought struck him then. One that made his blood run cold.

She could be carrying his child.

There was actually a really good possibility she was carrying his child. Lord knew he'd done his best to knock her up over the last couple of days, and she'd said it was the right time of the month for her to get pregnant.

Granted, if she *was* pregnant, the baby was no bigger than a grain of sand at the moment, but still.

No one hurt his woman.

No one hurt his child.

No one.

He turned without saying another word to Felicity and headed out of the bathroom and straight for the door of Ace Security.

"Where are you going?" Blake called out.

Ryder didn't bother to ask anything. He simply stood and headed straight for Cole.

"Parker," Cole said without stopping. "Sarah's in trouble, and I promised her that if anything ever happened, I'd find her. And I can't do that standing around here."

"We're going to find her," Blake said.

"Go," Logan said, nodding. "You and Ryder check out her house and let us know what you find. We'll contact the Castle Rock PD and have them put out a BOLO for her car."

"She hasn't even been reported missing yet," Nathan argued.

Logan turned hard eyes on his brother. "They will *not* deny us this. We're not fucking around. Too many of our loved ones have disappeared, and there's no way I'm going to let them sit on their hands. Sarah is one of us, and she needs our help."

Nathan nodded immediately.

"Go," Logan repeated.

Cole didn't need to be told twice. He was striding out of the office within seconds, Ryder hot on his heels.

"I'll drive," the other man said succinctly.

Cole didn't argue. He knew he probably shouldn't get behind the wheel of a car right now. He'd drive too fast, too recklessly, and the last thing Sarah needed was for him to get in a wreck when he was on his way to find her.

Cole wasn't usually a praying man, but as Ryder raced toward Parker, he prayed that they'd find Sarah alive in her house. If she was hurt, fine, they'd deal with that, but if she wasn't there . . . he wasn't sure what he would do.

~

Sarah moaned and brought a hand up to her head. It hurt. Bad. But when she tried to roll over, she almost passed out once more at the pain that shot through her ankle. Groaning, she couldn't remember what in the hell had happened and why it felt as if she had knives stabbing into her leg.

"Rest," a deep male voice said. "I'll make you better."

Sarah's eyes popped open—and she stared up in horror at Owen. He was standing above her, smiling. He held out a plastic cup. "Here. Drink."

Moving slowly, trying to figure out what in the hell was going on, Sarah pushed herself to a sitting position. Her head spun, and her ankle throbbed. She reached out and took the cup Owen offered and saw it held what looked and smelled like orange juice.

"When I'm sick, OJ makes it better," he said proudly.

Sarah wanted to kick him in the face and run out of the room to get help, but something Cole had taught her in one of the many talks they'd had was to use her head in any dangerous situation. He couldn't tell her how to act and what to do in every scenario because all of them were different. Some women were able to fight like hell and get their abductors to give up and run away. But in other situations, when a woman fought, she immediately had her throat slashed.

Dealing with a kidnapper was a matter of sizing up the situation and doing whatever it took to keep him or her calm. And then when the opportunity presented itself, she could escape.

Looking around the room, Sarah didn't recognize where they were. It looked like one big room, with a kitchen on one end and two twin beds on the other. A wooden table with two chairs was behind the couch, but she didn't see a television anywhere. She was sitting on said couch, right in the middle of the space. An old couch. There were holes in the cushion next to her, as if rodents had made their home there once upon a time.

That thought made her shudder, but she pushed it back. Dealing with a few mice wasn't a big deal, not when the man standing over her was the bigger threat.

But Owen didn't look like much of a threat at the moment. He was still smiling down at her as if she were dancing a jig to entertain him or something.

"Go on. Drink," he ordered.

Sarah had no idea if the juice was drugged or not, but she was thirsty. She didn't know how long she'd been knocked out either. She tentatively took a sip of the drink and was happy when it didn't taste funny. "Thank you," she said softly.

If possible, Owen's smile grew. He nodded several times and repeated, "OJ makes everything better."

Sarah wasn't so sure about that. She looked down at her ankle and winced. It was swollen to twice its normal size. She wasn't wearing shoes, and she knew there was no way she could walk on it. She had a feeling she'd broken it, which would be bad. Very bad.

Tears threatened. If she could walk, she could be nice to Owen until he let down his guard, then she could run. But that was obviously out. Even moving her foot an inch had her wanting to scream with pain.

"Where are we?" she asked before taking another sip of the orange juice.

"My house," Owen said proudly.

"And where's that?" She needed information. If she could get to a phone, maybe when Owen fell asleep, she could tell 911 where to find her.

"The mountains."

Oh shit. Castle Rock was surrounded by mountains. There was no telling where they were.

"Where in the mountains? Are we near Denver?"

Owen shook his head. "We aren't near anything. This used to be Gran's house. Then it was my mama's. Now it's mine. Mama taught me how to get here. We can live here forever and ever. I can take care of you, and you can take care of me."

Sarah's head continued to pound, and she felt sick. She glanced toward the one window and saw nothing but trees. "Owen, you have to take me back."

He frowned and shook his head.

"Yes, you do. My ankle is hurt really bad. I need a doctor."

"No!" he yelled, scaring the shit out of Sarah. "I brought Mama to the doctor, and she *died*! No doctor!"

"It's okay, Owen," Sarah said as calmly as she could. "I don't have what your mama did. I'm not going to die."

"No! No no no no no!" he chanted, pulling at his hair as he paced in front of the couch she was sitting on.

Sarah had never seen a grown man have a tantrum, but that's exactly what Owen was doing right in front of her eyes.

"No doctor! No leaving! We're gonna live here forever. I love you, and you love me. We're married like Mama was. She said you'd take care of me! You aren't leaving. *Ever.* You'll cook for me and clean. I'll help. We'll play games and live happily ever after just like in the books!" Owen's voice had gotten louder and louder until he was practically yelling.

Tears formed in Sarah's eyes, but she immediately nodded and agreed. "Okay, Owen. No doctor. Calm down."

"Don't tell me to calm down!" he yelled. Then he leaned over and pointed a finger in her face. "You aren't leaving. I gave you presents! We love each other! I watched you. You're nice and quiet. I like that. We could've lived in your house together, but then you started packing. You were gonna leave me! I won't let you."

"You watched me?" Sarah asked, shaking.

"From the top of your house."

Suddenly, it all came to her. "You were living in my attic?" she whispered in horror.

Owen smiled and straightened. He nodded. "Yeah. I was real quiet. Like Mama taught me. You bought food for me and had boys' clothes too. I came down when you left the house. I brought the clothes and stuff with me. Things for you too." He rushed over to a corner of the room where a few boxes were stacked.

Sarah recognized them as being from her own house. He pulled out some of Mike and Jackson's clothes that Owen obviously thought she'd bought just for him. Then he pulled out some sort of hideous muumuu covered with garish flowers.

"You wear Mama's dress!" he said with glee.

"Oh God," Sarah gasped under her breath.

"And food!" Owen rushed over to the kitchen and opened a cabinet filled with canned food. "I went shopping on the way here and also brought food from your house for us. It'll last ages!"

A thought struck Sarah. "What happens when we run out?" she asked. "I'll need to go get us some more." If she could get him to take her to a store, she could alert a clerk that she'd been kidnapped.

Owen shook his head. "You make a list. I'll go. I'm a good helper."

Her hopes dashed, Sarah stared as Owen came back to the couch. He sat on the cushion next to her, and she inhaled sharply when his movements jostled her ankle and pain shot up her leg.

He patted her chest as he spoke. Not in a sexual way, but in a child-like gesture that Sarah knew he meant to be reassuring, but in reality was scary as hell.

"Me and you. We're married now. Till death do us part."

And with that not-so-reassuring statement, Owen got up and sat on the floor in front of the couch. He pulled a toy train set in front of him and began to play, occasionally mumbling something under his breath as he did.

The tears fell down Sarah's cheeks unheeded. She leaned over, placed the half-empty cup of juice on the floor, and carefully scooted down until she was lying flat once again. Her head throbbed, and the pain in her ankle was almost unbearable.

Closing her eyes, she prayed that Cole had meant what he'd said. That he'd never stop looking for her. Because she had a feeling she was going to be here a very long time unless he found her.

～

Cole stood in the middle of Sarah's living room and turned in a circle, trying to find some sort of sign about where she'd gone. There were boxes everywhere because she'd been in the middle of packing, and it was impossible to tell if anything had been disturbed or if this was how she'd left it. Cabinets in the kitchen were open, and various belongings were scattered along the counters and floor.

He and Ryder had already searched the house and hadn't found Sarah. That was both good and bad. Good because it meant she hadn't been lying here, scared and hurt, hoping someone would find her. Bad because they had absolutely no idea where she was.

"I can't find her purse," Ryder said as he came into the living room.

Cole nodded. "Her car is gone, so that makes sense."

"But I did find this," Ryder said, holding up Sarah's phone. "I already called Alexis and told her not to bother trying to trace it."

Cole stared at Sarah's phone, and his hopes sank. He'd prayed she had it with her and could be traced that way. He reached for it and clicked the "Home" button. When he'd chastised her for not having it locked, she'd just laughed and said she had nothing to hide and wasn't doing anything illegal, so it didn't matter if anyone was able to use it or not.

He clicked on the text-message icon and swallowed hard. He could see all the texts he'd sent when he'd been trying to get ahold of her. All unanswered.

He checked her emails. Most were junk. There was one from him and one from one of the nurses she worked with, checking on her. He shook his head in despair. If she'd only bought the cameras for the front porch, they might've been able to download the video and see who took her and what direction they went in, but she hadn't. They'd talked about it, and decided since she'd delayed this long, and was moving into the studio apartment in a few days, it was no longer worth it.

Stupid. So fucking stupid of him.

Sighing, Cole put the phone in his pocket. He'd give it to the cops and see if they'd be able to find anything on it, but he had a feeling they'd come up empty.

Looking at Ryder, Cole asked, "Where is she?"

The other man came over to him and put his hand on Cole's shoulder. "Do *not* give up," he ordered. "I've been in your shoes, and it sucks, but you can't doubt that we're going to find her."

"You know as well as I do that the recovery rate for people who aren't found in the first forty-eight hours isn't good," Cole told his friend.

Ryder's hand tightened on his shoulder painfully. "I don't give a shit what statistics say. This is *Sarah*. She's tough. You've taught her everything she needs to know in a situation like this. Besides, you and I both know this isn't a normal case."

Cole fought down the nausea that had been a constant companion ever since he hadn't heard from Sarah that morning. "What do you mean?"

"Owen Montrone isn't like the scumbags we usually deal with."

Yeah, Owen may not have the mental capacity of an adult, but that didn't mean he couldn't hurt Sarah. There were plenty of cases where men, and women, with low IQs hurt those around them. He nodded at his friend anyway.

He was sure he wasn't that convincing, but Ryder didn't call him on it.

"Come on. We need to take another quick look around, but don't touch anything if you can help it. The house could be a crime scene. I told Logan to call the Parker PD, so I'm not sure how much time we have before they arrive."

It was good that the police were coming, but it also made things more real. Sarah was gone. Vanished. Poof . . . disappeared into thin air.

Clenching his teeth together, Cole inhaled deeply through his nose. He couldn't help Sarah if he was freaking out. He had to get his shit together and see if he could find any clues that would help point to where that butthead had taken her.

It didn't take him and Ryder long to find their first clue.

The spot on the hardwood floor was small. Tiny. Ryder had almost stepped on it when Cole had yelled at him to freeze.

Blood.

There was no way to tell whose it was from looking, but Cole knew down to the marrow of his bones that it was Sarah's.

It was in the upstairs hallway. It was only the one spot, but one was enough. Looking around, Cole tried to figure out why. Why here? What was she doing in the middle of the hallway? If she'd seen Owen, why hadn't she run?

Then something else caught his eye, and he remembered what she had planned to do the night before.

Pointing, Cole said, "Ryder, the attic. The stairs are right above us. Sarah had been putting off going through the boxes that were up there, but she told me she was going to tackle that last night."

Grimly, Ryder nodded and reached for the string that was hanging down from the hatch in the ceiling. A wooden ladder was folded up inside, and the two men pulled it down. Ryder put his arm out when Cole moved to climb the stairs.

"Let me."

Cole hesitated. He wanted to protest. Wanted to tell his friend that it could be *his* woman up there. That Sarah needed him. But he understood why the other man wanted to go up first.

He was protecting him in case Sarah's lifeless body had been stashed in the attic.

He understood, but didn't like it.

Ryder climbed up the rickety ladder slowly. His head popped over the edge of the attic floor—and after a few seconds, he swore long and low.

"What?" Cole asked urgently. "Is she up there? Do I need to call 911?"

Ryder looked down at Cole and shook his head. "Give me a minute. And whatever you do, do *not* come up here. Understand? It's important, Cole."

"If Sarah is up there, I'm coming up," Cole growled.

"I don't think she is. But if I find her, I'll call down. Okay?"

"What's wrong?" Cole asked.

"Give me a minute," Ryder repeated and held Cole's gaze.

Reluctantly, he nodded. "Fine."

Ryder didn't respond, just stepped up, and Cole lost sight of him as he entered the attic. Cole kept his head tilted back and stared at the space where his friend had just been standing.

True to his word, Ryder was back within a minute. He slowly started climbing back down the ladder.

"What? What's up there?" Cole asked impatiently.

"Boxes. Lots of them," Ryder told him.

"And?"

"You aren't going to like this," Ryder warned.

"I don't like any of this already! Sarah's missing," Cole hissed. "We both know that fuckhead took her. Whatever's up there can't be worse than not knowing where Sarah is, if she's hurt or scared, and what he's doing to her. Whatever's up there can't be worse than what I'm imagining in my head. Just fucking spit it out!"

Ryder held Cole's gaze for a second before saying, "There's evidence that someone's been living in the attic."

Cole blinked. "What?"

"If I had to guess, I'd say the reason we couldn't find Owen Montrone is because he's spent the last couple of weeks living in your girlfriend's attic."

Cole was wrong. It was worse than anything he'd imagined in his head. Much worse.

∼

Sarah slept off and on for most of the day. She'd wake up to find Owen sitting near her, watching her with wide, scared eyes. He'd give her more orange juice and pat her on the arm or leg, and tell her he would watch over her . . . which wasn't exactly comforting.

When night fell, Sarah realized wherever they were wouldn't be easy to find. Somehow Owen, with his low IQ, had managed to bring her somewhere off the beaten track. Somewhere Cole and his friends couldn't immediately find her.

Every time she woke up, she hoped it would be to find Cole holding her in his arms, telling her everything would be all right. But that hadn't happened. She was still here.

Taking a deep breath, she knew she had to start figuring out what to do. Cole was looking for her, of that she had no doubt. She didn't even want to think about how pissed off and scared he probably was. She had to concentrate on saving herself. She wanted to stay huddled on the couch, but that wasn't going to get her back to Cole, and it wasn't going to magically solve her problems.

At the moment, the biggest issue was her ankle. It was bad. Very bad. She wasn't a doctor or a nurse, but she'd seen enough broken bones being set to know that was what she had to do. It was going to suck, there was no doubt about it. But she couldn't really feel her foot and knew if she didn't at least try to make sure the bones were put back where they were supposed to be, she could lose the foot altogether . . . or her leg. If the blood flow was being cut off or constricted, she'd be in big trouble.

"Owen?" she asked.

He was puttering around in the kitchen. Sarah's stomach growled, but she knew if she ate anything, she'd probably throw it up when she set her ankle.

"Yes?" Owen asked, almost skipping over to her side.

"Are there any painkillers around here?"

He frowned as if he didn't understand.

"Did your mom take any pills? Do you have them here?"

He smiled. "Oh! Yeah, hang on." He went into the bathroom located off the main room and reappeared in seconds. He had a fabric bag, which he held out to her.

Sarah nodded and loosened the tie around the top. Rummaging around in the bag, she found a treasure trove of narcotics. Aubrey had obviously been in a lot of pain toward the end of her life, and there were more than enough painkillers for Sarah to choose from.

Hating to do it, knowing taking them would alter her mental state, but knowing she wouldn't be able to do what needed to be done otherwise, she pushed one of the OxyContin tablets out of its bubble pack and into her palm.

Looking up at Owen, she asked, "Can I have some more orange juice?"

"OJ! Yes!" the large man said with excitement. "It'll cure what ails ya!"

Sarah nearly smiled as he hurried back to the kitchen to fill her plastic cup. His mom had obviously told him that all the time, because it was clear Owen truly believed it. He returned in moments, and Sarah took the pill without hesitation.

"Owen help some more?" he asked.

"No, I'm okay for now."

"Good." Then he turned and went over to the table, where he'd spread out a puzzle earlier, and hunched over it once more.

Putting her head back on the arm of the couch, Sarah tried not to cry. She was scared to death. So far, Owen hadn't done anything violent toward her. Yes, he'd essentially kidnapped her from her house, but he hadn't hurt her. No, she'd done that to herself by falling off the ladder. She'd hit her head hard enough for it to bleed, and she thought she had a slight concussion, but in the scope of everything else wrong at the moment, that wasn't even a concern.

Sarah felt stupid for not realizing the extent of Owen's disability when she'd cared for his mother in the hospital.

She'd always prided herself on being nice, on being able to figure out what people needed even before they needed it. But she'd completely missed the boat when it came to the Montrones. She thought Aubrey was just being a normal mom when she'd said that her son was special. She'd nodded her head in agreement when she'd talked about needing to find someone responsible and giving to help look after him when she was gone. Sarah hadn't meant to imply that *she* would be that person, but maybe Aubrey had taken it that way? She wondered if she'd told Owen that Sarah would look after him after she died. If she'd planted the seed inside her son's head in the first place.

When she began to feel like she was floating, Sarah realized the potent painkiller was kicking in. The feeling was nice. For the first time since waking up in the cabin, she didn't hurt. Well . . . not as badly as she had been.

But she couldn't fall asleep, not until she did what needed to be done.

Sitting up, ignoring the way the room spun, Sarah stared down at her foot. She leaned over and carefully pressed on the lump she saw on the side of her ankle . . . and almost screamed out in pain.

Damn.

That was a bone. And it wasn't supposed to be sticking out the way it was. This wasn't going to be fun.

Looking over at Owen, she saw that he was still engrossed in the puzzle. It was now or never.

She took a deep breath, pressed her lips together, and did what she had to do.

Chapter Fifteen

"Dammit! It's been three days!" Cole yelled in frustration and anger as he ran a hand through his hair. "Where is she?" He was standing in the back of Ace Security, along with Logan, Blake, Nathan, and Ryder. Even Grace, Alexis, Bailey, and Felicity were there. Little Nate and Ace were in a playpen off to the side, happily babbling to each other and ignoring the tension in the air.

"We're getting close," Logan reassured him.

"Not close enough!" Cole shouted.

Felicity came over to him and put a hand on his back.

Cole knew he should calm down, be more rational, but he couldn't. "He's had her for three days," he told Felicity, his voice breaking. "She has to be scared to death and wondering why I haven't come for her."

"Everyone's doing everything they can," his best friend replied.

"What if it's not enough?" Cole asked in anguish. "What if he kills her, and she dies thinking I didn't love her enough to find her?"

"She knows you're looking for her," Felicity admonished.

Cole turned around and stared at his friend. "How? *How* does she know that? We're no closer to finding her today than we were three days ago. The bastard was living in her attic, and we had no idea! There's no telling how long he was up there, and now he's taken her!"

Felicity reached up and took Cole's face in her hands. "I'm *positive* she knows you're looking as hard as you can for her because I was in her shoes. When Joseph had me, I knew without a doubt that Ryder was doing everything in his power to get to me. And you. And Logan, Blake, and Nathan. She *knows*, Cole, and you have to hold it together so you can think straight and find her."

Cole closed his eyes, squeezing them even tighter when he felt Felicity's arms go around him. Then he felt another pair of arms go around him from behind. Then another from his left and, finally, a pair from his right. He was surrounded by his friends' women. It was appreciated, but the only feminine arms he really wanted around him right now were Sarah's.

After a moment, he opened his eyes and took a deep breath. The women all stood back. "Thanks, guys," he said softly. "I'm okay now."

"She's smart. She won't antagonize him," Grace said softly.

"Sarah's the nicest person I've ever met," Bailey chimed in. "I swear to God, no one can resist her. She'll do whatever it takes to keep him calm."

"If she gets the chance, she'll escape," Alexis added. "I have no doubt of that."

Cole knew the women were trying to reassure him, but everything out of their mouths just made him more anxious, thinking about what she might be going through.

"You ready to look at everything again?" Felicity asked.

Cole couldn't help a small, begrudging smile. Leave it to his BFF to pull his head out of his ass. "Yes," he told her. "From the beginning. We're missing something. I know it."

Felicity nodded and reached for his hand. She towed him back to the table he'd pushed away from to have his little temper tantrum.

"Give me the file on Owen," Cole said. "The man has the mental capacity of a ten-year-old. It shouldn't be this hard to find him."

The other men nodded at Cole and bent their heads back to the papers in front of them or their computer screens. They were missing something. The cops were too. Owen Montrone didn't simply disappear into thin air. He was somewhere. He'd obviously taken Sarah's car, or forced her to drive them somewhere. The BOLO hadn't produced any hits, so they had to assume the car was either hidden or had been destroyed somehow. Owen might be only ten mentally, but he was also the sneakiest person ever, or the luckiest.

Neither thought made Cole feel any better.

~

Three days. It had been three days, and Sarah was still in this cabin with Owen.

The day after she'd set her ankle had been hell. Every time she'd woken up, she'd forced down an Oxy and passed back out.

Today had been better. Not good, but better. She hadn't been eating or drinking much, but this morning, she knew she had to do what she could to get better. Meaning, she had to start eating and drinking to get her strength up. The last thing she wanted was to still be living in this cabin with Owen a year from now. And if she didn't get off her ass and start trying to get stronger, that might be what would happen.

She knew the fact that Cole and the guys from Ace Security hadn't found her yet wasn't a good sign. After spending three days with Owen, she also knew he was very definitely mentally deficient, but he was crafty. She hadn't been around many children in her life, but she'd met this one kid in the hospital. He was sneaky, and he did everything he could to manipulate those around him. He could cry on cue, and he threw tantrums when they served him best. She'd learned quickly that even though he was young, he knew exactly how to get what he wanted.

The same thing was obviously the case with Owen. He'd set his sights on her, and had somehow hidden his tracks well enough that it was difficult to find him.

But Cole wouldn't give up. Sarah knew that without a doubt. He wouldn't stop until he found her.

She put a hand on her belly. She didn't know if she was pregnant yet, but the last thing she wanted was to have a child in this cabin in the middle of nowhere, with only Owen and his overeager wish to help for company.

Though she knew some women lived in captivity for years. Look at Amanda Berry and the other girls from Cleveland, who'd been kidnapped and abused for more than a decade. And Morgan Byrd. She'd been kidnapped and hidden in the Dominican Republic for a year.

But Ryder's friends from Colorado Springs had found her, and she'd survived everything that had been done to her—so Sarah could too.

She'd already found she wasn't as scared of Owen as she had been before he'd kidnapped her. Between naps, she'd gotten to know him a little better. She didn't exactly trust him, but he hadn't hurt her, and every time she'd woken up, he'd been concerned about her and wanted to know what he could do to help.

He played a lot with the toys strewn about the cabin. It looked like a toy store had exploded in the middle of the place. Legos were everywhere, along with picture books, a train set, puzzle pieces, and there was even a huge homemade dollhouse in the corner of the room. It looked similar to the one Owen had sent her, but it was obviously not the same one.

He'd also given her more presents.

Most were things she recognized from her own house. He'd obviously left the attic when she wasn't there and pilfered things. He'd given her stuffed animals that she recognized as being hers from when she was young, and he'd even happily presented her with a few books he'd held out proudly.

Books that her dad had read. The very books of Jackson's that she'd thought she'd given away.

She was glad to know she hadn't accidentally gotten rid of them, but was horrified that Owen had been through her house and taken whatever he'd wanted.

But instead of yelling at Owen, because he certainly wouldn't understand why she was so upset, she'd merely taken the presents and thanked him.

"What do you want to do today?" Owen asked eagerly when he saw that she was awake.

"What do *you* want to do?" Sarah asked, trying to ignore the way her ankle throbbed. After pushing the bone back into place—at least she *hoped* she'd put it back where it should be—she'd wrapped it with pieces of a thin blanket she'd managed to rip up. It was crude, and she knew if she didn't get to a hospital soon, it probably wouldn't heal right, but it was the best she could do under the circumstances.

Owen's eyes lit up. Every time she'd woken up, he'd asked her the same thing, and she'd blown him off, taken another pain pill, and fallen asleep. It was time to start trying to do what she could to get Owen on her good side, once and for all. Besides, she was bored. Even though she'd slept a lot, there was absolutely nothing to do in this cabin. There was no television, and she hadn't seen a radio either.

"Go fish!" Owen yelled, obviously thrilled she was going to play with him.

"Okay. But my ankle is still hurt, so we'll have to play over here on the couch," Sarah told him.

"Yay!" Owen said, and immediately started getting the room ready for their game.

Earlier, he'd brought her a peanut-butter-and-jelly sandwich for breakfast. It actually tasted good, which was a little surprising, as the last time she'd had the kid's meal was years and years ago. She hadn't expected to enjoy it as much as she did. Glancing over at the kitchen, Sarah saw that it, too, was a mess. Owen could obviously only handle the simplest of meals and didn't bother trying to clean up after himself. Later, she'd see if she could convince him to try to tidy up both the living area and the kitchen. The last thing she wanted was more rodents and critters moving into the cabin.

"After a game, the kitchen needs to be cleaned," she said firmly, testing him.

Owen pouted, but nodded.

"And your toys are everywhere. It would be easy to trip and fall over them."

His eyes got wide. "It hurts when I fall and hurt my knees."

Sarah nodded, and her hopes rose. She'd noticed that the man-boy did almost anything she told him to. He'd gone to bed when she told him to. He brought her whatever she requested, and when she did have to use the restroom earlier, he'd carried her easily, left her alone when she'd told him to, and carried her back to the couch.

If she did have to be there long enough for her ankle to heal, maybe she could eventually convince him to take her into town . . . there had to be something close. He'd said that he'd gone shopping. If she could get him to take her with him, she could find someone to help her, or maybe they'd recognize her. She knew that Cole and Ace Security had probably plastered her face all over the news.

If she could only get out of this cabin, she could be saved. She knew it.

~

Cole stared at the papers strewn across the table. He'd looked at them until his eyes had crossed, and he was no closer to finding Sarah than he'd been five days ago.

Five days. *God.* He'd been so sure they'd figure out where Owen had taken Sarah in a few hours. He'd been so sure that with Owen's low IQ, he'd never be able to hide for long. But they'd been wrong.

Cole hadn't slept more than an hour here and there. How could he when he had no idea if Sarah was sleeping?

He hadn't eaten anything other than what Felicity and the others had forced on him. How could he when he had no idea if Sarah was being fed?

He hadn't showered and didn't care if he stunk. How could he enjoy that luxury when he had no idea what conditions Sarah was living in?

The only reason his gym was still running was because of Felicity. She'd taken over without prompting.

But Cole didn't care about that either. He didn't care if he lost every penny of his savings; he only wanted Sarah back in his arms, safe and sound.

Even the police were losing hope. He'd heard it in the detective's voice the last time he'd come into the offices to talk with all of them. The police thought Sarah was probably dead. In most cases, kidnappers almost always killed their victims after a few days of holding them in captivity. But Cole had a feeling that wasn't the case with Sarah. He felt it in his bones.

If not for the support of the Anderson brothers, he knew he'd have gone crazy by now. Logan and the others had been tireless in their quest to find Owen. Ryder had even contacted his mysterious ex-handler down in Colorado Springs for help.

But they hadn't found hide nor hair of the man . . . or Sarah.

They'd looked over every gift the man had left for her. Thanks to her pictures and notes, they'd had a thorough list. From the cookbook, jewelry, and even clothes, to the notes he'd written to her . . . nothing had stuck out, and every lead they'd followed had been a dead end. There had been boxes and boxes of papers found in Aubrey Montrone's house, and they'd at least glanced at them all, but it had been impossible to read every single one word for word. The woman had been a pack rat, and finding the one needle in the haystack that would lead to wherever Owen was holed up was turning out to be impossible.

Nathan was sitting at his desk, his eyes glued to his computer as he continued his search. Logan was on the phone with a reporter, and

Blake was organizing a search party to continue looking around the neighborhood where Sarah's house was located.

The women were at Grace's house. Sarah's kidnapping had brought back Grace's own nightmares of her son being taken, so she hadn't wanted to be separated from her babies. Cole couldn't blame her. So the women had started spending their days at her house. Keeping her company and doing what they could to help in the search from there. They had a few boxes from the Montrone house and were sifting through them much more thoroughly than their men had time to do.

Ryder was sitting across the table from Cole, staring down at more papers they'd looked at a hundred times before.

Cole stared almost sightlessly at the mess in front of him. He felt like shit, but nothing seemed to matter as long as Sarah was missing. He'd promised. He'd told her that if she ever disappeared, he'd find her. And here he was, sitting on his ass while she was hidden, possibly going through hell.

Sighing, he blindly reached for the nearest piece of paper and forced himself to focus. The answer was here . . . somewhere. He just had to be awake enough to find it.

Cole wasn't an investigator. He was just a guy who liked to work out and had somehow been lucky enough to make a living at it. But he'd learned a lot by watching and paying attention to the Andersons. They'd looked at things he wouldn't have thought twice about. They'd taught him to question everything.

Not only that, but they'd had a long discussion about Owen's mental status. He was basically a kid. And kids thought differently than adults did. If Cole was going to find Sarah, he had to think like Owen. Which was extremely tough, because looking at the asshole in a picture they'd taken from the Montrone home made it hard to remember he was developmentally disabled. His large stature and scruffy beard made him look like a middle-aged man who could, and would, hurt anyone who stood between him and what he wanted.

And the man wanted Sarah. For what purpose, Cole didn't know.

But he couldn't have her. Sarah was his. From the top of her head down to her pretty little toes, she was *his*.

Cole read down the piece of paper he was holding. It was the list of things Sarah had received from Owen. Mentally, he paired her list with the pictures she'd emailed to Ace Security.

Cookbook. Check.

Note. Check.

Coat. Check.

Peanut butter. Check.

Letter. Check.

Jewelry. Check.

Flowers, Candy, Lego set . . . check, check, and check.

The list went on and on. Some of the items were bizarre, like the bedpan with the can of chicken soup inside. But others simply seemed like a gift a boy would give to a girl, like the dried wildflowers, and the pine cone he said he'd found and thought was pretty so he'd wanted to give it to Sarah.

Cole was about to put the paper aside and concentrate on something else when a gift on the list caught his eye.

Dollhouse.

His brows furrowing, Cole stared at the word. He didn't remember reading about this present before. Did they have a picture of the dollhouse? He didn't think so, because someone probably would've said something about it.

Rummaging through the papers, he tried to find the folder that held all the pictures of the presents she'd gotten.

"What's up?" Ryder asked, watching him riffling through the contents of the table.

"Where's the folder with the pictures of everything he sent her?" Cole asked.

Ryder helped him look for a moment and pulled it out from under a stack of other papers. "Here."

Cole took it and quickly flipped through the contents. Then he did it again, slower. Then he did it a third time, with the paper containing the list of gifts. He checked off each one, matching the pictures to the list in his hand.

When he was done, the only thing they didn't have a picture of was the dollhouse.

"Where's the dollhouse?" Cole asked Ryder.

"What dollhouse?"

He pointed to the list. "Right here. She wrote that she'd received a dollhouse. Where is it?"

Ryder sat up straighter. "No clue."

"She didn't take a picture of it?" Cole asked.

"I don't know. I don't remember seeing one. It might've gotten erased if she had."

"She had to have done something with the dollhouse," Cole said, feeling adrenaline course through him for the first time in days. "It's not in her house or up in the attic. We would've found it."

"Don't get your hopes up," Ryder said, but Cole could tell that even he was excited at the prospect of something new to look into.

A dollhouse wasn't normally something a boy would give to a girl . . . unless it had some sort of meaning for him. They'd already puzzled out the significance behind most of the other gifts. Other than a few items that seemed to be picked as sweet gestures, like the flowers and jewelry, all the rest of the presents had one thing in common—they could all be used in some way for Sarah to take care of Owen.

The jar of peanut butter was perhaps something he liked to eat.

The cookbook so she could cook for him.

The coat so she would stay warm.

The bedpan was obvious, as was the chicken soup.

But what did a dollhouse have to do with anything?

Unless . . .

Could it *really* be that obvious? Had they overlooked the one thing that was practically screaming at them from the get-go?

Then something else occurred to him. "Ryder," Cole said, "there was a tax payment on the bank statements somewhere, right?"

"Yeah, I think so. Why?"

"Was it for the house in Castle Rock?"

Ryder nodded.

"Are we sure?" Cole asked. "Because I've been thinking . . . what if Aubrey had a second house? I mean, if Owen was giving Sarah gifts that had deeper meanings, things that would help her take care of him, wouldn't a house be a huge part of that? A *dollhouse*? Even if Aubrey paid off a second house, she would have been paying taxes on it. What if Owen's taken Sarah there? There are hundreds of small cabins up in the mountains west of here. It'd be a great place to hide out."

"Shit. You're right. And the dollhouse has to mean *something*. I'll take another look at the tax records and see if we can get more information on the property they were paid on. You can track down that dollhouse and see if there's anything we can get from it."

Cole nodded. He still didn't exactly feel great about the search for Sarah, but he was at least feeling a little more hopeful now that they had something new to go on.

"Hang on, sweetheart. I'm coming," he said softly as he got to work trying to figure out what Sarah had done with the dollhouse Owen had given her.

～

As the sun rose on the seventh day of her captivity, Sarah took a moment to pray that today was the day Cole would find her.

Surprisingly, living in the cabin with Owen hadn't been *all* bad. Besides the fact she couldn't walk because of her ankle and, of course, the boredom, Owen had been extremely attentive. He did what she asked of him without complaint, including cleaning all the dishes he'd dirtied in the first few days after he'd brought her here.

He'd carried her to and from the bathroom, leaving her alone to do her thing. She hadn't been able to stand in the kitchen to make meals for them, but he'd done his best to follow her directions to the letter. Owen had been so proud when he'd managed to make a simple macaroni-and-cheese dinner.

They'd played card games, Go Fish being his favorite, as well as a ton of board games. She'd even helped him put together a puzzle that he'd been struggling with.

The only time Sarah had seen Owen lose his cheery disposition was when she asked if he would drive her into town. He'd frowned and shaken his head violently.

"No! Someone will see and take you away!"

Sarah had backed off immediately, but her heart had sunk. Owen knew as well as she did that the only way he'd be able to "keep" her was if she remained a secret.

Short of crawling out of the cabin and into the forest, and for who knew how many miles, it looked like she was stuck.

"Good morning!" Owen said happily as he sat up on his bed next to her. The twin beds had been a relief; knowing he didn't expect to sleep with her or next to her was one worry off her plate. The mattress wasn't very comfortable, but after he'd gotten her a pillow from the couch and helped her prop up her ankle, it had been better than the sofa.

"Morning," Sarah said. She was missing Cole more than she could say, and was beginning to think it would be a lot longer than she'd thought before he would find her. But she wasn't going to give up.

"Go Fish this morning?" Owen asked.

Sarah sighed. She was so sick of the card game, but it was much better than War, because at least it ended. She'd made the mistake of agreeing to play War with him the day before, and five hours later, she thought she'd scream in frustration when it still wasn't over.

Someone had stocked the cabin with a ton of kids' games. There was a whole closetful—Sorry!, Chutes and Ladders, Pictionary, Mouse Trap, Clue Junior, Shark Bite, Apples to Apples, Battleship, Trouble, HiHo! Cherry-O, and Let's Go Fishin'. She had played them all with Owen and preferred Go Fish. It was simple and easy, and she didn't have to think too hard. Besides, the man-boy was a sore loser, and it was easier to cheat to let him win in Go Fish than some of the other games.

"Sure. We can play Go Fish," she said wearily.

"Yay!" Owen said, clapping joyfully. "But first, Owen needs to take care of Sarah."

Sarah nodded and braced herself for his touch. He might act like a kid, but every time he picked her up, she was terrified he'd drop her. Or decide he wanted to touch her like an adult touched a woman. Besides that, her ankle was still extremely painful. She'd stopped taking the Oxy, afraid of becoming addicted, and had switched to plain Tylenol. It wasn't as effective, but at least it took the edge off.

When Owen left her in the bathroom so she could pee and clean herself with a washcloth, she stared in the mirror. Her hair was a mess; she hadn't washed it since she'd arrived. The huge muumuu she was wearing hid her body from view, but she knew she'd lost weight. The stress of the situation was taking its toll.

All things considered, Sarah knew she was still lucky. Owen hadn't hurt her. He was actually somewhat sweet when she forgot that he was keeping her in the cabin against her will. He'd told her about his mom and how much he missed her. He talked about his life with her, and Sarah realized exactly how much Aubrey had done for her only child. She'd obviously loved him, and had probably been terrified for him when she'd found out she was dying. It didn't excuse her for making her son think he could drag someone off into the woods and live happily ever after, but after spending time with Owen, Sarah at least understood.

But she missed her life.

Missed her new friends.

Missed Cole.

God, she missed Cole.

For the first time, she had true empathy for Owen. For what he might feel missing his mother. Of course, Cole wasn't dead, and Owen was keeping her from him.

Hating how she vacillated between feeling sorry for Owen and being terrified she'd never see Cole again, Sarah took a deep breath. She placed a hand on her belly and closed her eyes. "Please find me soon, Cole," she whispered. "I'm ready to go home."

"Thank you very much," Logan said into the phone as he nodded at the others. "I'd love for you to send a picture of it to me. Yes . . . I'll be waiting . . . I appreciate this so much . . . If I have any other questions, can I call you back? Great. Thank you . . . I hope we find her too. Bye."

He hung up the phone and said, "The lady at the hospital found the dollhouse! Sarah donated it to the children's ward. It's been in one of the playrooms ever since."

"She's sending a picture of it?" Blake asked.

"Yeah."

Cole paced. He tried like hell not to get his hopes up, but everything else had been a dead end. Ryder was still looking into the tax payments on Aubrey's accounts, but otherwise, they were stumped. They'd been searching for a week, and nothing had panned out. They'd had some close calls where they'd thought they were on the right track, but then each lead had fizzled out, or the cops had followed up and found nothing. At this point, Cole was ready to go rogue.

Ready to go door-to-door, head up into the mountains, whatever it took to find his Sarah.

He hadn't found her only to lose her now. They had years to look forward to together. He wanted to grow old with her and watch as their children, grandchildren, and great-grandchildren gathered around them at the holidays. He wanted that chaos, wanted to see the smile on Sarah's face as she basked in the glory of her family.

"The picture's here," Logan said as his phone chimed with an incoming email. "I'm forwarding it to everyone. Hang on."

Cole stared down at his phone impatiently as he waited for the email to come in. The second it did, he clicked on it and downloaded the picture.

At first glance, the dollhouse was nothing special. A two-story cabin with a bunch of wooden furniture in it and two small dolls, with a couple of bigger Barbie dolls as well. He figured the Barbies were additions by whatever kid had last played with it.

"It looks like a normal dollhouse," Nathan observed.

Cole blocked out the disappointment he heard in his friend's tone and zoomed in on the picture.

Everything in the dollhouse looked handmade, which had the hair on the back of Cole's neck standing up.

Apparently the others noticed as well.

"This isn't some dime-store dollhouse," Logan said.

"Nope. Hand-fucking-made," Ryder agreed.

"I'm enhancing the picture now," Nathan said.

"I'm going to head over to the hospital to see this thing up close. I'll send back more pictures, and if I can find a signature or mark from whoever made it, I'll send that too," Blake said, already standing.

"If we can find out who made this, we can hopefully get more information on who bought it," Logan said, the excitement easy to hear in his voice.

"And many times artisans have an inspiration for their creations," Ryder added. "He might've modeled this after a real cabin or house."

"If we can find a signature, I can search the name on the internet," Nathan said.

With every word that passed his friends' lips, Cole's hope rose. They'd had so many dead ends and so much bad news over the last seven days, even this little thing seemed momentous.

"I'll call Alexis on my way to the hospital," Blake said. "Tell her and the other women to be on the lookout for any reference to woodworkers or handcrafted products. There's an entire box of random receipts. Maybe we'll get lucky."

They would. Cole was sure of it.

This was it. This was what they'd missed all along. He had no idea how he knew it, but he did.

Running a hand through his mussed hair, he couldn't help but get excited. It had been a long week. Seven days that felt like seven years. But he'd soon have Sarah back in his arms, and the son of a bitch who'd taken her would pay.

"I'm calling the detective," Logan said, pushing away from the table with his phone up to his ear.

Cole knew they had to keep the police informed about what they were doing for their own safety. The last thing any of them wanted was to be charged with obstruction, and they couldn't head off and act on any tips without including the cops. But Cole wanted to. He wanted to run with whatever information Ace Security found and get his Sarah back. He didn't want to wait an extra second.

But they'd need the law on their side.

If shots were fired, and Owen was taken down, none of them wanted to be charged with murder. And if Sarah needed medical attention, they needed an ambulance at the ready.

But all that took time.

And Cole didn't want Sarah to spend one more second at that man's mercy than she had to.

"We're gonna get her back," Ryder said softly from next to Cole.

He nodded.

They were. They totally were.

~

The sun had gone down on her seventh day at the cabin.

One week.

She'd been there one week. In some ways it seemed like forever, but in others it seemed like just yesterday when she'd found Owen in her attic.

She thought about Cole. About their phone calls and texts. About how attentive he was in bed. How it felt to be held tightly in his arms.

Tears formed in her eyes, but she fought them back.

She wouldn't cry. Cole was looking for her, and he'd find her. She couldn't doubt that.

Thank God she'd decided to give him a second chance after he'd blown her off at his gym. If she hadn't . . . Sarah shivered.

If she hadn't, no one would be missing her. Her work would have wondered what happened and why she hadn't shown up, but the cops probably would've just assumed she was a grown woman and could go where she wanted, whenever she wanted. At least for the first couple of days. After that, they probably would've started to investigate, but who knew if they'd be able to connect all the dots to Owen and this cabin in the middle of freaking nowhere.

It was fate.

Cole belonged to her just as she did to him. He'd find her. He had to.

"One more game!" Owen begged.

Sarah wanted to tell him it was bedtime. If she did, she had no doubt he'd pout, but he'd do as she said. He'd change into his footy pajamas—which looked extremely weird on the overweight forty-four-year-old man—brush his teeth, and climb into bed.

But it was early, and Sarah wasn't ready to be alone with her thoughts so soon. She knew she'd lie awake and get distraught over her situation. She was better off playing another game of fucking Go Fish than drowning in her own misery.

"One more," she agreed.

"Yay!" Owen exclaimed, bouncing on his butt on the end of her bed, making her wince as the vibration of the mattress caused her ankle to throb.

He really wasn't a bad person. He'd taken her against her will, but he hadn't beaten her, hadn't abused her, had actually been extremely worried about her. He was generally a happy person, if overly emotional at times.

It was obvious he didn't understand that what he'd done was wrong. He was happy in his knowledge that he'd done what his mom had wanted for him. He'd "married" Sarah, and she would take care of him for the rest of his days.

Sarah had to hope that Aubrey didn't really understand her son would take her suggestion as gospel, and actually kidnap Sarah and take her into the mountains.

The cabin was clean now. She'd made a game out of Owen picking up all his toys. Every time he filled one of the large toy bins along one of the walls, she'd play a round of Go Fish. When he swept the floor and cleaned the kitchen countertops, she'd sing a song for him. And when he cleaned the dishes in the sink and put them away, she'd read him a book. Positive reinforcement seemed to work best with Owen, and Sarah had already gotten very good at it.

"Do you want a snack before we start?" Owen asked, the hope in his voice easy to hear.

Sarah couldn't help but chuckle. She knew he wasn't asking if *she* wanted a snack, but was asking because *he* wanted one.

"Sure. But not popcorn. Last time you made a mess trying to pop that stuff on the stove. I think a can of peaches should tide you over." There were times, like now, when Sarah almost forgot Owen was in his midforties. Every emotion was easy to see on his face and hear in his voice.

Owen pouted, but he nodded and climbed off Sarah's bed. The motion once again jostled her ankle, and she inhaled deeply, trying to breathe through the pain.

It wasn't getting better. Even though she'd splinted the hell out of it, her ankle still throbbed in agony every minute of every day. If she didn't get it taken care of, she was probably going to end up crippled for life.

She pushed the thought aside. Minute by minute. That was the only way she was getting through this. She couldn't think about what her life would be like if she was still here a year from now.

Trying to get comfortable, Sarah propped the pillows behind her back and attempted to relax. She still had another hour to go before she could take another Tylenol. She'd been taking them every four hours just to keep the edge off how much she hurt.

A scraping noise outside the window to her right suddenly made her freeze.

Her eyes went to Owen in the kitchen part of the cabin, but he obviously hadn't heard anything. He was humming under his breath as he struggled with the can opener on the peaches.

Not daring to look over, in case Owen saw her, Sarah's heart kicked into overdrive.

Had Cole found her? Were the police surrounding the cabin right now?

And if so . . . what would Owen do when he figured out that the nice little life he'd set up for the two of them was about to come to an end?

Or what if it was just an animal? Another mouse trying to find a way in to stay warm?

Sarah had no idea what had made the sound, but she prayed as hard as she could that, after a very long week, she was about to be rescued.

Chapter Sixteen

Cole stood out of the way behind a tree and stared at the small cabin in the woods. It was dark now, and it had been a very busy four hours since they'd located the dollhouse at the hospital.

Blake had gone to the hospital and examined the dollhouse. He'd found a signature on the bottom. Nathan had tracked down the artist and learned that he used to live in a small town in the mountains west of Castle Rock called Twin Cedars. It wasn't much of a town, not anymore. There was a gas station and a small mom-and-pop grocery store, and that was about it.

A call to the artist verified that he'd indeed made the dollhouse. He'd custom-made that particular piece for Aubrey Montrone years ago. He'd specifically remembered it didn't match the cabin she owned, which she'd always wished was bigger. So when she'd commissioned the dollhouse, she'd sent a picture of the cabin and told him to use it for inspiration, but asked that he embellish and make it larger, with two stories instead of one. The artist also volunteered that he'd made a second piece, a smaller dollhouse, for Aubrey about twenty years ago, as well.

Then the man told Nathan that he'd seen Aubrey's son in the only local store a week or so ago.

The artist had been there visiting his friend, who owned the place, and recognized Owen from a picture Aubrey had apparently shared with him when she'd ordered the smaller dollhouse. Owen hadn't said much, and had bought a very strange assortment of food. Mostly canned and boxed food. Nothing fresh. Things that would last a long time.

When Nathan had asked if the man had seen the car Owen was driving, he'd said yes. He'd gotten into a gray Galant.

Cole had made a fist pump in the air at hearing that. The man hadn't seen anyone else in the car, but that didn't necessarily mean anything. Owen could either have already stashed Sarah somewhere, or she could've been lying down in the back seat. Cole refused to even consider the possibility that she'd been in the trunk at the time, or that Owen had already hurt or killed her.

Everything had begun falling into place. Ryder made a few calls and, within an hour, had uncovered a connection between Aubrey and the tiny town. Her parents, Owen's grandparents, had lived there for a few years a long time ago and had moved to Castle Rock when it was obvious the small town wasn't prospering.

But they'd owned a cabin up there. One that had passed to Aubrey.

And Ryder had finally found proof of the woman paying taxes on the house and property for years. Records they'd overlooked because they were mingled among all the financial data for her home in Castle Rock. For some reason, the cabin hadn't been listed in any of Aubrey's legal paperwork or her will, which was why no one had known it existed.

But Owen obviously did.

Twin Cedars was about an hour's drive from Castle Rock, but the Anderson brothers and the two police officers they'd convinced to come and check it out with them had made it there in forty-five minutes.

Finding the road to the small cabin was more of a challenge, but eventually they'd found the dirt track off the main thoroughfare. They stopped their two vehicles far enough from the cabin so as not to alert anyone inside that they were there, and they walked the rest of the way on foot.

Ryder and one of the officers headed to the right side of the cabin while Logan went to the other side to make sure Owen didn't try to escape out one of the side windows. The other detective walked silently up to the door and stood there for a long moment, listening.

Cole couldn't stand still. He wanted to burst into the room and take out the asshole who had taken his woman away from him.

"Easy, Cole," Blake said softly.

"I need to get in there," he hissed back.

"And you will. Just let them do their job."

That was the thing. No one knew how Owen would react when confronted. Was he armed? Had he already hurt or killed Sarah? Would he hold her hostage once he found out the cops were there? The unknown questions were haunting Cole.

There was a window at the side of the cabin, and Logan signaled something to Blake and Nathan, who were standing with Cole. Blake then passed along the signal to Ryder and the cops.

"What? What was that?" Cole asked impatiently.

"Logan has a visual," Blake said.

That was it. Cole wasn't going to stand back and watch, hiding behind a damn tree. He didn't know what a "visual" meant. Didn't know if that meant Sarah was fine or his friend had seen her body.

Without another word, Cole hunched over and ran toward the front door of the cabin. He heard Blake swear behind him, but he wasn't waiting around anymore.

He was about twenty feet away when the officer at the front door picked up his foot and kicked it open, then entered, holding his weapon up at the ready. A scream tore through the air, and a panicked yell. The officer's loud voice barking orders added to the chaos.

Cole pushed himself to run faster than he'd ever run in his life.

∾

One second Sarah was mentally preparing herself for another game of Go Fish, and the next, everything was complete chaos. She would've thrown herself to the floor and rolled under the bed, but with her ankle as it was, she could do nothing but sit there and stare at the commotion.

The door to the cabin suddenly burst open, and a police officer rushed inside, holding his weapon.

Owen moved faster than she'd ever thought him capable, and before she could blink, he was standing in front of her bed. His legs and arms were outspread, as if that would keep the cop from taking her away.

"No!" Owen yelled. "Go away!"

"Step away from the woman!" the police officer retorted, pointing his gun at Owen's chest.

"No! She's mine! I found her fair and square!" It was obvious Owen was stressed and panicking.

Sarah leaned over to see around him—and gasped when she saw Cole fly into the cabin through the open door. He was followed by Blake and the rest of the Anderson brothers. The cabin quickly became crowded as it filled with her pissed-off and concerned rescuers.

"No! No no no!" Owen said, and he came around the bed and grabbed Sarah by the upper arm, pulling her into his side.

Gasping in pain, Sarah did her best to get her good knee under her to hold her weight. Her broken ankle was jostled, and blackness began to creep in from the sides of her vision with the pain. She forced herself to stay conscious.

The police officers pointed their weapons at Owen, and the Anderson brothers fanned out around the cabin, leaving Owen with no way to escape.

Taking a deep breath, she held up her free hand, trying to calm the intense, chaotic scene.

"Everyone, chill!" she yelled.

Obviously surprised, the officer who'd been barking orders simply stared at her.

Knowing if she looked at Cole, she'd start bawling, Sarah turned and looked up at Owen instead.

"It's time for me to go," she said gently.

"No! We're staying!" Owen said stubbornly. "We're gonna live here and take care of each other forever."

"What happens when we run out of money?" Sarah asked, proud that her voice only cracked a little bit.

"I get money every month. We'll be fine," Owen said, not looking down at her, but staring belligerently at the officers instead.

She'd seen him act like this when he didn't get his way before. One day he'd wanted to play Go Fish for the thousandth time, and Sarah had told him no. He'd pouted and crossed his arms and yelled and blustered for thirty minutes. But she'd worn him down and convinced him a game of Sorry! would be just as fun.

She just had to be patient now too. Of course, Owen had a lot more to lose this time, and he knew it.

"Owen, my ankle really hurts," she said softly. "It's broken, and I need to see a doctor."

"*No.* No doctor!" Owen said, but his protest wasn't quite as strong as it had been.

"I know you want to take care of me, but some things have to be looked at by experts."

"I'll take care of you," Owen whined stubbornly.

"Sarah—" Cole started.

But she shook her head and didn't take her gaze from Owen. Cole sounded closer. So close, she wanted nothing more than to let him take over. Tackle Owen and force him to let her go. But if she didn't get this situation under control now, there was no telling what would happen to the developmentally disabled man.

"Owen, look at me," Sarah ordered.

He shook his head. "They'll take you from me if I do."

He was probably right. Sarah turned to look at the police officers. "Please, put your guns down. Owen won't hurt me."

"I'm not sure—" the man who'd burst into the room started, but Cole interrupted him.

"Do as she says."

Slowly, both police officers lowered their guns. They didn't holster them, but at least they weren't pointed at them anymore.

"See? They aren't going to hurt us," Sarah told Owen.

His hand tightened on her arm. "I don't want to go," he whined.

"I know. But sometimes things happen in our lives that we don't want."

"Like Mama dying?" Owen asked sadly.

"Exactly. I've had a good time with you here in your cabin," Sarah told him. She wasn't *completely* lying. She didn't want to be here, but all things considered, it could've turned out a lot worse. "But I have to go back to my home. To work. I need to help other people's mamas in the hospital. Remember how I helped your mom? Other people need me too."

Owen's gaze flicked to her face, then immediately went back to the men standing in the cabin. The Andersons hadn't said a word, but it was more than obvious they were ready to pounce the first chance they got.

"I need you." Owen's voice lowered to almost a whisper. "Mama said that I can't live by myself. That I need someone to take care of me just like I took care of her. I want *you* to take care of me."

As scared as this man had made her over the last few months, Sarah suddenly felt very sorry for him. He was just a little boy living inside a man's body. He didn't understand how the world worked. His mother, the person who'd looked after him for his entire life, had died, and he was lost, hurting, and scared.

That didn't mean he couldn't be a danger again. If he took a shine to someone else he thought might be able to care for him, he might think it was okay to kidnap her too. And that would be horrible. She wouldn't wish the terror she'd experienced on anyone.

"What if I helped find you someone who could take care of you?" Sarah asked. "I bet there are other men and women out there just like you, who need taking care of too. You could all live together and look after one another."

She knew there were group homes out there for people like Owen. She and Cole had even talked about them once. They had house monitors who helped the residents live semi-independently. She had no idea how much they cost or where they were, but she knew without a doubt that Cole and their friends from Ace Security would help find one for Owen.

But she couldn't get him there if he did something stupid and crazy in the next five minutes. She had to convince him to let her go. To not hurt her or anyone else . . . and not get shot in the process. The last place Owen Montrone needed to be was in prison. He wouldn't last a day.

"Look at me, Owen. Please," she pleaded.

Slowly, Owen looked down at her. His eyes were wide, and she could see the fear in them. She moved her hand slowly until she cupped the side of his face. His beard was scratchy against her hand, and she wasn't exactly thrilled to be touching him this way, but the nurturer inside her couldn't deny him the gentle gesture. "We've had fun this week, yeah? But it's time to go. I'm always going to be your friend, but I can't take care of you the way your mama did. I can help you find someone who can."

"Promise?" he whispered.

"I promise."

"I know just the place," Logan said quietly.

Both Sarah and Owen turned their heads to look at him.

"I know the woman who runs it. She's amazing. There are four other residents, just like you, Owen, who live with her now. They have their own rooms, and they go to work every day, and then they come home, and she makes them a big dinner."

"I liked when I worked," Owen said matter-of-factly. "I was good at it. I swept the floors and took out the trash. There were lots of people to talk to."

Logan nodded. "I bet you could get a job like that again. And then you could go home and play cards with your new friends, and the nice lady who lives in the house will make you all sorts of good food."

"Like pizza?" Owen asked, sounding much more interested now.

"Exactly," Logan agreed.

Owen turned back to Sarah. "But who will take care of you if I leave?"

Sarah opened her mouth to answer, but Cole beat her to it.

"I will."

Owen looked at him and narrowed his eyes. "I've seen you."

Cole nodded. "You have. I love Sarah. She means the world to me . . . and I'll do whatever it takes to keep her safe."

Sarah tried not to wince. She knew Cole was threatening Owen. Hopefully he wouldn't recognize the words for what they were.

"I love her too."

"I know you do," Cole said, in a voice that was way gentler than Sarah would have thought he could use with the man who'd kidnapped her. "But she's going to have a baby with me, and I need to keep her close to make sure she *and* the baby are okay."

Tears sprang to Sarah's eyes. Neither of them knew if she was pregnant yet or not, but ultimately it didn't matter. They both knew Cole would do whatever it took to keep her, and her child, safe.

"A baby?" Owen asked.

Sarah nodded. She hadn't looked at Cole yet, more convinced than ever that if she did, she'd lose it. She needed his arms around her, telling her she was safe, more than anything. But Owen still had his hand on her arm, and she really didn't want him to get hurt.

Owen grinned. "I like babies." Then the smile left his face. "I'm scared," he told her.

"I know, but you don't need to be. Logan and the police officers will make sure you're safe."

His eyes went to the cards that were now strewn about the bed and on the floor. "We didn't get to play Go Fish."

"We can play when I come and visit."

"Promise?"

"I promise." She was making a lot of promises to this man-boy, but after spending a week with him, she understood him a hell of a lot better.

"Okay," Owen said. And he let go of her arm so suddenly, Sarah teetered.

But the second she thought she was going to fall over, she felt Cole's arm snake around her waist, holding her safe and secure.

Logan and one of the police officers were there too. The cop took hold of Owen's arm, much as he'd been holding her, and Logan made sure to put his body between him and Sarah.

Owen met her eyes, and he looked sad and regretful. "I didn't know you had a baby in your belly, Sarah."

"I know you didn't."

"I didn't mean to hurt you," he added.

"I know that too."

"I can't wait to see your baby and play Go Fish!" And just like that, he was back to being the carefree little boy.

"Me either. Go with the policeman and Logan now, Owen. They'll take you to a place where people will play all the Go Fish you want, and they'll take care of you and let you take care of them right back. Okay?"

"Okay. Bye!"

Sarah didn't get a chance to say goodbye before she was cradled in Cole's arms. She buried her face between his head and shoulder and held on to him as hard as she could.

"Sarah?" he asked, his voice tortured.

"I'm okay," she managed before bursting into tears. She hadn't cried in almost a week, but seeing Cole and being in his arms broke her.

"Is she gonna press charges?"

Sarah heard the officer's question and immediately shook her head. Through her tears, she said, "Owen doesn't belong in jail. He honestly doesn't understand that what he did was wrong."

"Fuck, I love you," Cole said. He didn't try to convince her to change her mind. Didn't yell and tell her she was insane. He simply held her tighter against him. She heard him say, "Let me know when they're gone."

She didn't understand the words for a second, then realized Cole was talking to the others still in the room. She didn't pick up her head when she heard Blake taking pictures with his phone. She didn't move when she heard Nathan swear at finding the towel in the bathroom she'd used to clean the blood from her head wound. And she refused to move when Ryder tried to talk to her about how badly her ankle was hurt.

She couldn't do anything but sit on the bed and cling to Cole, so damn happy he was there and that he'd found her.

Cole didn't try to speak, obviously as overcome with emotion as she was. But she only got to enjoy being with him for another minute or so before Cole pulled back. He looked into her eyes, drinking her in, as if seeing her for the first time. And in a way, he was. They'd gotten a second chance. One they were both very aware they were lucky to get.

"Are you really okay?" he whispered.

Sarah nodded. Her eyes wouldn't stop leaking, but she barely even noticed. "He didn't hurt me. Not once. I climbed into the attic, and he startled me. I fell. Caught my foot in one of the rungs of the ladder and hit my head when I landed. Didn't wake up until I was here. I would've run, but with my ankle, I couldn't."

Cole's eyes went to her wrapped ankle, then back to her face. "I was so scared."

She nodded and whispered, "Me too. But you promised you wouldn't stop looking for me. So I sucked it up and waited for you to show."

"Sorry it took so long," he said.

Sarah gave him a weak smile. "I love you."

He put a hand on her stomach. "I love you too, angel."

Covering his hand on her belly, she blurted, "I want to shower."

He smiled, but said dryly, "Let's get that ankle fixed up first."

"It's gonna need surgery," she told him. "Which means I won't be able to go home for a while." Sarah wasn't an idiot. She'd seen enough bone breaks to know that hers was bad. If she didn't need surgery, it would be a miracle.

"They're gone," the remaining police officer informed them.

"This is gonna hurt," Cole warned her.

"I know," Sarah said. And she did. Every time Owen had carried her into the bathroom, it had hurt like hell. But she'd endure any kind of pain if it meant getting out of this cabin and going home with Cole. "I can take it."

Cole kissed her temple, and the feel of his warm lips against her skin made everything within her melt. Having him near was better than a thousand Oxy pills.

"Hang on," he said, and Sarah braced herself when he stood.

It *did* hurt. But she swore the pain was less than in the last week, because she was in Cole's arms. He carried her out of the cabin, her prison for the past seven days, and simply smelling the fresh mountain air felt amazing. She hadn't realized how stuffy the cabin was until right this moment.

She relaxed fully into Cole's arms and closed her eyes as he carried her down the dirt driveway toward where she assumed the car he'd arrived in was waiting.

∽

Hours later, Cole sat next to Sarah's hospital bed. He was exhausted, but refused to leave her side. She'd been right—she'd needed surgery to fix the broken bones in her ankle. Luckily, the breaks were fairly clean, and the doctor said he didn't think there would be any lasting damage.

While she'd been in surgery, Logan had called to let Blake know Owen had already been placed in a group home for mentally disabled adults, up in Denver. Since Sarah wasn't pressing charges, Owen could hopefully settle in quickly and live his life.

It didn't seem fair to Cole, but he understood Sarah's decision. Even agreed . . . to a point. If it had been anyone other than *his* woman taken, he wouldn't have hesitated to make the same decision. But he was so torn. He couldn't forget the agony of the last week. The not knowing if Sarah was alive or dead. If she was being tortured or violated. The fact that she was fine didn't do much to make him feel better about her being kidnapped in the first place. Not yet. Maybe not ever.

But his woman was the way she was, and he wouldn't change one thing about her. She wouldn't be his angel if she were vindictive and vengeful.

He shifted and rested his hand on her belly . . . and smiled.

Sarah was pregnant.

He'd told the doctor it could be a possibility before she'd been taken back for surgery. After hearing it had been less than two weeks since she could've conceived, the doctor had warned them that it was probably too soon to tell, but when he'd confirmed the test was positive, Cole couldn't stop beaming.

In a week or two, they'd repeat the test, just in case it had been a false positive, but Cole knew it hadn't been. Sarah was going to have his baby. They were going to be a family.

He had a ring in his pocket, and he'd make Sarah his wife as soon as reasonably possible. He had to call his parents and brother and let them know, as well as figure out a hundred other details, but the sooner he made things official, the happier he'd be.

Cole had already talked to Blake, who was going to arrange to have Sarah's things moved into Cole's apartment. There was no way she was moving into that studio apartment now. Nope, she'd be right by his side so he could pamper both her and his child for the rest of their lives.

Sarah's eyes fluttered, and Cole waited patiently for her to fully wake up and remember where she was. He hated the way her body stiffened, as if she thought she was still back in that cabin, but when he squeezed her hand, she relaxed.

Turning her head, she saw him sitting by her side. "Still here?" she asked groggily.

"Where else would I be?" he asked.

"At home? In bed? Like a normal person?"

"I'll go home when you do. I'm not letting you out of my sight."

She rolled her eyes, and Cole knew he'd never seen anything more beautiful. Even after a week in captivity, no shower, and having just undergone surgery, she was still the most enchanting woman he'd ever seen.

His hand was on her belly. Her hand came up and covered his. "Why am I not surprised you knocked me up the first time you took me without a condom?" she asked. "I'm not sure this bodes well for the future of my figure."

Cole grinned, brought her hand up to his mouth, and kissed the back of it. "You're going to be beautiful pregnant. And I want to give you as many babies as you can handle. And when they become too much, I'll hire a nanny."

"What if I said I wanted twelve kids?"

"Then I'll hire two nannies," Cole said immediately. "I want you to have the family you were denied growing up. I want to surround you with all the love you deserve. You can have babies until the doctor says it's not safe or whenever you say you're done. We'll go and talk to the program manager at the Adoption Exchange as well. I know there are some amazing older kids who need someone like you to love them. Like us. You're going to be the best mother any kid could ever have, and I can't wait to see the influence you have on them."

Her eyes teared up. "I love you," she whispered.

"And I love you," he returned. He leaned up and kissed her forehead, then briefly touched his lips to her cracked and dry ones. "Go back to sleep," he ordered.

She tightened her hand in his. "You'll stay?"

He smiled. He knew she wouldn't want him to go. They'd almost lost each other, and they both knew what a close call they'd had. Sarah didn't want him out of her sight any more than he wanted her out of his. "Of course, angel."

She closed her eyes, and he thought she was asleep several moments later, until she murmured, "Do you want a boy or a girl?"

God. He couldn't decide. Both. He wanted both. A girl with Sarah's luxurious hair and even-keeled disposition, and a boy with her eyes. "I don't care," he told her.

"Boy," she said firmly. "We need a boy first so he can look after his little sister."

Cole nodded. Yeah, he could go for that.

∽

Thirty minutes later, Felicity stuck her head in the door of Sarah's hospital room. She'd wanted to see Sarah and tell her she was glad she was all right.

But the sight of her best friend stopped her in her tracks. Cole was sound asleep. One hand was resting on Sarah's stomach, and the other was gripping her hand tightly. His head was on the mattress by her hip, and even though his body was twisted in the chair and he looked uncomfortable, she wouldn't dream of waking him up.

Slipping out of the room, she quietly shut the door. Seeing Sarah could wait. The satisfaction on Cole's face was all she needed to see to know they'd both be all right. She'd been worried about him over the last week, but she knew without a doubt that all was well in his world . . . finally.

Epilogue

Sarah stood against one of the walls in the large gym, smiling as she watched her man on the other side of the room. He'd offered to get her a drink, but of course he'd been stopped by just about everyone while on his errand and was now surrounded by the men from Ace Security as they shot the shit.

Rock Hard Gym was having another of their famous "black light" nights, and it seemed as if the entire town had shown up.

Sarah was standing with Grace, Bailey, Alexis, and Felicity, chatting while their men took a break from checking IDs and walking around the gym to make sure everyone was safe and happy.

"How's the ankle?" Felicity asked Sarah.

She stuck it out in front of them and wiggled it back and forth. "Good as new. Joel calls it my bionic leg."

Bailey laughed. "I swear he and Nathan are obsessed with science-fiction shit. It's crazy."

"They only put in a few pins, right?" Grace asked.

Sarah nodded. "Yeah, but I might've exaggerated when I was telling Joel all about it."

Everyone laughed.

"You look good," Alexis told her.

Sarah smiled and rested a hand on her belly. She'd just started to really show, and every day seemed better than the last. "Thanks. I feel good."

"Well, I feel like shit," Bailey complained, resting her hand on her own protruding belly. "I'm ready to have this kid. If I hadn't already had the ultrasound, and if I hadn't made the doctor promise that there was only one kid inside me, I'd swear there were at least two."

Sarah pressed her lips together and looked at the floor.

"Sarah?" Felicity asked. "You have something you want to share?"

Shit. She and Cole had decided to keep this to themselves for as long as possible, but she'd always been horrible at keeping secrets.

She shrugged, then smiled. "We're having twins."

"No shit?" Bailey asked.

"Oh my God, really?" Felicity breathed.

"That's so cool!" Alexis said, practically jumping up and down with excitement.

"I'm so glad I'm not the only one," Grace said with a small smile.

Everyone hugged Sarah, and she couldn't help but laugh. She was so happy it was almost scary.

"Tell us all the details," Felicity urged.

"We were going to wait to find out the gender, but the doctor was concerned by how big I was getting. So we agreed to let him do a more thorough examination. Turns out there was a reason I was so big—there are two little buggers in there!"

"Holy crap. I bet Cole about lost his mind!" Felicity said.

Sarah nodded. He had. He'd been so excited that he'd taken her straight home to "get acquainted with his babies," as he'd put it. She'd tried to remind him that he'd been "acquainting" himself with them for weeks now, but he'd ignored her.

The way he'd made love to her, so tenderly and gently, had made tears fall down her face. Then, being Cole, the slow lovemaking quickly turned carnal, and he'd taken her hard and fast, vowing to keep her knocked up and filled with his babies for the next ten years.

"He totally bragged that he had the most potent sperm in three counties," Sarah admitted with an eye roll.

The other women all laughed.

"That sounds like him," Felicity said with a chuckle. Then she bit her lip and looked at Sarah with a strange expression on her face. "I know you and I aren't officially related, not like we are"—she gestured to the other women—"but I feel as if Cole's my brother, so that makes you my sister-in-law. And if you're my sister-in-law . . . then that would make our kids cousins."

It took a second for her words to sink in, but when they did, Sarah smiled huge. "Are you saying what I hope you're saying?"

Felicity nodded. "It's early. Eight weeks today, but still . . ."

There was more screeching from the women and more hugs given out.

Alexis held up her hands when everyone was done congratulating Felicity. "Don't look at me. Blake and I are going to wait a few more years. We want to enjoy the fact it's just the two of us for a while longer."

"I hope you've got good birth control," Grace said dryly as she patted her flat tummy, "because it seems those Anderson boys have very potent sperm."

"You are fucking kidding me!" Alexis said in mock disgust as everyone laughed and started the congratulatory hugs once more—this time with Grace.

Sarah stood in a circle with the women who had become as much her sisters as her friends, and she couldn't help but remember what her life had been like just six months ago. She'd been lonely and simply going through the motions. Now here she was, married to the love of her life, pregnant with twins, and celebrating bringing new lives into the world with some of the nicest, and toughest, women she'd ever met.

She and Cole had decided to wait on adopting any children until she'd had these first two, but that was definitely on their agenda for the following year as well. They'd already put in their application and had their background checks completed, so it was just a matter of finding the right child.

Her house had sold almost immediately, and Cole had insisted the money from the sale go into an account in just her name. He'd said he never wanted her to feel dependent on anyone, even her husband. He wanted her to have the freedom that money represented, the independence Mike and Jackson would've wanted for her.

He'd also unreservedly supported her decision to hyphenate her new last name, especially after reading the beautiful letter her dads had written for her future husband . . . for Cole.

Sarah glanced back over at her husband, who was still standing with the Anderson brothers on the other side of the gym. He saw her looking at him and raised a brow, as if asking if she was okay.

She nodded and blew him a kiss. Cole lifted his chin in return.

Sarah turned back to her friends, happy she was here with them, but counting down the minutes until she could go home with her husband. The further along she got in her pregnancy, the hornier she became. It was no wonder Cole wanted to keep her pregnant. He certainly benefited from the hormones coursing through her body.

Besides, she had a special surprise for him tonight. She'd finally decided on what she wanted for the tattoo she'd agreed to get after losing that bet with Felicity all those months ago.

Cole had refused to allow her to get inked while she was pregnant, and Sarah knew she'd only have a small window to get the design inked on her body after the twins were born, before Cole probably knocked her up again . . . not that she was complaining. She wanted to share the design with him. He was going to be floored, and she couldn't wait to see his reaction.

∾

"I see our women have finally shared the good news," Logan said dryly to his brothers and Cole.

Everyone laughed. Logan, Blake, Nathan, and Ryder had never been tighter. When the triplets had first come back to town and started up Ace Security, they were basically strangers. But living near each other again, not to mention the shit they'd been through with their women, had brought them closer together. And bringing Ryder into the fold had cemented their bond.

Cole knew Logan had told his brothers the day after Grace had taken a pregnancy test, even though she'd made him swear not to tell a soul until at least the eight-week mark. The same had happened with Ryder. He'd been so excited to share the news that he'd knocked up Felicity, he also hadn't honored his promise to keep it a secret.

As a result, the five men had already congratulated each other and reveled in the fact that their children would grow up together.

Cole hadn't shared that Sarah was going to have twins yet; he was still reeling with the news himself. He had no idea how he'd gotten so lucky. Sarah was the best thing to ever happen to him, and while he was thrilled about the twins, he was also scared to death. He might've told Sarah he'd give her as many children as she wanted, but it was a little daunting to have two at the same time.

Vowing to have a long talk with Logan later about raising twins, he looked back over at the group of women standing on the other side of the gym.

He saw Sarah looking at him, and he raised a brow at her. When she smiled and blew him a kiss, Cole gave her a chin lift in return and turned his attention back to the men at his side.

"You heard anything about Owen?" Blake asked.

The topic of his wife's kidnapper was enough to put a damper on Cole's excitement. "Yeah, the lady who's in charge of the group home emails me every week with updates. Apparently he's doing really well. He likes working a couple of hours a day at a local diner near the house, and he's gotten really close with one of the other residents. She says they play Go Fish for hours every night."

The other men all grinned, except for Logan. "How are you doing with Sarah's visits to him?"

Cole sighed. They'd had their one and only fight a few months back, about her desire to check on Owen. He'd relented when he realized it was something she had to do in order to move on from her ordeal. But he'd made her swear that she would never, *ever* go to the home without him. He'd been afraid that seeing Owen would bring back bad memories for her, but it seemed he was wrong. Seeing him happy and flourishing in the group home had made the few nightmares she'd still been having disappear.

"I fucking hate it," Cole told Logan and the others. "But Sarah needs this. I think a part of her feels guilty for being scared of him, and another part feels as if it's her duty as a decent human being to check on him."

Ryder put his hand on Cole's shoulder in sympathy, but didn't say anything.

"I think as time goes on, and she gets busy with her baby, the visits up there will happen less and less," Logan offered.

"I'm hoping so. I love Sarah exactly how she is, and I fucking love that she doesn't have a mean bone in her body, but seeing her anywhere near him still gives me the creeps."

"Have you told her?" Nathan asked.

Cole shook his head. "No. It's my problem, not hers. But . . . she knows anyway. I didn't sleep well after we got home the last two times we went up to see him." He'd lain awake, holding Sarah in his arms, and relived the nightmare week he'd spent not knowing where she was, if she was even alive. And when his demons got too bad, he'd woken her up and taken her hard. Reassuring himself that she was there with him. Safe and healthy.

"I'm hoping, eventually, Owen himself will forget about her. The last time we went up there, it took him a moment to remember who she was, which I kind of thought was a relief."

"Talk to her, man," Blake suggested.

Cole shook his head. "No. I can handle it. I want what Sarah wants. And if she needs to see him, to keep the promise she made to him, then that's what I'll make sure happens."

The men were all silent for a moment, and Cole knew they understood. He knew down to the marrow of his bones that the men standing in front of him would do whatever was best for their wives. No questions asked. No hesitation. Call them pussy whipped or obsessed . . . none of them cared. They loved their wives deeply, and nothing would change that.

"On another note, you gonna show her your new tattoo tonight?" Ryder asked.

Cole smiled. "Yeah. I had my last sitting a few days ago, and that was mostly for some touch-up work."

"I can't believe you've avoided letting her see it for so long," Nathan said with a shake of his head.

Cole shrugged. "She falls asleep easily. The pregnancy has made her tired all the time. It's been easier than you'd think. And when we have sex, I just let her ride me, then fall asleep on top of me." He grinned. "I put a shirt on after she's out."

The others just nodded and grinned back. Cole had never been the kind of man to talk much about his sexual exploits, but he was close to these men, and they'd had more than one conversation about sex in the past.

Ryder lifted his chin, indicating the women. "Looks like their little powwow is over. We meeting in the morning to work out?"

The five men had started getting together a few mornings every week to go running, then lift weights at the gym before starting their day.

"I'm in," Nathan said.

"Me too," Blake added.

"See you then," Logan agreed.

The four Andersons looked at Cole.

He took one look at his wife, her body beautifully rounded with his babies, and thought about how horny she'd been lately. That, combined with what he was going to show her later, made up his mind. "I'm gonna have to skip it. I'll catch up with you guys later, though."

Everyone chuckled and slapped him on the back and shoulders.

"Have fun!" Logan told him.

"I intend to," he told him, then turned to meet his wife halfway across the floor.

~

Sarah sat on the edge of their bed and nervously stared at Cole. He'd been quiet on the way home, even though he'd rushed her out of the gym as if he couldn't wait to take her to bed. Since they'd gotten back to their apartment, he'd been acting very mysterious.

"I love you."

Sarah stared at him. *Oh shit.* This wasn't starting well. "I love you too," she returned.

"I've been keeping something from you."

Sarah frowned. "You have?"

"Yeah. I mean, I'm pretty sure you're gonna like it, but I wanted it to be a surprise."

"I don't like surprises," Sarah replied, telling him something he already knew.

Cole winced. "I know. That's why I'm kinda nervous about this one."

The last time he surprised her, he'd slipped an engagement ring on her finger while she'd still been asleep in the hospital. She'd woken up to it, oddly heavy on her hand, and to Cole telling her they were going to get married that afternoon. That he'd arranged for the priest from the hospital to come up to their room and marry them. She had been excited and happy, and had agreed. Even though she didn't like surprises, that one was pretty darn awesome.

And for the last five or so months, he'd been good, hadn't sprung any over-the-top gifts on her and hadn't done anything like, say . . . go down on one knee—which he did at their wedding reception after she'd gotten out of the hospital, surprising her by singing that goofy song made famous in the movie *Top Gun*, "You've Lost That Lovin' Feelin'." It wasn't even close to being a wedding song, but when all four of the Andersons had joined in, she'd laughed at their antics until she'd cried. She didn't even care that the song was about someone losing their loving feeling—it was hysterical. That moment was one of her favorite memories from the reception.

After that, Cole hadn't kept anything from her that even remotely resembled a surprise. Including making sure she knew before he'd talked to the manager of the apartment complex with all the security, begging him to give them a three-bedroom place that was opening up.

But he'd also introduced her to a friend of his who was a member of the gym . . . and who happened to be a Realtor. Sarah had told Cole she didn't think she was ready to live in a house again yet, and he'd agreed, but he hadn't hidden the fact that he was talking to the Realtor and browsing online for houses.

Sarah wasn't an idiot; she knew they'd eventually need to move out of the apartment and get a house of their own . . . especially with the twins on the way, adopting, and who knew how many children after that.

He wouldn't have decided to buy a house anyway and surprise her with it . . . would he?

"What'd you do?" she asked with trepidation.

Instead of responding with words, he turned his back to her and took off his shirt.

The second she realized what she was looking at, her breath caught.

She'd always admired the tattoos on Cole's arms and chest. She'd even teased him about the compass next to his junk, while secretly thinking it was hot as hell. She couldn't imagine him any other way.

She knew Cole had been getting a tattoo on his back—of course she did, it was huge—but he didn't want her to see it until it was complete. And he hadn't told her it would be finished anytime soon.

"I wanted to surprise you. I went in a few days ago and had it finished up. I think it's pretty amazing, don't you?"

Sarah hated the vulnerability she could hear in his tone, but simply couldn't find the words to express what she was feeling.

She'd seen part of the outline when he'd first started getting it done, but at his request, she'd done her best to not look at it, even after he'd had several more sessions. But now that it was done—the tattoo was an absolute piece of art.

And besides that, Cole had put *her* on his back. Not her image, per se, but she knew immediately that was what she was looking at regardless.

An angel covered his skin from shoulder to shoulder. She had hair the same length as Sarah's, wings expanded. The feathers looked so incredibly real, Sarah had to reach out and touch him to make sure he hadn't gotten them glued onto his skin somehow. The angel's arms were outstretched, and she was wearing a beautiful, flowing gown. She had on an old-fashioned nurse's cap, and in front of her appeared a plethora of images: dogs, cats, a homeless man lying on the ground covered in a blanket, a woman on crutches with a child peeking out from behind her leg, and a baby in a bassinet.

He'd even included the logo of the Adoption Exchange, the agency she'd been adopted from so long ago.

Over one of the angel's shoulders were two men. They were cheek to cheek, smiling and holding hands . . . and looked just like her dads.

Over the angel's other shoulder was another man. Cole. It looked exactly like him. The figure wasn't smiling; he was holding an arm out, as if holding back anything and anyone who might want to go through him to get to the angel.

It was intricate, and so amazingly beautiful, Sarah didn't know what to say.

Tears formed—damn hormones—and she couldn't stop them no matter how hard she tried. Cole turned and took her in his arms, and she wanted to push him back around, tell him she wasn't done looking at his tattoo, but the second she was wrapped in his tight embrace, she knew she didn't want to be anywhere but right where she was.

"It's beautiful," she hiccuped.

He chuckled. "So these tears are because you like it?"

Sarah shook her head. "No. They're because I *love* it. It's the most gorgeous thing I've ever seen, and I don't think I'll ever be able to live up to the meaning behind it."

"You already have," Cole said softly. "You're an angel to everyone you meet. I've seen you hug men and women who looked like they hadn't showered in weeks and not flinch. You can make babies stop crying, and kids are giggling minutes after meeting you. You're the best thing to happen to the patients you're assigned to, and they damn well know it. I will do *anything* to protect you from the shit in this world. I've got your back so you can do your thing, angel."

She looked up and took his face in her hands. Tears continued to fall down her cheeks, but she couldn't stop them. "I'll never deserve you," she told him.

"Wrong," Cole disagreed. "We deserve each other."

"Damn straight," she said with a small smile.

Cole kissed her for several minutes, then pulled back, breathing heavily. He held out one arm and showed Sarah his forearm. There was a small heart tattooed there that she hadn't noticed. It was a dash of red in the midst of the black ink that covered his body.

She looked up at him in surprise. "That's new too?"

"Yup. This heart is for you . . . because you hold mine. Every baby we have will be added to this one. You and our future children are my everything. You mean more to me than anything or anyone else. I know I promised to love you in sickness and in health, but I want to make sure you understand. The thought of losing you scares the shit out of me. I won't let you leave me. If you did, I'd shrivel up and die. I mean that. I'll never take you for granted, and I'll always bend over backward to give you anything and everything you need or want."

"I'm not going anywhere, and all I need and want is you," she whispered.

"And you've got me."

Sarah took a deep breath. "I decided what I'm getting tattooed. As soon as I can, after these babies arrive."

"Yeah?" Cole asked, his nostrils flaring. She loved that he got turned on thinking about her with a tattoo. They so hadn't been her thing . . . until she'd met Cole. Now she couldn't wait to get inked. Especially after seeing his tribute to her and their love.

She pulled out of his arms, which wasn't that easy since he was reluctant to let her go, and went over to the dresser on her side of the bed. She pulled out a piece of paper, nervous now. When she'd seen what the artist had drawn, she'd loved it, but after seeing his, she wasn't so sure.

"Show me, angel," Cole urged.

Sarah came back to him and held out the piece of paper.

He took the sheet and unfolded it as she said, "I'd planned on getting it on my shoulder blade. It's not as big as yours, but I figured I'll probably be a huge wuss, and it'll hurt."

When he didn't say anything, she asked nervously, "Is it too big? I can do something else."

Without a word, Cole dropped the paper and jerked her into his body. Sarah let out a loud *oof* when she landed against him, and before she could say or do anything, she was whisked up into his arms, and he was dropping her on their bed.

"Cole?" she asked, propping herself up on an elbow.

His hands were undoing the button of his jeans, and he grunted, "Strip. Now."

Smiling, Sarah felt her nipples get hard, and she immediately got wet between her legs. She loved it when Cole went all alpha on her. She got to her knees and pushed her leggings and panties down her thighs. She'd gotten her shirt up and over her head, but hadn't managed to get her leggings all the way off when she felt Cole's hands on her hips. He turned her as if she weighed nothing and weren't six months pregnant with twins.

He pushed until she was on her hands and knees in front of him. His fingers went between her legs and spread her wetness up to her clit. He began to stroke her exactly how fast and hard she liked it, and she moaned. "Cole . . ."

"Need you," he said. Sarah also loved it when he got so turned on, he couldn't speak in complete sentences.

Nodding, she lowered her head and pushed back against his fingers as he began to fuck her with them. She couldn't spread her legs apart very far because of her leggings, and she whimpered in frustration. Before she could beg him to let her finish getting undressed, he was pushing his dick inside her.

Then he was fucking her as if it were the first time . . . or the last. She wasn't sure which. Within a minute or two, Sarah knew she was going to come. Her pregnancy had made her extremely sensitive, and she never failed to come at least twice when Cole made love to her.

"That's it, angel. Come for me."

She felt her muscles fluttering around his dick and moaned in ecstasy as she exploded. As she knew they would, Sarah felt Cole's thrusts speed up after she came. One hand snaked under her to squeeze her nipple, and the other went between her legs.

"Shit . . . Cole . . . shit!"

She was beyond words as he fucked her to another monster orgasm. She felt him fill her up even as she twitched and writhed under him.

Instead of immediately falling to his side and taking her with him, as he usually did when he took her this way, Cole's fingers traced the small of her back. His touch made goose bumps form all over her body.

"Right here," he said softly. "You should put that tattoo right here."

Smiling, Sarah nodded.

"I want to see it every time I take you this way. I want to know it's under my hand when I walk beside you. I love the thought of having me inked on you. I love you, angel. You'll never know how much."

And with that, he gently fell to his side, taking her with him and keeping himself lodged inside her until the last possible moment. With her belly being as big as it was, it was harder to stay connected after they made love, but his hand gently cupped her folds. Holding her to him. She knew he was also enjoying the feel of his come dripping out of her, but she didn't call him on that.

Smiling, she could just see the edge of the paper with the design of her tattoo, lying on the floor where Cole had dropped it. She didn't need to see it to know what it looked like, though. She'd memorized the drawing, had described in detail what she wanted to the tattoo artist.

A man was holding a woman against his chest, his face not quite visible because his head was down. And it wasn't actually a woman, but an angel. The man's arms were covered in tattoos that closely matched Cole's. The angel had hair like hers, and her eyes were closed. She was snuggled into the man's chest, and the word *home* was written over and over, end to end, around the couple, in the shape of a heart.

"You're home to me," Sarah told Cole softly. "Wherever you are is where I want to be."

"I love you."

"And I love you."

As she knew it would, his free hand slipped to her belly, and she covered it.

She twined their fingers and smiled when she heard Cole snoring a minute later. Her leggings were still around her thighs, and Cole's hand was still covering her lady bits. She was lying in a wet spot, and her bra was digging into her ribs, but Sarah had never been more comfortable.

She had no idea what life would bring for her and Cole. They'd most certainly fight, and she'd probably cry when things got too crazy, but she knew without a doubt that no matter what, Cole would be by her side. He was her everything, just as she knew she was his.

Life was odd. One second you could be scared out of your mind and sure nothing was ever going to work out, and the next you were happier than you could ever imagine. Sarah couldn't wait to experience every second of life's roller coaster, with Cole right there next to her.

Sighing, she closed her eyes and let herself sleep, secure in the knowledge that when she woke, Cole would be there, protecting her, encouraging her, and most important, loving her.

Author's Note

For those of you who have been following this series closely, you know that this book was published quite a bit after *Claiming Felicity*. Initially, this was going to be only a three-book series—then, of course, when I was writing the fourth book, I realized I really needed to give Cole his happily ever after. I gave my editor at Montlake a sad, pleading face, and she agreed to add one more book to this series! LOL!

I appreciate the support from all of you for this series. I've loved being able to create this final addition. Enjoy!

About the Author

Susan Stoker is the *New York Times*, *USA Today*, and *Wall Street Journal* bestselling author of *Claiming Felicity*, *Claiming Bailey*, *Claiming Grace*, and *Claiming Alexis* in the Ace Security series. A lover of alpha heroes, Susan is also the author of the Badge of Honor: Texas Heroes, SEAL of Protection, and Delta Force Heroes series. Married to a retired Army noncommissioned officer, Stoker has lived all over the country—from Missouri and California to Colorado and Texas—and currently lives under the big skies of Tennessee. She is a true believer in happily ever after and enjoys writing novels in which romance turns to love. To learn more about the author and her work, visit her at www.stokeraces.com.

Connect with Susan Online

Susan's Facebook Profile and Page

www.facebook.com/authorsstoker

www.facebook.com/authorsusanstoker

Follow Susan on Twitter

www.twitter.com/Susan_Stoker

Find Susan's Books on Goodreads

www.goodreads.com/SusanStoker

E-mail

Susan@StokerAces.com

Website

www.StokerAces.com